# Bank on Nothing

RUSSELL GOVAN

© Russell Govan 2020

Russell Govan has asserted his rights under the Copyright, Design and Patents Act, 1988, to be identified as the author of this work.

First published in 2020 by Sharpe Books.

*For Alistair.*

CONTENTS

Chapters 1 – 41
Acknowledgements

# Chapter 1

Jack Laidlaw was laughing as his wife died.

Later, all of the more appropriate clichés would be trotted out, as they so often are when death visits.

*She never saw it coming. She didn't know what hit her. At least it was quick. She wouldn't have suffered.*

Most of them probably true. Some even providing a degree of comfort. Maybe.

It was the first Friday in November after the clocks changed. The whole day had seen murky drizzle and the early darkness was almost a relief. People, breaking free of doing what they had to, were looking forward to two days of doing what they wanted to.

Jack arrived at The General Havelock just before quarter to six. The Tube from Bank and the train from Stratford helped deliver him to the pub barely half an hour after he'd left the office. Rob, Pete and Bazza were there already. Jack ordered his pint and joined the others. The buoyant mood delivered by the infant weekend was heightened by anticipation of the arrival of Gadger around six. Gadger had been on a contract for the past four months, programming in Atlanta, and everyone was keen to see him again. He actually arrived at quarter past six. Jack remembered afterwards that Pete had said, "Fifteen minutes late. Typical of you, Gadge."

Howdys and hugs, hellos and handshakes, insults and smiles, and another round of drinks. Within ten minutes Gadger was holding court and he had his jesting trousers on. Wisecracks, corny one-liners, descriptions of American ridiculousness, tall tales and patent nonsense all helter-skeltered from him. His gestures, timing, facial expressions and mimicry were gifts that made the unfunny funny and the funny hilarious. Their table snorted and roared, giggled and guffawed. The merriment and decibel level suggested a much later hour, and that gallons had been sunk rather than just a few pints. Their table at The Golden Curry was booked for half past seven, leaving time for a couple more rounds at The General first. It was going to be a cracking night.

A mile and a half away Debs Laidlaw phoned the pizza joint

at ten past six exactly. Experience had taught her that the number was usually engaged between six o' clock and then. Large ham and mushroom, medium Hawaiian, both on standard bases, collection as usual – it was convenient, and quicker than delivery. She knocked up a quick salad of iceberg, rocket, cucumber, spring onions and cherry tomatoes – the same guilt-inspired accompaniment she always made to try to mitigate the dietary vandalism of the kids' weekly treat.

She set the table for three and shouted up to the kids that she was just nipping out to get the pizzas, back soon. She exited the front door at twenty past six, just like she had done on most Friday evenings for the last couple of years, and zipped her jacket right up to the neck. The drizzle wasn't heavy enough to warrant an umbrella.

The till receipt for £21.40 was timed at 18.27 pm, and the girl who'd served her remembered that she and Debs had briefly discussed who their favourites were for *Strictly* this season.

The dual carriageway of Woodford Avenue was still busy when Debs turned the corner into the tranquillity of Gaysham Avenue, where the very few cars actually on the road were all parked. She didn't register the sleek, expensive-looking car camped in the disabled bay outside the solicitors' office. She gathered pace slightly and dipped her head against the drizzle becoming rain, comfortingly warm pizza boxes cradled in her left arm. Leaving the commercial premises behind and passing the first of the neat semis and terraces. She soon passed the first entrance to Roll Gardens to her left on the other side of the road. The trees on the street had already lost half their leaves, and the rising wind was encouraging more to parachute down to join their siblings' pavement dance. Halfway towards the second entrance to Roll Gardens, at the long stretch of road marked with a single yellow line between street parking bays, a telegraph pole, a streetlight and another tree stood in tight formation. This was where Debs habitually crossed the road, and where she taught the children it was safest to cross.

She didn't look backwards as she stepped off the pavement. There was no traffic noise and no car headlights to alert her, and she was in a hurry to get home. The Tesla Model S struck her at over seventy miles an hour. In less than one second the front bumper had broken both of her legs, the bonnet smashed three ribs and the windscreen fractured both her skull and her right eye socket. Her body bounced over the top of the car and was a corpse before it landed on the road. Thirty feet in front of the body the Hawaiian also lay smashed face down, its box blown off in the wind. The ham-and-mushroom, still boxed and intact, rested just to the left on the pavement. Most of the houses around had lights on behind drawn curtains. No curtains twitched. No one came to his or her door. Six minutes later, another woman walking to her home discovered the smashed remains of Deborah Laidlaw.

## Chapter 2

"This channel is 78% secure. Adopt the appropriate protocol."
"Understood."
"Report please."
"Contact has moved offline to eyeball."
"How many eyeball contacts?"
"Just one."
"Successful?"
"Can't tell. Nothing to suggest it wasn't successful."
"Next steps?"
"I wait. I'm not in the driving seat."
"Understood. Be careful."
"Will do."
"Good luck and goodbye."
"Thanks. Goodbye."

## Chapter 3

Jack's mobile rang. He felt absent-mindedly for it in his right-hand jacket pocket, whilst still straining to catch the punch line to Gadger's anecdote about the Georgian chambermaid and the dead halibut. He was irked and puzzled at the same time as the screen showed the caller as 'Home.' "I better take this guys. It's the missus." He got to his feet slowly, waving away the good-natured jibes about being under the thumb and being out past his bedtime. He pressed 'accept' and placed the phone to his right ear. He recognised Fi's voice, but couldn't make out her words over the baboon troop at his table and the general pub hubbub beyond. Jack placed his left index finger in his left ear and pressed the phone harder against his right. "Fi sorry, it's very noisy in here."

Something about Mum, but still too difficult to make out.

"Hang on, Fi. I'm just going to step outside where it's quieter." He was shouting, despite it being him that was having difficulty hearing, "Almost there." He passed through the door and squeezed past two refugee smokers, one of who was rather incongruously drawing on a cheroot, and stepped on to the pavement. "Hi, Fi. Can you hear me?"

Despite the rain, wind and traffic noise, it was quieter than inside the pub. "Of course, I can hear you. Can you hear me?"

"Yes. Yes, I can hear you. Now what is it?"

"Mum's not come back with the pizzas and Ollie has stolen my Barbie Princess."

"Sorry, what? What about Mum?"

"She's not come back with the pizzas. And Ollie has stolen my Barbie Princess. He says he's going to cut her hair off. You need to tell him that he shouldn't."

"Have you tried ringing her?"

"Yes, but there's no answer."

Jack looked at his wristwatch. Nearly seven o' clock. "What time did Mum go out for the pizzas?"

"I don't know. But it was ages and ages ago."

"Think Fi. Was it ten minutes ago? Twenty minutes?"

"I don't know what time she went out. But it must have been at least half an hour ago." Fi was beginning to sound more worried about her mum and the pizzas than Barbie Princess. Jack knew that Fi had no real sense of time, but he was also pretty sure that when he was home on Friday evenings, they were all tucking in to their pizzas shortly after half past six.

He sighed inwardly, "Okay, Fi. I'm sure there's nothing to worry about, but I'll pop home now just to make certain. I should be about fifteen or twenty minutes. Mum will probably be back before me and you guys will be tucking into pizza when I get there."

"Okay Dad. Thanks. See you soon. Bye."

"Bye." Jack pocketed his phone, re-entered The General and made his way back to the table. "Sorry lads, minor domestic crisis. Got to nip home to sort things. But I'll catch you up at the curry house. Keep my seat warm." His announcement met with the conventional barrage of catcalls and banter reserved for lightweights and others similarly perceived as letting the team down. Jack grinned sheepishly, shrugged his shoulders and turned to make his way out.

Outside he was able to hire a hackney on the High Road almost immediately and less than ten minutes later the cab was at the junction of Shere Road and Gaysham Avenue. "Can't go no further, mate," the driver stated the obvious. A small gaggle of people, some hooded, others with umbrellas and a few unprotected from the rain, were gathered at the junction. Beyond them two uniformed police officers stood blocking the middle of the road. Further behind them there were at least three flashing blue lights. Jack paid the cabbie, jumped out and joined the dozen or so others strung across the carriageway in three distinct knots. He approached a tall bearded fellow, easily six four in his dark anorak, drawstring tied under his chin pulling his hood tight against his head. "What's the score mate?"

"Accident, mate. They've closed the street between here and Woodford Avenue. Woman over there reckons someone's been killed." He nodded towards a group of four Asian women.

A sudden surge of concern threatened panic, before relief

arrived with the realisation that this is what had delayed Debs. If the road was blocked off at both ends, she wouldn't be able to get back. He made his way towards the group of women. "Hello. Any idea what's going on?"

The unusual circumstances allowed normal protocol to be suspended and his forward manner seemed entirely appropriate. The four faces turned and he was confident, from the striking resemblance they shared, that this was a family. Three younger women whose ages he guessed as late teens, early and mid-twenties. All taller than the middle-aged woman who must be their mother. The teenager, pretty and bright eyed, was the first to respond, eager to share, "A woman's been knocked down."

Jack held his breath and her gaze, saying nothing.

"She's dead. They say she was carrying pizzas."

The better part of Jack Laidlaw's life died in that instant.

## Chapter 4

"Is it done?"

'Yes it's done."

"Everything went as we had planned it?"

"Yes, everything."

"Good. You've done well. I know that it can't have been pleasant for you."

"It needed to be done."

"There'll be no comeback?"

"I told you. Everything went to plan. There'll be no comeback."

"I'm sorry. I didn't mean to question you."

## Chapter 5

The next seconds, minutes, hours, days and weeks happened. They just happened. Sometimes Jack would appear to be in control, able to make decisions. But really he was on autopilot. Numb. Things that had to happen did so in spite of him.

Because Debs didn't die of natural causes there had to be an inquest. The Coroner opened it so that a burial order could be issued, as well as to confirm evidence of Debs' identity, before adjourning proceedings with the direction that they be resumed at a later date. Funeral Directors had to be appointed. The Co-op was local and had handled things when his Dad died, so were an easy choice. Choose a coffin. Decide on flowers. Burial or cremation? Not something they had ever discussed – burial. Find a church. Brief a vicar. Pick the hymns. Find a venue for the reception after the funeral. Choose the menu. Make sure people knew the funeral arrangements.Talk to work. Talk to Debs' work. Talk to the kids' school. Advise the bank and the mortgage company. Delete Debs' social media accounts. Countless meetings with police. A constant stream of visitors. Debs' family. His Mum. His brother. People from his work. People from Debs' work. Friends. Neighbours. Condolences cards to open, read and find somewhere to display as the space ran out.

Jack navigated the tricky seas of life immediately after death reliant on custom, the love of family, support of friends and the services of professionals. He was captain of the ship in name only, a figurehead bereaved and bereft, incapable of steering without help.

There were four occasions when the psychological armour his mind had garbed him in was pierced, when reality and realisation speared him. The first was almost immediately, when he identified her body. He was physically sick. Three times. In between, he almost choked as he sobbed and staggered, fell to his knees, tearing his right trouser leg. He sobbed and he howled. He actually howled, and the police and ambulance personnel present, used to grief but not inured to it, feared for him. A green-clad paramedic in her mid-twenties went to him and knelt by him, pulling his head to her bosom, hugging him tightly with all the love she could afford. Eventually, after a thousand years, his tears slowed and his breathing evened. As some kind of rational thought returned, his brain was girding his body for telling the kids.

That was the second time, so soon after the first. He would not have believed that any pain could have been greater than seeing Debs' body, but telling Fi and Ollie was worse. Their anguish seemed even sharper than his, the end of their worlds. And, as if in some perverse competition, their reaction caused his own grief to ratchet up still further, determined not to be outdone.

On the first Friday of December, three weeks after Debs was killed, he was at the police station. He'd endured the invasive process required to rule him out as a suspect. Watched the minutiae of Debs life sifted through in search for what? A lover? An enemy? What? He'd heard that CCTV had drawn a blank and that the burned-out Tesla was barren as far as forensics was concerned. One senior officer had told him that if this had been a professional hit it was impossible to imagine it being carried out more effectively. He had experienced all of this as a detached observer – interested, understanding, but not involved. But when Officer Kane said that every lead had drawn a blank, and then suggested that this might be kids who had been stealing high-end motors for joyriding – and it had gone wrong, reality popped the protective bubble again. The police were giving up. Putting their excuses in place. Withdrawing gracelessly. *The bastard who did it was going to get away with it.* Jack realised that, when it really mattered, justice was a chimera. His empty stomach convulsed and he retched bile.

The next day Jack took the kids to visit their Aunt May, Debs' sister in Chiswick. May was two years older than Debs, divorced, with twin eight-year-old daughters, Flora and Maggie. Jack liked May. Despite financial and health challenges, she was one of life's positive people, good company, energising and someone others liked to be around.

There was a strong family resemblance and she looked like Debs, although carrying much more weight and looking ten years older rather than two. The four kids got on particularly well – Ollie still sufficiently young not to mind being with three girls. The fun, laughter and evident happiness of Fi and Ollie was a testament to their resilience and made it possible to imagine that the healing process was underway for them at least. But when it came time to leave Ollie refused absolutely to go. Much cajoling and encouragement only had the effect of prompting tears. May knelt by her distressed nephew, "There, there Ollie. There's a good boy. You do know that you have to go home sometime."

"Don't want to."

"Why ever not?"

"Because. Because it's full of empty." There were tears in Ollie's eyes. Jack looked at his son, and then to Fi. He could see tears in her eyes too, and felt his own moisten. They all knew it was true. Their house was full of empty, and they didn't want to go back there. The heartbeat of their family had been cleaved out and its absence was a constant, raw, sapping presence.

## Chapter 6

"How long since she first contacted you?"

"I told you already. It was me who contacted her."

"How long?"

"Many months. At least six. I can easily check."

"What! You mean there's a trail? You really can't be that stupid!"

"Relax man, it's secure. It was you who set up the security."

"I've told you before. Nothing is secure. Nothing. Anywhere. Ever. Do you never listen?"

"I said relax. Nothing is secure from *you*. But you're on the inside."

"We agreed no unnecessary risks. And now this!"

"I keep telling you, relax. Chill. This isn't a risk. This makes us stronger. Even more certain to succeed."

"You and me and our two brothers were tight. We were secure. Then you do this!"

"Listen. I've thought this through. A sister gives us an extra dimension. Makes us stronger."

"You are an idiot. You know that the longer you make a chain the more you increase the risk of there being a weak link."

"Shut up. You might be older than me, but you're not smart at this stuff. She will make us stronger."

"You need to prove to me that she is secure, reliable."

"I will, I will. Relax brother, relax."

## Chapter 7

Despite the late hour, the night was still warm and sticky as Jack closed the front door behind him.

"How many have you had?"

"A few. Not that many. I guess I'm not that used to it any more."

"So who was there tonight?"

"All the guys. Rob, Chugs, Bazza and Pete. Lennie, Gadger and Tom."

"It was nice that they were all able to be there. Nice they made the effort."

"Yeah, it was good of them. But you're right as well when you say effort. It kind of felt like they were there out of a sense of duty."

He paused and she continued to focus on him. He certainly wasn't drunk but he'd had a few and his tongue had been loosened. She felt he might open up more about how he really felt, and bet on saying nothing.

The payback was immediate. "It was kind of awkward, Mum, you know? Even after a few rounds it was still like the guys were treading on eggshells. There was a bit of banter and Gadger had his usual ton of new, unfunny jokes that still make people laugh. But there was an awkwardness too. Maybe it was just in my head, maybe nobody else felt it. But it was the first time all eight of us had been together in one place since the funeral. And nobody mentioned the funeral. Nobody mentioned Debs."

"It's natural. People feel awkward. They don't know what to say. Especially men. Especially when it's a bunch of men together."

"I know. I know that. But it still felt awkward. At least I felt awkward. I think they did too. When it got to half ten and I said I'd better be getting back everyone seemed relieved. They were all keen to get back too for various reasons. In the old days before... before, there would have been all sorts of name-calling and insisting on at least another one for the road."

"I understand, Jack. But, like you say, it was the first time you'd all been out since Debs died and it will take time for things to start to feel normal again."

He looked over at her, perched on the dining chair, chin in hand and elbow resting in her other palm. She looked small, and old, and tired. Guilt flooded over him. She was seventy-two years old and had had a hard enough life of her own. A month after Debs had been killed it was obvious that he was struggling to cope and she had suggested moving in temporarily to help with Fi and Ollie. Just until he was "properly back on his feet again." That was seven months ago and she was still stuck here looking after her own youngest child and his kids.

"Were you waiting up for me, Mum?"

"No, no. Just lost track of the time." She was lying. She knew he knew. "But I will be heading up now. 'Night, Son."

"Goodnight, Mum. Have a lie-in tomorrow. It's Saturday – no rush to get the kids up."

He sank back into the consoling armchair and inhaled deeply as he listened to her arthritic steps gradually climb the stairs. A faint trace of burned cheese from the kitchen mingled with the scent of Persil from Fi's hockey kit drying on the clotheshorse.The dishwasher hummed and clicked its way through its eco-programme in the distance.

This was what he dreaded. Sitting alone in that room where he and Debs had spent so many evenings after the kids had gone to bed, chatting, laughing, cuddling and effortlessly being each other's best friends. Everything in the room reminded him of her. Indeed everything in the whole house did. Even things that had been introduced since her death, as he imagined what she would have thought of them. It wasn't a problem when there was someone else with him, but when he was alone memories and reminders of his loss were ubiquitous. The fact of her absence became a being alongside him - an unwelcome companion, mocking and taunting him for his loss.

He felt the familiar anger kindle within him. Hatred for the bastard who had mown Debs down and just kept driving. Exasperation at the inadequacy of the police and their ineptitude in finding her killer. Resentment at the lack of interest from the media, for whom her killing was ancient history and therefore no longer a story nor news. Once before, many months ago, the blaze had got out of control and as fury engulfed him he had started to smash things up. The terror on the uncomprehending faces of the kids, roused by the bedlam, had doused the conflagration in a torrent of shame. His Mum had moved in the next week.

He reached for the framed photo of the kids on top of the bookshelf and held it in front of him in both hands. This now routine practice had the established effect, as he immediately felt the anger ebb. He studied the faces. They both looked like Debs, but Ollie particularly so. Looking at this picture before going to bed was therapy. It neither denied nor belittled his anger and anguish, but it gave him meaning. They needed him and loved him, just as he needed and loved them.

He gently placed the frame back on top of the bookshelf and inhaled a huge sigh, bracing himself. Much as he hated sitting alone downstairs, he often did so much longer than he needed to. It was preferable to going to bed alone. Once in bed, in the darkness, there was nowhere to hide. The super king mattress that he and Debs never regretted spending a small fortune on was now a tundra, where he would spend unending broken hours fruitlessly searching for any kind of warmth and comfort. He walked over to the light switch and flicked it off. Turning through the doorway and left up the staircase, quietly in the dark so as not to disturb any sleepers, he made his ascent toward the empty bed.

Perhaps it was discussing Debs with Mum last thing. Whatever the reason, her absence felt even more acute than usual. He rolled on to his side, facing the void where she should be. He pulled her pillow to his face and inhaled deeply. Only the faint odour of washing powder, not unpleasant, but sterile. He remembered the night he'd gone to bed months ago and discovered Mum had washed the bed linen. Washed the hint of Debs' perfume and every other physical connection to her away. He cried a lot that night, although he never said anything to Mum.

Now there was no comfort and no connection. His imagination's pictures of her last conscious seconds returned, ready to begin their familiar torture. The unwelcome speculation about her thoughts and feelings in that final instant started its familiar loop in his mind. Tonight was particularly bad.

He sat up and reached for his mobile phone on his bedside table and brought it to life with his thumb. He scrolled to her number and rang it. Nothing. Shit! He'd let her battery run down. He slalomed across the bed on his side and reached into the drawer on her bedside table. His hand located her phone, with its charger attached, atop her knickers and ankle socks. He'd put it there along with her purse the day the undertaker had given them to him after her body had been collected from the coroner. When he had sorted through all the administrative details after her death he consciously didn't cancel her phone contract. He knew others might consider it ghoulish, but there was bittersweet comfort in occasionally hearing her voice. He had smiled wryly once in the car when the radio DJ played an oldie he'd never heard before *Hello this is Joanie*, where the singer repeatedly called the answer machine of his late girlfriend. Jack had taken the phone out of her drawer a number of times to put it on charge, but had forgotten to do so recently. The light from his own screen was enough for him to fumble Debs phone out of the drawer and plug the charger into the socket between the table and the bed. A buzz preceded the appearance of the charging icon.

He waited a few minutes for her phone to take on some charge then called her number again. Three rings, then her voice: *Hi. Sorry I can't take your call. Leave your name and number and I promise I'll get back to you. Bye.*

Jack pressed his phone hard against his chest, so that it was painful. He inhaled deeply to suppress an involuntary sob. He'd not called her for over a month. He wasn't sure if that was good or bad, and he didn't really care. Her voice message left him melancholic but at least this self-inflicted pain was less barbed than the involuntary images it chased away.

He was fully awake now. The icon on Debs phone showed

that it was 22% charged. He picked it up and studied it. The charger cord was easily long enough for him to handle it comfortably. Idly he tapped Fi's birthday in when it asked for the passcode. Both his and her phones operated by Touch ID but they each knew that the other also used the kid's birthdays as passcodes so that they could use each other's phones if the need ever arose. He realised that in all the time since she died, he'd never done anything with her phone other than charge it up so he could ring it and hear her voice. He pressed Contacts and scrolled through the familiar names. He was there, of course. And Mum. Her siblings May, Martin, Ricky and Harry. Chloe and Ella, her best friends. And so many other friends. Work colleagues. The plumber. The dance instructor. The bloody pizza shop. The garage. The window cleaner. It was her life in microcosm. Everyone she loved and everyone she knew. And every one of them familiar to him. He felt closer to her, reminded of how intimately he knew her life. Her phone connected her to him in a way its designers probably never imagined.

Then he came to Vic. No surname. Just Vic and a mobile number. Who was Vic? Was it a man? Or maybe a woman – Victoria or Vicky? He finished scrolling through the last few letters to confirm his belief that he knew everyone else in her contacts. He did. Everyone. Except Vic. She hadn't ever mentioned a Vic. Never. Jack racked his brains, but nothing came to him. Perhaps it was some tradesman or other that she'd used once. Or someone who insisted she have their number and she was too polite to refuse. But she'd have told him about someone like that.

He clicked on Favourites. It was just him – his mobile, his work mobile and his work landline. He smiled. He wasn't just her only favourite, he was her triple favourite. He pressed Recents. All the calls Debs had made on that phone in her last three months were there – the final one to the pizza place. There were lots of calls. Multiple calls to him, May, Harry, Ella, Chloe. And Vic. Seven calls to Vic in those final three months. All outgoing calls, none lasting more than a minute. All made on Tuesday lunchtimes. Who the bloody hell is Vic? Jack switched to Calendar. Debs had her mobile synced with her desktop and laptop, so everything would show on all three devices. But she wasn't a great one for noting things in the electronic diary. Going back several years there were sporadic entries for hairdresser appointments and numerous reminders about things to do with the kids schooling, like parent's evenings. Otherwise nada. The Calendar wasn't going to shed any light on Vic's identity.

He switched her phone off and placed it back on top of her bedside table to finish charging overnight. He lay back and closed his eyes. The conundrum that was Vic occupied his thoughts until blessed oblivion finally descended.

## Chapter 8

"This channel is 73% secure. Adopt the appropriate protocol."
"Understood."
"Report please."
"Significant developments. Four eyeballs in nine days. Two with Alpha and two more with Alpha and his brother Beta. Gamma and Delta have been mentioned, but no eyeballs there. Alpha is the driver I think, certainly more so than Beta."
"Can you confirm whether Gamma and Delta are IC4 or IC6?"
"I think they are IC6, but I can't confirm absolutely."
"We need to know."
"Understood."
"What do you make of Beta?"
"Bit other-worldly. Maybe on the spectrum."
"That tallies. How has he reacted to you?"
"I think he is OK with me."
"Good. Next steps?"
"Another eyeball with the pair tomorrow. I think I'll be going properly inside the tent."
"Excellent. Keep us posted."
"Will do."
"Good luck and goodbye."
"Thanks. Goodbye."

## Chapter 9

"I hate to admit it, but you were right."

"As usual."

"Seriously, she is fantastic. And she really seems to get it."

"Whoa! Do I detect a romantic interest?"

"Don't be ridiculous. She's way too old."

"And out of your league."

"Yes, very good. At least she and I play the same game."

"Shut up."

"Sorry. Anyway, I'm confident she can do this."

"Agreed. The others believe it too."

## Chapter 10

Jack couldn't concentrate on his work throughout the entire morning. He kept making stupid typos, and simple documents presented more of a challenge than normal - causing him to re-read to make sure that he had properly understood them. Lunchtime arrived and he consumed his tuna mayo baguette and latte on autopilot at his desk. All of the packaging was recyclable. He put the baguette wrapper inside the coffee cup and placed it at the corner of his desk, ready to take to the recycling bin when he next headed in that direction.

He put his hand into his left-hand jacket pocket and brought out Debs' phone. He hesitated briefly before keying in Fi's birthday to unlock it. Despite having just eaten he had an emptiness mewling in his stomach. Contacts. Vic. Call. The number rang three times before it was answered. "I wondered when you'd get around to calling. What's kept you?" The deep male voice paused. "Hello?"

"Is that Vic?"

"Who is this?"

"My name is Jack Laidlaw. Is that Vic?"

"I'm sorry. There's no-one of that name here. And I don't know any Jack Laidlaw."

"Who did you think was calling? You were clearly expecting a call from this number."

The briefest of pauses. "I am expecting a call from my sister. I do not have caller ID on this phone. I am sorry, but I think you must have dialled a wrong number." A click signalled the other party had ended the call.

Jack looked at the phone, as if expecting it to offer an explanation. This was bollocks. Every mobile phone has caller ID. He dialled the number again. A brief silence and then a disembodied voice advising him that the person he was calling was not available. He cursed under his breath and cradled her phone back in his hand before slowly easing it into his breast pocket. This wasn't right, but he was struggling to work it out.

"You okay, Jack?" He looked up to see Martha, leaning slightly forward against his desk – just sufficiently on the right side of the line that would constitute an invasion of personal space if crossed. Almost half as wide as her five-foot nothing height, dressed immaculately in navy suit and court shoes, complemented by an old gold neck scarf and matching brooch, she tilted her head quizzically. Dark hair scraped back into a small bun, eyes narrowed and Munsell red lips so tight as to be almost invisible, her whole demeanour broadcast compassion and concern. She was twenty-nine years old but dressed like his mother. She'd been a fixture in his team for six years, and had been a rock when Debs died. Martha was one of the good guys. "Really, are you okay?"

"I'm fine. I'm fine." He had delayed his answer too long.

"You don't look fine and you don't sound fine." Martha leaned in closer. "Has something happened?"

"No, not at all. I've just come over a little queasy. And my head isn't quite spinning, but it's not right. Kind of fuzzy, you know?"

"Do you think that maybe you should go home? Take the afternoon off?"

"Well, I'm not sure about that." Their eyes met, hers widening in tandem with an almost imperceptible nod. A brief silence.

"You've only one meeting this afternoon, and it's an internal with McCormack. I can easily cover it for you." The instruction presented as a suggestion sealed matters. "If you're sure you'll be all right you should probably just go now and I'll sort things here. Text or email me to let me know you get home safely."

"Thanks Martha. I'll be fine. I'll see you tomorrow." His departure towards the door to the lifts, jacket on and carrying his laptop case drew a couple of curious glances from the few staff not already at lunch. He didn't feel any need to acknowledge them, confident that Martha would manage the situation discreetly and supportively.

Ten minutes later he was seated on a stool looking out on to King William Street, nursing his Starbucks latté. Jack Laidlaw was not a shirker. The notion of skipping work for any reason would simply not occur to him. He might have been expected to feel guilt even though the queasiness and fuzzy head he had reported were hardly elaborations of the truth. But he didn't. His mind was the chaos of a party gone catastrophically wrong. Too many thoughts and questions crowded his head, but the most unwelcome of all – like the two funeral crashers who were at the reception for Debs – were the suspicions that clamoured for acknowledgement.

A casual observer would be unaware of his turmoil as Jack perched almost motionless, eyes closed, oblivious to the coffee and pastry aromas, and deaf to the gentle hubbub of busy lunchtime trade. After a full two minutes he opened his eyes, took a lubricating mouthful and reached for his phone. A quick scroll through contacts and press dial. Three rings. "Yes. Hello. Can I speak to WPC Konstavis please?" Pause. "When does she come on duty?" Another pause. "Okay, that's fine. She's my FLO. Please tell her Jack Laidlaw rang and that I'll call in to see her this afternoon. Thank you."

## Chapter 11

Jack came out of Ilford Rail Station at quarter past two. He crossed Cranbrook Road and walked the short distance downhill to turn left on to the High Road. The ten-minute walk along the busy street took him past the General Havelock. That reminder opened the door to admit guilt into the maelstrom of emotions already threatening to overwhelm rehearsals of what he wanted to tell Rachel. By the time he arrived at the three storeys of glass, blonde brick, and blue & white clad steel he was as discombobulated as he had been immediately after speaking to Vic. He paused, took a long slow breath, checked his watch and pushed the glass door open. A few steps inside and the officer on duty behind the desk hailed him, "Ah, Mr. Laidlaw! I take it you're here for WPC Konstavis? Please take a seat and I'll let her know that you're here." Jack recognised the officer and realised that it was him that he had spoken to when he 'phoned the station less than an hour ago.

"Jack! Good to see you." He had barely sat down before he was on his feet, shaking the hand proffered by Rachel. "Shall we go into a room? Can I get you a tea or a coffee?" She acknowledged his shake of the head, simultaneously reading him, smiling and turning to lead the way. He followed through the doorway into a small room, and took the seat she beckoned to as she closed the door behind him. Rachel took the other chair at a right angle to his alongside the small square wooden table. The room was sparse - a water cooler with plastic cups in the far corner, a box of tissues on the table, a green and black *Crimestoppers* poster on the back wall urging the reader not to get drawn into criminal damage, and a single naked light bulb bayoneted into the ceiling. There was a faint trace of bleach in the air and a ball of cotton wool in Jack's mouth.

"Are you sure I can't get you a drink?"

"Water, please." He watched mute as she filled a cup and handed it to him. "Thanks." He half emptied the cup in one go.

"You're welcome. How are Fi and Ollie doing?"

"They're both fine, thanks for asking. It was parents evening last month and the reports on both of them were really good."

"That's not a surprise. They're both lovely kids, and bright too. How about your mum? Is she well? Still helping out?"

"She's okay too. Feeling her age a bit, although she never mentions it. She's an absolute star."

"She's certainly that, Jack. A very impressive lady. And how about you? How are you, and what brings you here today?"

"Well." Jack paused and looked properly at her for the first time since they entered the room. Rachel was forty years old but looked thirty. Her uniform, clearly donned less than an hour ago and still immaculate, suited her olive skin tone. She was perhaps a stone-and-a-half overweight, but carried it well at five foot nine. Her large brown eyes, prominent Roman nose and full, wide mouth combined to produce a face that was both striking and attractive. Her expression married empathy with curiosity. She had been more helpful than he could have imagined in the immediate aftermath of Debs' death, and for some months after that. He regretted now that he'd broken off contact with her after she had become defensive of what he saw as PC Kane's inadequacy.

"It's all right, Jack. Take your time. How is it that I can help you?" Her voice was warm, the smile on her lips encouraging, as she gently lowered her chin and widened her eyes.

"I think I've got a new lead. There's this guy called Vic and I don't know who he is and Debs had been calling him and maybe seeing him and when I called him he blanked me and gave me some sort of cock-and-bull story about his sister and then refused to talk to me any more and I just wonder if he's got something to do with the reason she was killed."

"Whoa! Slow down, Jack. Let's just try to take this at a pace I can keep up with, and maybe understand. Take a drink of water then – slowly – tell me what you know about this Vic fellow, and how you came to know it."

"Last night I was playing around with Debs' phone." He paused and looked her in the eye. "I never cancelled her contract. I wanted to be able to hear her voicemail message."

"I see. I can completely understand that."

"I was going through her contacts and came across this guy called Vic. I had no idea who he was."

"Well you can hardly be expected to recognise every single one of the contacts on Debs' phone."

"You're wrong. I did recognise every other contact. And if things were the other way round Debs would recognise every single one of mine. Even if she didn't know them personally, she would know who they were. We knew everything about each other. No secrets."

"Okay, I see."

"So then I was checking through her call history. There weren't any calls from him to her, but she'd called him. Seven times in her last three months. Always on a Tuesday lunchtime and never for even as long as a minute."

"Okay." He had her complete attention now.

"So today is Tuesday. I waited until lunchtime and called him. You'd have done the same. Anyone would. Anyway he answers and says he's been wondering why I haven't called. So I ask him if he's Vic and he doesn't answer and I tell him who I am. He says he's not Vic and that he's never heard of me. I asked why he said he'd been wondering about why I hadn't called and he gave me some bollocks about expecting a call from his sister and then he hung up and then he wouldn't answer when I rang back I and I think that means there's something bloody suspicious about the bastard."

"Stop! Slow down, Jack. So you called the number in Debs' phone and asked to speak to Vic?"

"Yes. Well I rang his number and he said he had been wondering why I hadn't called. Then I asked him if he was Vic."

"And he said no."

"That's right. And he said he'd never heard of me."

"And he said that he answered the way he did because he thought you were his sister calling him?"

"That's what he said. But it's crap. It was just some bullshit to try to fob me off."

"Then you tried to call the number again and he wouldn't answer?"

"That's it."

"Well, that certainly sounds a bit odd. What do you make of it? What does your gut tell you?"

"That's the trouble, Rachel. I don't know what to make of it. I barely slept last night going over and over in my mind wondering who the hell Vic was. Then when I called the number today I get this crap. I honest-to-God don't know what to make of it all. That's one of the reasons I'm here – to see what you think."

"All right, I understand. Take another sip of water, and here – take one of these." She pushed the box of tissues towards him and he realised the moistness he felt in his eyes must be obvious. He took two tissues, blew his nose and tried to surreptitiously dab his eyes. "There are will be a finite number of possibilities within a range here. At one end of the spectrum we need to take Vic at his word, and accept that he doesn't know anything about you or Debs. At the other end he absolutely knows who Debs is and is blanking you because he has something to hide. Or it could be any one of multiple shades of grey in between."

"Do you think she was having an affair with him?" A betraying bead manoeuvered down his right cheek.

"Jesus, Jack! Where did that come from?" The shock on Rachel's face was genuine. "Look you're upset, you're sleep-deprived and you're emotional. Just slow right down and think about this. You and I talked about Debs a lot. You two were like that." She held up her crossed index and middle fingers. "From the way you described your relationship, I wouldn't think that was remotely likely. Also, remember that we've investigated this case to the nth degree. If Debs had been having any sort of affair there is no way that we wouldn't know about it." Her right hand reached across the table and rested gently on top of his left. "I can see how you've jumped to that conclusion, but that's exactly what you've done – jumped to a conclusion. You're overwrought and not thinking straight. You really mustn't torture yourself in this way." There was a pause as she waited for him to dab his eyes again before focussing on hers. "Listen to me, Jack. If Debs was having an affair we'd have known about it."

Even as he inhaled slowly and deeply, he could feel her words blowing away some of the horrors that had been pitching camp in his brain. "Thanks. Thanks, Rachel. I'm sorry it came out like it did and I'm sorry for landing it all on you. It's just that I didn't know what to think – or how to stop imagining the worst. I didn't know who to talk to."

"That's fine, Jack. That's what I'm here for. You did the right thing confiding in me. Besides, we both know you need me too."

Jack tensed as he returned her gaze, and he could feel a tightness in his throat. "Yes, I need you. Will you do it?"

"It's a perfectly legitimate line of enquiry. To be honest, I suspect it will already have been covered off as part of the investigation earlier. After all, we did have access to Debs' desktop and laptop before – all the contacts were probably checked then. But yes, of course. We'll check out the number."

"And?"

"And if there's anything - *anything* - that you need to know I will tell you. You have my word on that."

The tension easing was tangible throughout Jack's body, an involuntary yet pleasant shudder coursing through him. "Thank you. Thank you for listening, for helping, for understanding. I'm sorry I was so off hand the last time we met. I know you were only doing your job – sticking up for your colleague, and there was no way I should have been that rude."

"Jack, it's fine. Like water under the bridge, or off a duck's back, or whatever. It's what I'm trained for. You're the person who's lost his wife and not been given satisfactory answers. You had every right to be unhappy."

"You're being very gracious. We'll say no more about it, save to say again that I really appreciate everything. One final question – how long do you think it will take?"

"Not long – a few days at most. As I said, I'll let you know. Now, is there anything else?" as she stood to signal the meeting was concluding.

"No. Thanks again, and I'll wait to hear from you." He extended his right hand and they shook gently before she led him to the door and an exchange of goodbyes. He exited the building less burdened than on entry. But an insistent niggle still gnawed at the back of his head. If Debs could keep a secret from him, it was unlikely that anyone else – even the police – would be able to uncover it.

## Chapter 12

He could see Jalal making his way towards him and remembered they had an appointment to investigate a complaint that Mullins had registered with them.

Jack switched his mind back to work and his screen to secure mode as he flicked his eyes up to Jalal, "You ready then?"

Jalal was standing beside Jack's desk and nodded his assent. He was just less than five foot ten, slim-built with thick raven hair fashionably short at the side, longer and swept back on top. Deep set dark brown eyes over an elongated nose with a pronounced bridge sat above a small mouth. He sported a short, thick, immaculately trimmed black beard. His pale grey suit was clearly very expensively tailored, complemented by a crisp white shirt and tasteful claret paisley pattern tie. Jalal was a man who clearly took great pride in his appearance.

He seemed a very serious young fellow, and Jack had mused that he had never seen him smile. Of all of his team, Jack felt he knew him least well. Jalal had been recruited by Mike and HR when Jack was still absent in the aftermath of Debs' death. Nevertheless, his diligence and high productivity marked him out as a star performer in the team, and his air of professionalism was a decided asset to the department.

Jalal kept pace with Jack along the corridor as they headed towards the staircase. "Mullins has complained that the walls on both flights between the first and second floors have been badly scuffed. God knows how that can have happened. Everything of any size that needs moving should go in the service lift."

"The service lift was out for planned maintenance last Tuesday," Jalal reminded him. "Maybe something happened then."

They reached the cantilever staircase and began to make their way down. The staircase was another of the bank's many architectural treasures. Located in the front hall of the bank, it had been completed just before the Second World War during the Sir Herbert Baker re-building of the Threadneedle Street premises, and at one hundred and sixty-five feet was amongst the longest in Europe. As they descended Jack looked over the bannister and his eye was drawn, as it always was, to the original Roman mosaic pavement that Baker had placed at the bottom of the stairwell. Being Facilities Manager for such a unique institution posed many challenges, but Jack enjoyed his job and was happy to have to deal with the idiosyncrasies that came with the territory. What he was not happy to deal with was additional work and expense caused by thoughtless idiots. "Bloody Hell," he cursed as they turned down from the second floor and saw the damage to walls at the bend of the first flight downwards. The pale cream paintwork was badly marked by a number of black streaks three to five feet up, and there was a nasty eighteen-inch gash where something had gouged the plasterwork. "Something pretty big and heavy has done that."

"Not obvious what, though," observed Jalal, crouching to inspect the damage more closely. "I'll get on to the contractor when I get back to my desk. This can be filled, dried and sanded today, then repainted after hours. Be perfect again by tomorrow morning."

"You're right. Okay, nothing more we can do here. Let's check out the graveyard next." Jack led the way down the final flights of stairs and along various corridors towards the garden court area outside. The bank had very quickly outgrown its first building in Threadneedle Street in the eighteenth century and purchased the church of St Christopher-le-Stocks next door to provide room for expansion. The church was deconsecrated and demolished, but the graveyard was left in place and later became the bank's Garden Court, although many insiders like Jack still referred to it by its earlier name. As they stepped into the fresh air Jack turned to Jalal. "So what exactly is the issue?"

"The Governor's PA emailed to say he'd commented that the leaves on the mulberries looked unhealthy."

"Better have a look then." Jack led the way to the path that bisected the lawn. On each side of the path at both ends were mulberry trees. As with so much else at the bank, they were both decorative and symbolic. The earliest form of paper money was produced in seventh century China and printed on paper made of beaten mulberry bark. The trees in the graveyard were emblems of the origins of paper money.

It was obvious even as they approached that there were large brown spots on the leaves of all four trees. Jack paused between the first two trees and inspected the one to his left. "Bacterial blight," he pronounced with authority.

"Wow. How do you know that? Are you big on gardening or something?"

"No. Seen it before a few years back."

"So, can it be treated?"

"It was the last time, but this looks a bit worse. When we get back upstairs I'll get you the number for the arboreal specialists we used. Are you happy to liaise directly with them?"

"Yeah, of course."

"Okay, great. Let's head back in then. I need to prep for my meeting with Rob from Finance this afternoon. He's not happy about the tenders we've received from the lift people." Jack turned to retrace their path, then stopped as he felt a butterfly tap on his right shoulder.

"Jack, could I have a chat with you?"

Jack turned to look at him. "Yes, of course. What is it?"

"It's …" Jalal broke eye contact, looked towards his feet and then quickly around over each shoulder. He looked back to Jack. "It's kind of difficult to talk about."

Jack nodded, encouraging Jalal to go on.

"Is there somewhere private we could talk?"

"I'm sure we could find a meeting room somewhere. There are bound to be some free on the fourth floor."

"No. Sorry. I mean, is there somewhere we could talk off site?"

Jack could see clearly that the younger man was troubled. "Yes. Yes, of course. Shall we go somewhere for a quiet drink after work and have a chat then?"

Relief was visible on Jalal's face immediately. "Yes. Yes, please. That would be great. Thanks Jack."

Six hours later Jack and Jalal eased themselves into their seats opposite each other in the coffee shop. The counter was at the far end of the long, narrow premises. On either side high-backed leather bench seats ran along each wall from the front to the back. In front of each were a dozen octagonal white faux marble topped dark wooden tables fixed to the floor via sturdy pedestals. A single low-backed black plastic and chrome chair was available at each two-person table. Large industrial style lights hung low from the high ceiling, set just above seated head height. The floor and some of the side pillars along the wall were covered by a hardwearing brown and beige crocodile skin patterned carpet.The air was filled with the piquant bouquet of freshly ground coffee and the gentle babble of a dozen different, quiet conversations. The walk there had been punctuated by small talk about the events of the day and had taken less than five minutes. Now, as Jalal cradled his espresso and Jack adjusted his cup of latte that Jalal had insisted on paying for, it was time to get to the point. "Right then, what can I do for you?" Jack smiled lightly, tipping his head slightly forward and to the side as he looked at his companion.

Jalal seemed to be girding himself. He looked down at his lap, inhaled deeply and gradually looked back up. "I find this kind of thing difficult. I'm a very private person, that's why I didn't want to talk at work. I don't want people to see me talking to the boss, speculating about my business." The words were coming out slowly, just audible in a voice only slightly above a whisper.

Jack nodded in encouragement, "It's okay, take your time."

"Thank you. And thank you for making time. It's my Mum." He hesitated and Jack could see his eyes were moist. Another deep breath, "My Mum has cancer. Very aggressive. Very aggressive. She's going to be having lots of treatment. It's likely that I'll need some time off to help her, but I won't know when beforehand. It's also likely that I'll be a bit distracted at work and Idris said that I should tell you. He's telling his boss today too. I know there isn't anything you can do and I don't want any kind of fuss, but I felt you needed to know."

With the dam broken the words had flooded out, and now Jalal paused. Jack eyed him sympathetically. "I'm really sorry to hear that. Really sorry. Look, don't worry about the job. At times like these family must come first. Whenever you need any time you just take it and let me know. We'll cope fine. And if there's anything else, anything else at all, you just let me know." Jack's words were heartfelt. "And of course I'll respect your privacy. If you want to tell anyone else about things its fine, but they won't hear it from me."

"Thanks, Jack. Thanks." Jalal's composure had returned, his head no longer bowed, and he looked Jack in the eye. "I knew I could count on you."

"Really, it's nothing. I'm just sorry there isn't more that I can do to help. By the way, on that last point – is it okay for me to discuss this with Bob? Not that I plan to. I ask just in case he raises it with me." Jalal had mentioned his brother Idris, a year or two older than him and reputedly a superstar in the IT department. His boss was Bob Malcolm, a colleague Jack regarded as a good friend.

Jalal continued with eye contact, "Of course. Idris says Bob is a good guy, but a bit of a chatterbox sometimes. It's fine for you to talk to him if he wants. Thanks for checking." His eyes flicked momentarily upward over Jack's shoulder, as though something had attracted his attention.

"As I say, it's nothing."

Jack's phone rang inappropriately loudly and his hand automatically moved towards his left-hand jacket pocket. Jalal looked at his wristwatch and then back to Jack, whose hand was fumbling in his pocket. "Jack thanks, I didn't mean to keep you. I know you've got the kids to get back to. I'd better go and let you take that."

"No, no. It's fine." Jack waved his right hand to indicate there was no rush as he struggled to check caller ID in his left.

"No, honestly." Jalal had already risen. He leaned forward, touching Jack lightly on his right shoulder. "Thank you. I really appreciate your support. You better answer that. I'll see you in the office tomorrow." With that he smiled, turned and started to make towards the exit.

Jack focused on the 'phone display. *Unknown*. He pressed

green to accept and lifted it to his ear.

*"Is that Mr. Jack Laidlaw?"*

"Speaking."

*"Good. How are you today?"* Clearly spoken, with an accent Jack found hard to place, other than Northern.

"I'm very well, thank you. Who is this please?"

*"Mr. Morrison, I am calling you in connection with your mortgage lender misselling you Payment Protection Insurance. I wanted ..."*

"Stop right there. I don't have PPI and I've never had PPI. How did you get this number?"

*"I'm sorry. There must be an error in our records."*

"Sorry, how did you get this number?" But the caller was gone. Jack looked at his 'phone, mildly irritated. This was a work issued 'phone. His Mum, the kids and their school had the number along with colleagues and business contacts. Nobody else. He'd never had any personal nuisance calls on it before. There were plenty of unsolicited callers looking to do business in a professional capacity, but never personal. The raw emotion Jalal had shared, the abruptness with which the conversation ended and the unexpected nature of the call that had interrupted the conversation combined to somewhat throw Jack. He rose from his seat to leave and clumsily barged another customer who stumbled under the unexpected assault on her balance and fell forward. The woman's left hand grabbed the seat of a chair on the way down, her right thrust in front of her towards the floor, and she managed to land on her knees without sprawling her full length. The bag she was carrying landed in front of her and a purse, a set of keys and a small packet of tissue papers spilled out. As she fell the woman had let out a little yelp of surprise and a few heads had turned. Jack leaned forward in a futile and unseen gesture of help, "I am so sorry. Can I help you?'

"I'm fine, I'm fine." She didn't turn to look at him, instead staying on her knees and reaching forward to retrieve the scattered contents of her bag. Instinctively, Jack reached down for the tissues and proffered them to his victim.

The woman returned her purse and keys to her bag and turned

to accept the tissues. For the first time she looked up at Jack, "Thank you."

"I'm so sorry. I wasn't looking. Can I help you up? Please?" Jack offered his right hand, which she grasped and used for leverage to pull herself to her feet. She swayed slightly unsteadily. "Are you all right? Perhaps you should sit down for a moment?"

"Yes," she turned towards the chair Jack had vacated, "perhaps. Just for a moment. I think I may have got up a bit too quickly." She sat down, placing her bag in her lap. Jack took the seat opposite her, "Can I get you anything? Coffee? A glass of water?"

"No. Thank you, no. I'm fine."

Jack looked closely at her, checking to see that she was indeed fine. Her hair was thick raven, cut boyishly short. Large brown eyes, high cheekbones, a long, thin nose and a wide mouth with full lips graced a flawless olive complexion. Careful, subtly applied make up enhanced nature's gifts and Jack registered for the first time that the woman was genuinely beautiful. He took her to be five or so years younger than him, maybe even late twenties, and was trying to work out what, aside from her beauty, was intriguing about her.

Their eyes met. Her expression became quizzical. "Do I know you?"

"I don't think so. No. Well, at least, I don't think that I know you."

Her face was a study in concentration, appraising him. "Are you from Ilford?'

"Yes. Well Gant's Hill, but yes, near enough." Wrong footed.

"Jack? Jack something?"

"Well yes actually. Jack Laidlaw." Bewildered.

"Valentines High School."

"Yes. Yes that's right. Look, I'm embarrassed because I knocked you over just now. And now I'm even more embarrassed because it looks like I should know you. Please. Help me out here. Put me out of my misery." He raised his eyebrows, inviting her to take pity.

She broke into a wide smile, flashing perfect teeth. "Jack

Laidlaw. That's right. I don't think I'd have got your second name. And I don't think you'll remember me at all. Ayesha. I'm Ayesha Alfarsi. We were in the same year at Valentines High."

Jack stared at her in a manner that would have been downright rude, were it not legitimised by their conversation. Only mildly perturbed on the surface, he was frantically dredging his memory banks, desperate for some recollection that might provide a fig leaf. The name did ring a vague bell, but that was all.

"It's all right, Jack," still smiling. "It's the best part of twenty years ago. I left Valentines when I was sixteen. My family moved because of my Dad's job and I had to do sixth form at my new school."

"I think I do remember your name, but …."

"But you don't remember me." No chiding or disappointment. The tone was kind, gentle. "The last time you saw me I would have been in school uniform, hair down to my shoulders, big heavy black framed specs and with more metal and plastic in my mouth than teeth. I'll be honest, I'm relieved that you don't recognise me."

Jack was struggling to reconcile the attractive woman opposite him with the barely remembered girl that she was describing and he was trying so hard to remember. "Ayesha Alfarsi. You were smart. Really smart. I remember that. And you captained the hockey team. And the netball team."

"Yes. Yes, that's right. I'm flattered you think I was smart. And I'm flattered you remember me. You were captain of the football team."

"No, afraid not. I played in the team, but Sammy Nelson was captain. You don't remember Sammy, do you?"

"Tall kid? Gangly, red hair?"

"Yes, that's right. That's him. Now he really could play. Went on to have a career as a pro. Played in the lower leagues for a while."

Both were leaning forward, animated by the pleasure of shared recollection.

"What are the chances?" Ayesha stopped, four words a perfect summary.

"I know, I know. I've only ever been in this place twice before. And I only came in just now because a work colleague wanted a chat."

"I've never been in here before. I fancied a coffee and this was the first place I passed. It looked okay, and so here I am," another wide, easy smile.

"Anyway, you mentioned a work colleague. I take it you work around here?"

"Well yes, actually. I'm with the Bank of England, the Old Lady herself."

"Sounds like you've done all right for yourself. Well done."

"Don't get me wrong, I'm not some high-flying City type. I'm responsible for FM – facilities management - for the bank. It's not remotely glamorous, but it is a job I enjoy. What about you?"

'I'm what people seem to call 'between jobs' at the moment. I've been working abroad for a while, but want to come back to the UK. I've only been back just over a week, and I'm looking for work. That's where I've been today – having an interview."

"How did it go?" Jack hoped she didn't notice his surreptitious glance at his watch.

"Fine, I think. They said they'd get back to me within a week. Do you need to be somewhere?"

She'd clocked him. Jack's default mode was honesty, "Sorry, yes, but not yet. I need to get home in time to take my son to Cubs, but I don't need to rush off just yet."

"Well, if you're sure?" She paused for Jack's confirmatory nod. "So you have a son. A family? How wonderful. Do tell."

"Ollie, my son, is six. Full of mischief and fun. Fi is nine and the apple of her daddy's eye."

"They sound great. And what about their Mum, your wife. Or partner, maybe?"

"My wife, Debs," Jack hesitated. He had never had to discuss it with anyone who didn't already know. Friends, family, work colleagues, the police, neighbours – they all knew what had happened to her. "My wife Debs died last year."

Ayesha leaned closer. Unconsciously, her hand reached across the table and her fingers rested gently on the back of

Jack's hand. "Oh, Jack, I'm so sorry."

"It's okay, it's okay. I just realised, I think you might be the first person I've mentioned it to who didn't already know. It seems strange. You'd think I'd have had to tell someone else before now."

"I really am sorry. Had she been ill? Or maybe you'd rather not talk about it."

"She wasn't ill. She was," another pause, "she was in an accident. But, yes, let's not talk about it."

"No, no. You're right. Look, you're making me feel really guilty about making you late getting home to see your children. I really shouldn't delay you."

"Have I scared you off, talking about my troubles?" Jack attempted a half-hearted smile.

"Not at all. I just really don't want to be the cause of Ollie missing Cubs."

"Honestly, I'm okay for a few more minutes. I know the train timetable off by heart. Anyway, enough about me. What about you? Are you married, or with someone?"

"Me, no. Afraid not," smiling again, "I'm a confirmed old maid."

With her looks, Jack mused, she would only be an old maid through choice. "I must say I find that hard to believe."

"Believe it or not, it's true," a quick glance at her watch to divert the conversation. "Look Jack, this has been a most unexpected, pleasant surprise. But you've got a train to catch, I've got a tube to catch and it looks like they're getting ready to close up in here anyway. Maybe we can catch up again sometime."

"Yes, yes that would be good," Jack fumbled for the 'phone from his jacket pocket, "maybe we could exchange numbers?"

"Good idea."

"No. Actually ehm, well yes we should exchange numbers, but we should firm something up too. You know how these things work. You meet somebody, agree it would be good to meet again, and then never do. Shall we agree something?" Jack looked at her expectantly, "Unless you'd rather not? Oh God," his voice trailed off, strangled by indecision and sudden embarrassment.

"What is it?"

"Sorry, I'm rambling. I'm being presumptuous and putting you in an awkward position."

Ayesha leaned forward and again put her fingers on top of his hand. "Jack, I'm a big girl. I said I thought it was a good idea to exchange 'phone numbers, and I meant it. I also think you're right, and that we should firm up on something. Most of my family and friends are in Manchester, so it would be good to have someone to talk to in London."

"Great," relief coursed through him like a cocaine hit, "how about tomorrow?"

A fleeting look of surprise was banished by another of her frequent smiles, "Oh, okay then. Why not?"

"Sorry, am I doing it again?"

"What?"

"I'm railroading you again, sorry. I'm not usually like this, honestly."

"Jack, it's fine. Really. Tomorrow works for me, and I think it could be fun. So relax. No one's being railroaded."

"Okay. If you're sure."

"I'm sure. So where, and what time?"

"Oh, how about Braithwaites? And does seven o' clock work for you?"

"Seven works fine. Where is Braithwaites, and what is it?"

"Sorry. It's a bar on Panton Street, just round the corner from the International hotel. We could meet there for a drink and then go on for a bite somewhere. If that's all right with you?"

"Sounds like a plan to me," another huge smile. "Now we both have connections to make and you've got to be home for your son. We better be going." She got to her feet; bag clutched in both hands, and turned towards the exit door. Jack followed, taking care to ensure that he didn't bump her again.

Once out on to the pavement they exchanged goodbyes and a final confirmation of arrangements for the following day before heading in opposite directions towards their respective stations. After twenty or so paces Jack paused, looked back, and watched until Ayesha disappeared round the corner. He cursed himself as he realised they had forgotten to actually exchange 'phone numbers. Or perhaps Ayesha hadn't forgotten. Maybe she hadn't wanted him to have her number. Maybe he would never see her again. Shit.

In bed that night he found his mind kept returning to Ayesha Alfarsi. He felt guilt at his disloyalty to Debs. It was just an old acquaintance from school, nothing more. He resisted the temptation to Google her name or search for her profile on Facebook. But the thoughts crossed his mind. Eventually, as always, he managed to fall asleep.

## Chapter 13

Jack looked at his watch again. He felt awkward, perched on a tall black leather-and-chrome barstool, beside the glass-topped bar, under lit by blue neon. He'd been there for fifteen minutes already and was still a further ten minutes early for the seven o' clock rendezvous, assuming that Ayesha was actually going to come. He'd never been to Braithwaites before and had suggested it on the spur of the moment based on an overheard conversation at the bank between two girls in their twenties, where one had described it as "classy". Rather than elegant, he had formed the view that it was chichi and overpriced. Sparse, muted lighting delivered gloominess rather than sophistication, and the fact that the background music comprised Nat Cole classics being sung by an anonymous cover artist was just cheap. The superior attitude of the white DJ'd barman would have irked Jack even more, had he not been feeling so nervous about seeing her again. A bunch of eight or so office drones, the only other customers, joshed and chattered leaving noises as they exited their booth in the far corner and headed towards the door. Jack silently lamented their departure as he imagined dispiritedly how she might react to meeting him in an empty bar.

"Jack, Jack!" A tap on his shoulder caught him unawares, causing him to turn. "Jack, I thought it was you."

"Hazza! Good to see you. You took me by surprise." Jack looked down from his perch at Harry, at twenty-two the youngest of Debs' three younger brothers. He had always been Debs' favourite and so had also automatically been Jack's favourite too. Jack slipped off the barstool and leaned forward to shake Harry's hand, only to be pulled into a man hug by his much shorter counterpart. As they each stepped back, Jack was struck by how much Harry looked like Ollie, all fair hair, big teeth and smiles.

A couple of the others Harry was with were loitering by the door, waiting. Harry turned, "It's OK guys, just catching up with my brother-in-law. See you all on Monday." Turning back, "So, how are you? You're looking well."

"I'm fine, Harry. I'm good. You're looking good too. You won't believe how much Ollie looks like you now."

"Yeah?" Harry beamed, then glanced down quietly at his moccasins before looking back up, eyes apologetic. "Look Jack, I'm really sorry I've not been round since the funeral. I keep meaning to, but then something always seems to come up."

"It's not a problem, Harry, honestly. I remember what it's like to be twenty-two and young, free and single – so no pressure to come round. Of course you're welcome anytime. The kids would be delighted to see you. Me as well. But really there's no pressure."

Harry seemed relieved and his smile returned. "I will get round soon, I will. It'd be good to see the kids again, and I'm sure they must miss their favourite uncle."

"You're not catching me out like that!" A pause, as a thought formed, "Harry, does the name Vic mean anything to you?"

A quizzical tilt of the head and a slight furrowing of the brow. "As it happens, yeah. There was a lad who used to turn out for our five-a-sides. Mind you he's a proper weapons-grade mentalist. Used to kick anything that moved – always in trouble. He got banged up a year ago. GBH on some geezer outside a nightclub. Why you asking?"

"Oh, nothing really. Bit of a long shot. I found the name Vic in Debs' contacts and didn't recognise it. Just wondered whether you could shed any light on it."

"Sorry, no. Except I'm pretty sure it's not the bloke I've just mentioned. Debs would definitely not approve of him. Anyway, what are you doing in this place?"

"Oh, I'm just meeting someone." A sense of guilt, and a quick glance at his watch combined to almost choke him as he saw it was less than three minutes before seven. "Was that work colleagues you were with?"

"Yeah. We always stop off for a few jars after work on a Friday – you know how it is. Anyway, who is it you're meeting?"

"Just a friend. Not anyone you'd know."

"Well, I hope they get here soon."

"What do you mean? Why?"

"Don't you know about this place, Jack? It's cool as an after work boozer for a couple of hours, but then it's where top end hookers and escorts meet up with their clients to have a drink before heading off to the International round the corner. The hotel doesn't like meet-ups in its bar so they get together here instead then go round there and book in as Mr. and Mrs. Whatever."

Jack's blood chilled as he listened, then glaciated as he saw Ayesha dazzle through the doorway. She was wearing a short navy jacket over a white cotton tee shirt, above a pair of pale mint jeans. Navy four-inch heels matched her handbag and boosted her height to five foot ten. Her complexion was as perfect as he remembered, and her hair possibly even more lustrous. Her whole appearance a marriage of subtlety and style.

Harry's eye followed Jack's gaze, and confusion spread over his face as Ayesha stepped gracefully toward them, smiling. "Jack, I hope I haven't kept you waiting."

"No. No, not at all. You're right on time."

"And I see you already have company." Ayesha nodded and smiled down at Harry.

"Oh, yes. Sorry. This is Harry – Debs' youngest brother."

"I'm very pleased to meet you, Harry." Ayesha proffered her hand, which Harry shook softly and quickly.

"Well look, I'd best be off now. The old folks will be wanting to know what's delayed me." He looked Jack in the eye as he spoke, and then turned.

"Please don't go on my account."

"I was just going anyway – honestly. I must dash. Jack, you look after those kids and tell them I was asking after them." Harry smiled and was gone.

Jack looked at Ayesha. She tipped her forehead slightly and fixed him with an inquisitive eye. "Are you okay, Jack?"

"Sorry. Yes, yes, I'm fine. It's just that I haven't seen Harry since the funeral, and then this place, and then you. And I wasn't even sure that you were coming…" The stream of consciousness spilled out and he immediately reproached himself inwardly. "Sorry, I'm babbling. God, what a terrible impression you must be getting."

"It's fine," she smiled gently taking his right hand lightly in her left. "You don't need to worry about making an impression. And if it makes you feel any better, I was worried that you might not be here after us not actually exchanging 'phone numbers in the end. Now, shall we have a drink here or just head off to the restaurant?"

Relief and gratitude jigged for joy in his heart and he smiled back at her. "Let's go," he said. "I'm led to believe that we probably don't want to be here after happy hour."

"I'm not sure what you mean," fixing him with a quizzical eye, "But I'm hungry, so that sounds good."

"I'll explain to you later. But first things first. What do you like to eat? Italian, Indian, Greek, French, Chinese – something else?"

"Can I be cheeky?"

"Sure, go on."

"There's a Lebanese place I passed on the way here from the tube station. I had a quick glance at the menu in the window and it looked really good."

"Sounds great – lead on."

She held his hand lightly in hers as she led him, laughing easily and naturally as he explained about Braithwaites. Despite it being Friday night and the restaurant already over three quarters full, they were able to get a well-positioned table for two in a corner of the further back of two separate dining areas. A profusion of plants, seating on different levels, mosaic-tiled walls and subtle lighting combined with exquisitely dressed tables to provide an ambience that managed to be elegant and exotic whilst also feeling intimate and relaxed. The waiter left them with the menus and wine list, which Ayesha talked Jack through. There was no superiority or showing off involved, but it was clear that she knew what she was talking about.

"So, you're a fan of Lebanese food then?"

"Absolutely. I've been working in Paris for the last three years and, despite what everyone says about French cuisine, the best food I had there was Lebanese. There were two outstanding restaurants that I would alternate between each week. I absolutely love it."

"I've had Lebanese a few times and I do enjoy it, although I'd be lying if I said anything other than I'm a true Brit at heart. I can't see past a really good lamb bhuna."

A smiled response, "I'm partial to Indian food too. In fact there's not much that I don't eat really, although I'm much more of a savoury girl than sweet."

"Cheeky," he grinned. "Anyway, Paris? Sounds very glam."

"It was. I had an apartment in SoPi," she registered his blank look, "South Pigalle, just below Montmartre, in the north of the city. It's very lively – loads of gourmet shops, bars and restaurants, as well as some fabulous monumental architecture. It also had the Metro nearby, which meant I could commute to work in La Défense in under half an hour."

"And what was work?"

"I'm an economist. I was doing economic modelling and forecasting for an insurance company there. Quite interesting work, and enjoyable. But not that glamorous." The conversation was interrupted by the waiter enquiring whether they were ready to order. Deferring to Ayesha's unmistakeable expertise, Jack was happy to make the same selections as her; a mezze selection for starters and Lahem Meshwi for mains, with a Chateau Musar.

"So, what made you decide to come back? You said you were job hunting."

"No one thing really. A combination of a whole lot of factors just meant that now was the right time to come back to the UK. Anyway, enough about me for now. Tell me about you."

"What do you want to know?"

"I don't know. Everything you think is important in twenty seconds."

Jack grinned and took a deep breath. "I got an opportunity to join the FM team at the Bank of England, which sounded a bit off the wall. But I took it as a way to get back to London from the sticks and found I absolutely loved it. Got promoted to run the department after five years and I've been doing that ever since. Met Debs the week I started at the Bank and we were married within six months. Two fantastic kids: Fi who's nine going on nineteen sometimes, and Ollie who is six. I like football, architecture, sci-fi and rock music. Oh, and I'm nearly thirty-six years old and I live with my Mum." Pause for another theatrical deep breath. "How did I do?"

"Eighteen seconds. Well done."

"Okay, your turn now."

"I think I've probably got two second's worth at most."

"Come on now, fair's far. Your time begins now!" Jack flourished his watch over the table before bringing it right up to his nose.

"Right. When I graduated, I got taken on by one of the big US consulting firms and spent three years training with them. I discovered that the insurance sector was surprisingly interesting and joined Chartered Municipal. I was based out of London, but spent almost all of my time on assignments abroad. I stayed with CM for over seven years, before I decided to move to France. That's where I've been for the last three years. And now it's back home to the UK for a new chapter. Oh, and I like tennis, Jane Austen, Sudoku and most classical music. How did I do?" Ayesha nodded towards Jack's wristwatch.

"Sorry, you've over-run by almost two seconds. Not really acceptable I'm afraid, but I suppose it shows that you've had a more interesting life that I've managed."

"Oh, come on now! How can you accuse someone who's spent the last ten years working in insurance of being interesting?"

They both laughed and Jack could sense the mood was good. The conversation rolled easily and the jitters he had experienced when anticipating potential stilted small talk were totally banished. The starters arrived and proved as delicious as Ayesha had promised. But it was the wine that was the real revelation.

"This stuff is fantastic,' Jack held his glass between them. "I've never tasted anything quite like this."

"I'm so glad you like it. It's my favourite red wine in all the world, and not really like anything else I've tasted either. It's a real Marmite of a wine – love or hate, with no in between. It also varies considerably between vintages, which is reflected in the price. This is one of the better years, but still not too pricey."

"I defer to your obvious expertise. What I can say with one hundred per cent confidence is that I am in the 'love it' camp. Where exactly is it from?" he picked up the bottle to study the label. "Lebanese. Makes sense, I guess, given we're in a Lebanese restaurant. I had no idea you could get wine from the Lebanon. Especially not wine as fantastic as this."

"I think it's from the Bekaa valley. They do some other wines, including a white I think, but this is the one for me. Anyway, enjoy." Ayesha raised her glass in salute and Jack responded in kind. They continued to chat easily and evenly, neither dominant, and each attentive to what the other had to say. Old school mates, music, food, holidays, politics, reading preferences, football, travel and university anecdotes fox-trotted between them. The Lahem Meshwi arrived, simple and succulent, along with another bottle of wine.

Jack, who was drinking more quickly, topped up both glasses from the new bottle for the second time. "This is a fantastic meal. Really delicious. Great choice."

"The secret of the most successful meals is the conversation and the company. Good food is just a bonus."

Flattered, and emboldened by wine, Jack fixed eye contact, "Do you mind if I ask you something?"

"Go ahead."

"In everything we've talked about, discussed, you've never mentioned anyone, you know, 'special'."

For the first time, there was a pause. Ayesha's chin tilted down slightly, she held his gaze with her eyebrows slightly raised, but said nothing.

"Oh God, I'm sorry. That was very forward of me. I'm really, really sorry. I shouldn't have asked."

"No, no it's okay. It's a perfectly natural question and I know that it must seem strange that I haven't said anything about 'relationships', particularly when you've been so open about Debs and your feelings. I've avoided speaking about it because – I don't know – maybe I feel awkward discussing it."

"Then please don't. As I say, I shouldn't have asked."

"No honestly, it's fine." Another pause. "It's kind of a quirk of mine that I have to be honest. Always." She looked at him for understanding and was grateful for his nod of encouragement. "I think it's to do with how I was brought up - *Always tell the truth Ayesha*. It's all very well in principle, but sometimes it's better or easier to say nothing. And that's generally what I do if it avoids confrontation or awkwardness. But then there are times, like now, when I realise that I have to be more open."

"You really don't have to say anything, honestly."

Ayesha put down her cutlery, picked up her glass in her right hand and took a small sip. She placed the glass back down, lowered both hands into her lap, breathed in deeply, glanced down at her hands, and then up at Jack. "I was married. Charles – Charlie – Thorburn. I met him at CM. We joined at around the same time, both regarded as high-fliers, often sent on the same assignments. Within two years we were married, CM's 'golden couple', with the world at our feet. Except it didn't stay that wonderful. We tried for kids and discovered that I can't have them. I suppose that put some kind of strain on our relationship. Anyway, one afternoon I arrived home a day early from a job in Madrid to find him in bed with someone I had regarded as a close friend. That was it. I had to get out. I had to get out of that marriage. I had to get out of CM. And I had to get out of London."

Jack could see the pain her story caused her and understood why she hadn't volunteered it earlier. He felt he should reach out to her but, like a seasoned priest in the confessional, he sensed there was more to come and stayed silent.

Ayesha continued to switch her eyes from him to her hands and back. "So I moved. I took a job with an anonymous French insurer – career suicide – and moved to Paris. My Spanish was passable, but my French was good. Also, Charlie's French was poor, so CM rarely assigned him to France. I was much less likely to come across him professionally if I was in France. CM didn't hold me to my notice period. Three weeks after I caught Charlie, I had my apartment in SoPi and was in my new job. I met Gaston, and six weeks later he moved in with me. We both knew, that way you just *know*, that we were each other's soul mates. I loved him with an intensity and a joy that almost made me burst. I had never known happiness like it and I even felt grateful to Charlie for driving me out, otherwise I'd never have met Gaston. We had the happiest two years of both our lives. Then one day I got a 'phone call at work to say that he was dead. Just like that, completely out of the blue. Running up some stairs on his way to work. Heart attack. He was thirty-two years old and in perfect health – or so we thought. The post mortem showed that he had a congenital hole in his heart and could have gone at any time." A brief pause, eyes closed, and a victory in the contest to maintain composure. "I didn't handle it well at all. I suffered a bit of a break down. My employer supported me really well and I did go back to work eventually. But I had already decided that I would be going back to the UK when my contract ended. Everything about being in France just reminded me of Gaston and what I had lost."

Ayesha's voice was even, calm almost. But there were tears in her eyes and Jack's hand instinctively reached out to her. She took it and squeezed.

"Ayesha, I am so sorry."

"Trust me to bring the mood down," she sniffed and attempted a smile. "I'm sorry to get so worked up. I thought I'd compartmentalised it and was dealing okay with it – but obviously not."

"I do have an idea of what you've been through. And I know how hard it can be to talk about it."

"I know you understand. I've just surprised myself at how raw it still feels when I talk about it."

"It's like not talking about it means it's not true. Then when you do speak about it, it makes it all real again. I do know, and I'm sorry for raising it."

"No, it really is all right. Everyone says that it's good to talk about it. I saw a counsellor in France and she said that talking about it would be painful at first, but that it would help me if I did. And actually, now that I've told you, now that you know, it does feel like a bit of a relief."

Jack continued to hold her hand over the table. He had seen a grief counsellor himself for almost four months and she had been a godsend. Although he himself was still healing, he did understand how powerful and helpful talking therapies could be. She squeezed his hand firmly for a second, then let it go, withdrawing her own. "Anyway, we said to each other that it would be fun to catch up properly. We seem to be overdosing on the catching up, but maybe neglecting the fun. Let's talk about something more cheerful. Tell me all about Fi and Ollie - they must be fun at those ages."

Normal service was resumed and the conversation returned to its previous lighter tone. But the depth of understanding and compassion was greater on both sides. Ayesha was beautiful, exotic, *very* smart, kind, funny and charming. But she was also damaged and vulnerable in a way he recognised too well. She had opened her heart to him, really still a virtual stranger. He felt privileged, and connected to her.

The sense prevailed that both wanted the evening to continue and they indulged themselves with baklava and numerous coffees before eventually settling the bill, which Ayesha insisted they go Dutch on. They left a generous tip and exited the restaurant into the mild evening and quiet streets.

"You need to head that way for Bank and I go this way for Mansion House," Ayesha indicated the opposing directions with nods of her head.

"I'll walk you to Mansion House first."

"That's very gallant of you, but really there's no need."

"I rather think there is," Jack feigned mock outrage. "I am Sir Galahad, fine lady, and for the sake of your reputation – and mine for that matter – I insist that I escort you to your station. I regard this mission as much my destiny as pursuit of the Holy Grail."

Ayesha's resistance liquefied into laughter. They had both been taught, separately and more than two decades previously, by the same gifted Arthurian-legend besotted English teacher. "All right great knight, this weak and feeble maiden is honoured to accept your valiant protection." She offered her left hand. Jack lunged forward on to one knee, took her hand in his and kissed it, simultaneously turning his other arm in an exaggerated flourish. Ayesha struggled to help him back to his feet, both of them weakened by wine and laughter. In other circumstances the whole episode could have been unbearably cheesy, but the alcohol, the mood and their shared experience made it natural and funny. Giddy and giggly, hand holding and high spirits accompanied their banter as they completed their leisurely stroll. The journey to the corner of Queen Victoria Street and Garlick Hill was over too soon.

"I've had a really great evening Jack, thanks."

"Me too. I can't remember enjoying myself – and laughing – so much in ages."

"We should exchange numbers. Keep in touch. Maybe arrange to do something else together again?"

"I'd really like that."

"Here's my 'phone," Ayesha passed it to Jack who keyed his number in and returned it. She called him and ended it immediately, so her number was in missed calls and the exchange was complete. "Is it easier for you to call me?"

"Probably, yes. When would be best for you?"

"I don't want to seem like a saddo Jack, but I'm pretty new back in town, unemployed and at a loose end lots of the time. Any time that's good for you is good for me." She leaned forward on her tiptoes and kissed him on his right cheek. A slight adjustment, and they were kissing fully on the lips. The kiss lingered for just a few seconds – long enough without being too long.

Ayesha stepped back, eyes holding his, smiling hope and happiness and promise. Rumbling from below signalled the approach of a train. Another step backwards, "I better run. Promise to give me a call." Jack nodded, returning her smile, and perished just a little as she turned and dashed down the stairs.

He turned, took a couple of dizzy steps, and leaned on the brown-flecked marble effect fascia of the station wall. The alcohol already in his system was turbocharged by the tsunami cocktail of dopamine, oxytocin, phenylethylamine, epinephrine, norepinephrine and endorphins. He could run a four-minute marathon. Swim the Channel even quicker. And outsprint Usain Bolt backwards. He felt euphoric, invincible. He felt happy. The thirty-minute tube journey from Bank to Gants Hill took thirty seconds.

In bed that night, Jack's efforts to find sleep were once again thwarted by thoughts of Ayesha, even more pervasive than before, filling his mind like groundcover. He replayed scenes from the evening over and over, always ending with the image of her smile as she turned to go for her train. The feelings of guilt about Debs were still there, but more muted, smothered and choked by the new arrival. Another seed had also taken root, Jack's very own magical beanstalk. When he awoke the next morning, he would find that it had grown into the realisation that he had a chance to be genuinely happy again.

## Chapter 14

"This channel is 82% secure. Adopt the appropriate protocol."

"Understood."

"Report please."

"Things appear to be going well. I am comfortably inside the tent now. I have their confidence sufficiently that I am integral to their plan and have engaged with the mark."

"And what *is* their plan exactly?"

"They haven't shared that with me yet. I'm not sure how clear they are in their own minds. It may be that they're waiting to see how successful my engagement with the mark is."

"And how successful will it be?"

"It will be fine. No worries on that score. The research and briefings were excellent. I am very credible."

"Good. So why don't you know more about their plan."

"As I said, I'm not sure how clear they are about it yet – at least not the details. Also, it's me who's on the inside. I'm the one who has to decide what to ask and when. It's my judgement."

"Of course. Sorry."

"It's okay. This is just going to take time. I need to further integrate myself with them by developing my engagement with the mark to the extent that I become indispensable."

"Understood. Keep us posted."

"Will do."

"Good luck and goodbye."

"Thanks. Goodbye."

## Chapter 15

"So it is going well?"

"Yes brother, like I told you it would. Relax."

"And our sister is … all right?"

"Yes. She's fine. She really doesn't mind."

"But how can she compromise herself, her values, like this?"

"Don't be so naïve."

"How am I being naïve?"

"We all have to handle conflicting priorities from time to time. When that happens, we have to decide which priority best serves the greater good and go with that. That is all our sister is doing."

"That's what we're doing too, isn't it?"

"Yes. Yes it is."

## Chapter 16

Jack was contemplating getting himself a coffee when his desk 'phone rang.

"Bet you're thinking about having a coffee."

Jack smiled as he recognised the distinctive, sonorous voice. "You must be a mind reader, Bob. Or maybe I really am as predictable and boring as you keep telling me."

"Oh come on now, I mentioned it once – in a very particular context – and you keep harping on about it. Leaving that to one side, do you fancy some company with your coffee."

"That'd be nice actually. Yes. I'll call by the coffee cart on the way down and meet you in the canteen. Skinny latte isn't it?"

"As always. I'll see you there in five."

Jack collected the skinny latte and a cappuccino, and made his way to the canteen. He picked a table by the wall and took his seat facing the doorway so he could catch Bob's eye when he arrived. He didn't have to wait long as, less than thirty seconds later, Bob Malcolm strode through the doorway and waved to signify he'd seen Jack. He was tall, around six two, and lean. His grey hair was thick and cropped short. Crisp Cambridge blue shirt with a navy tie. Understated white gold tiepin and matching cuff links in double cuffs. Silver buckled black leather belt for aesthetic purposes only. Razor creased navy and chalk pinstriped suit trousers. Brioni black leather Derby brogues. And a huge smile. He carried his fifty-one years lightly and could easily pass for ten years younger. His positive outlook and cheerful disposition made him one of those people that others enjoy being around, and Jack liked him enormously. They originally met when Bob had been running a multi-disciplinary project team that Jack was assigned to in his first week at the bank. Despite the notable gap in both age and rank they had formed a friendship that had endured and grown over the years. Jack and Debs had been guests when Bob married his long-term partner, Edward, in June 2014. Bob and Edward had been mourners at Debs' funeral.

"So, how is the world's greatest CIO?" Jack pushed the skinny latte across the table as Bob took his seat.

"Thanks. Can't complain. Continuing to make my own humble contribution to the good of the people of the UK by supporting monetary and financial stability. And how about you old chap, how is the world of canteens and toilets?"

"I can safely report that the nation's economic well-being will not be undermined by poor sanitation or a lack of decent grub at this bank."

"Relieved to hear it. Jolly good show." Bob's voice softened, "And how about you dear boy? How are you?"

"I'm well - really well, thanks. I've just started seeing someone recently. It's very early days, but things are going well."

"I see. Well, I can't pretend not to be surprised, but I'm pleased to hear it. Do I know her? Does she work here?"

"No, you don't know her and she doesn't work here. She's someone I was at school with that I bumped into unexpectedly."

"And she's someone who makes you happy. I can tell by your smile when you talk about her. Does she have a name?"

"Ayesha. Ayesha Alfarsi. It's early days but yes, she does make me smile."

"Good. I'm delighted. When you think the time is right let me know and Edward and I will have you both round to dinner."

"That's very kind – thank you. I'll have a chat with her and let you know."

"Splendid. And how are Fi and Ollie?"

"Both well thanks. They still miss Debs of course, and there's the odd tough moment from time to time. But generally they are in really good form and both seem happy."

"That's good to hear. You know that if there's ever anything Edward or I can do to help out that you only need ask."

"I know that Bob, and I really appreciate it. But we're fine just now."

"Excellent. Well, I suppose we should probably also have a quick chat about a different pair of siblings."

"I take it you mean Idris and Jalal. Terribly sad news about their mother."

"Absolutely. Do you know how she's doing? Idris told me the news, but hasn't said anything more to me since. One doesn't wish to pry for fear of causing upset, but equally it's important he knows that we care and will be supportive in any way we can."

"I'm afraid I don't know how she's doing. My situation's the same as yours. Jalal told me about her condition but hasn't mentioned it since. I don't know Jalal as well as I'd like, but I do know that he's very private and that he finds discussing this really hard. I had a discreet word with Martha about Jalal and she's agreed to keep an eye out for him too. She'll feed back if she sees or hears anything."

"They're an interesting pair. Idris has worked for me for almost three years now. It was a real coup for us to get him. He'd been in the retail-banking sector, which one would have thought would put him out of our price range, but we got him anyway. He is the most prodigiously talented software professional I've come across in my three decades in the industry."

"I knew you rated him highly, but I hadn't appreciated it was to quite that degree."

"One has to protect one's jewels. Idris worked part-time last year on a project some of my team were working on jointly with others from the Information Security Division. Next thing I knew the buggers were trying to poach him."

"I can imagine your horror at the prospect of your star joining Hannah Hamilton's Infosec mob," grinned Jack. Hannah Hamilton was Bob's talented high-flying counterpart who had achieved the dizzy heights of Chief Information Security Officer at the age of just thirty-eight. Her meteoric career was built on ability, prodigious hard work, great personal charm and the ability to attract some of the most gifted and able people to join her team. She mainly recruited from outside, but also had a track record of cherry picking from Bob's division.

"Quite. Hannah obviously knows about Idris already, but there's no point in me broadcasting to all and sundry just how brilliant he is."

"Is he really *that* good?"

"Yes. Yes, he is. Strictly entre nous, I have a theory." Although no one else was seated anywhere near them and they could not be overheard, Bob leaned forward and lowered his voice. "I've been doing a fair amount of reading and a little bit of research. I think Idris might be a savant. I'm not qualified enough to speculate whether he has autism or Asperger's Syndrome, but I suspect that he has one or other of those conditions."

"What, like the Dustin Hoffman character in *Rain Man*?"

"In some ways yes, and others no. What I mean is that Idris is incredibly talented in the same way as that character, but he is unlike him insofar as his social skills are very much less limited. I strongly suspect that he's what is regarded as very highly functioning. That is, at first glance or on first meeting him, you wouldn't be able to tell that he's anything other than perfectly normal. However, once you've met him a few times or spent a reasonable amount of time in his company, you begin to pick up little hints."

"Little hints like what?"

"Idris isn't great socially. Typically he doesn't maintain eye contact when you speak to him and he often seems to fail to read other people's faces and gestures. It's really rather difficult to describe precisely, but the best way I can think of is to say he's just like everyone else except not quite. Does that make sense?"

"I think so. I think most of us know people a bit like that. It's quite a leap from there to thinking he's a savant though."

"That's a fair enough challenge. Part of the problem is the incredibly diverse range of ways that savant syndrome can manifest itself. You mentioned *Rain Man*. The real Rain Man was a chap called Kim Peek. He was born with severe brain damage. His doctor told his father to put the boy in an institution and forget about him on the basis that he would never be able to walk, or to learn anything. Fortunately his father ignored the advice. Kim lived to the age of fifty-eight and struggled all his life with basic motor skills. He had difficulty walking, couldn't button his shirt and always scored well below average on IQ tests. But what he *could* do was simply astonishing. He read something like twelve thousand books and was able to remember everything about them. He would read two pages at once – left eye reading the left page and right eye reading the right. It would take him three seconds to read two pages and then he would remember everything written on them. He could recall facts from over a dozen subject areas as diverse as geography, history and sport. He remembered every piece of music he ever heard."

Bob was clearly animated by his subject and his voice speeded up slightly as he spoke. Jack raised a finger in an attempt to interrupt and signify that he 'got it', but Bob's enthusiasm for his subject made him uncharacteristically oblivious to the prompt. He continued, "More recently there's the case of a man called Daniel Tammet. He's actually from your neck of the woods originally – East London, although I believe he lives in France now. He has extraordinary language and mathematical skills. He first became famous when he was able to recite Pi to over twenty thousand decimal places from memory. He says that he is able to 'see'," Bob made quotation marks in the air with his fingers, "every whole number from one to ten thousand. Every one of them has their own unique, distinctive shape, colour and texture. He speaks ten or eleven different languages. Back in 2007 he was challenged on a TV documentary to learn Icelandic in the space of a week. Seven days later he was able to give a successful interview on Icelandic television in the local language."

Bob paused again, providing an opening for Jack. "Okay, I can see you're passionate about this and that you've done your homework. But I still don't get the link to Idris."

"Savants are incredibly rare. However, they are sufficiently fascinating that quite a lot is written about many of them and I've read about dozens of them. It seems that in many cases, although not all, there is a link to brain damage in some form or another. I pulled Idris's personnel file from HR on the pretext of needing it for his appraisal and found that he suffered from epilepsy as a child. I suppose that was the clincher for me. His ability to address extreme technical challenges is unparalleled, in my experience. I don't know how he does it, and he isn't able to explain it. When he's confronted by a problem that I would regard as impossible to solve he always comes up with the goods. Sometimes it can take him just a couple of hours, sometimes days and occasionally a few weeks. But he always comes back with an answer. And it's a complete, worked-through, finished answer. Not a Beta version or a test solution – something that does what is required and just works first time. It's remarkable. Jack, it's like me saying to you: I need you to make this coffee cup float in the air," Bob held his half-drunk cup in the air between them. "Then, you coming back to me, say a week later, with a floating coffee cup. He really is able to do the most incredible things."

"I can see why you don't want Hannah to get him."

"Indeed. But this goes beyond departmental politics. This fellow has an exceptional talent and he needs to be deployed where he can do most good for the bank."

"Which of course just happens to be your Information Service and Technology Division, rather than Hannah's Infosec Division."

"Absolutely. Got it in one. Always said you were a bright one," Bob flashed a quick smile before adopting a more sober expression. "Seriously though I think we need to keep an eye out for Idris – and Jalal too. I've no idea how they're handling this or how they'll be affected when their mother dies, other than badly of course. What I mean is that, particularly with Idris being the way he is, I find it difficult to know how he's coping. Do you get any better insight with Jalal?"

"I'm afraid not. He's a very private kind of a guy. He didn't even want to tell me about his mum when we were in here. We had to go offsite for a meeting, and even then I could tell how uncomfortable it was for him. Not just the fact of his mum's illness, but having to confide in me about his private business. To be honest, Bob, I like him well enough and I'm glad to have him on my team, but – as I said - I don't really feel that I know him that well."

"I see. I know what you mean. You'll be aware that he project managed the relocation of the Plan & Design and Build & Maintain teams while you were off after Debs died."

That was another reason Jack liked Bob – the ease with which he would still mention Debs. "Yes, I know he handled that."

"And handled it really well. He was incredibly professional and followed through on every detail. I probably had either formal or informal meetings with him every day for a fortnight. His planning, organising and communication were all out of the top drawer. But despite all of the regular contact, and plenty of positive feedback from me, I never felt like I really connected with him at any sort of personal level beyond the professional."

"Interesting. And reassuring that it's not just me."

"I did spot that he's gay."

"Sorry?"

"Let me rephrase that. I'm pretty sure that he's gay, although I don't think that he's come out yet. Thinking about it now, he may not even have reconciled himself to it."

"Are you really sure about that."

"As sure as I can be. I might be wrong, but I saw enough of him to feel pretty confident. I only mention it because of what else is going on. If he is gay but isn't ready to be open about it or acknowledge it, then it's nobody's business but his. However, if he's got issues around his sexuality and he's got the stress of his mother's illness, it might mean that he's just that bit more vulnerable."

"You could be right. Thanks for mentioning it. Obviously, I won't say anything to Jalal, but at least I can bear it in mind. Looks like all we can do is keep a watching brief and be there for them whenever they need it."

"I think that's right. I'd wondered if you had managed to get closer to Jalal than I did, and if that might have been a route to getting a better understanding of how Idris is coping – but that's obviously not the case. We should just agree that if either of us learns anything useful we should let the other know."

"Agreed."

"Now then, I can't be sitting around chatting to you all morning. I'm a big, important chap you know. People to see. Solutions to provide. Worlds to save." Bob stood up grinning, empty coffee cup in his left hand. "Glad to hear you're doing all right, that you're happy," he whispered. A kingfisher-quick wink, a turn, a toss of the paper cup into the bin and he was gone.

## Chapter 17

Jack mused on how good life was. Work was going well. The kids seemed happy and were earning good reports from school. Mum's health seemed to be holding up. He had agreed to go back to the football with the lads again tomorrow, although he'd told Ayesha a white lie about that when she'd suggested going for a meal in the evening. Now Jack was enjoying his lunchtime grub at his favourite greasy spoon, in the company of the beautiful woman he was smitten with. He'd gone to lunch with Bob, then Ayesha phoned unexpectedly and explained she was nearby. Jack invited her join them and Bob, ever the diplomat, had made his excuses and left the two lovebirds together.

Jack watched Ayesha survey their environment. The café was narrow. Basic wooden tables, each partnered by four vinyl-cushioned chairs, were spaced with military precision end-on along each wall, maximising the cramped square footage. The slender passageway between ran from the red painted glass-panelled entrance door to the serving counter at the rear. There were a further pair of two-seater tables in the middle at the rear, where the space widened slightly. They were seated at one of those. The walls were as magnolia as could be, with a sombre wooden dado rail running at table height. The square tiled floors nodded to the ceiling, with its 1980s office-style dropped rectangular tiles interspersed with fluorescent lighting. A couple of coffee and tea themed prints and three large rectangular mirrors, surely chosen to complement the bland anonymity of their surroundings, were the only adornments on the otherwise naked walls. Included in the condiments on each table was a tomato shaped ketchup dispenser, complete with congealed sauce around the green leafstalk pouring spout. Every seat was taken and the thrumming chatter and sound of cutlery on china meant that individual conversations could take place with a surprising degree of privacy. "I didn't know places like this still existed. Well, certainly not in the City."

"I know. Fantastic, isn't it?"

"Hmmm," Ayesha smiled and continued with her evaluation of the surroundings. The clientele was a mixture of builders in hi-viz jackets and safety boots, and office workers in various garbs that complied with the broad guidelines for City uniform. The air was savoury and warm, despite the entrance door being propped open by a strategically placed fire extinguisher, as the high external temperature was exacerbated by the heat of cooking and over forty bodies crammed into the confined space. "Yes. Yes, it is. It's real, isn't it? You get a lot of places trying to be retro and ending up being kitsch. But you can tell this place has been around for ages."

"The real giveaway is that the food is good and honest, and the prices are rock bottom. But now you've discovered my guilty secret."

"I beg your pardon?"

"This place. Bob and I try to sneak off here at least once a fortnight and indulge in all the fantastically unhealthy food that we're not meant to eat any more. When you called to say you'd finished early and were in Finsbury Square I was in two minds about telling you where I was."

"Good job you did. If I'd found out you were two minutes away and didn't tell me – well, let's just say I wouldn't be pleased." She sipped at the latte that Bob had insisted on purchasing and fetching for her when he gallantly vacated his seat, protesting that he was already late back for a meeting and that she must take it to keep Jack company.

"Noted," Jack returned her smile. "Now then, tell me about the interview. I take it that it didn't go well?" He took a slug of Fanta from the can and gestured with his fork for her to continue, before spearing a couple of chips and dipping them in the sauce of his lasagne.

"Not well at all I'm afraid. The woman who was meant to interview me had been called away on some sort of family emergency. I ended up being seen by the office junior." She paused. "No, that's not fair. Some poor young fellow was fielded to conduct the interview. He was easily ten years younger than me and clearly terrified. It was all he could do to spin the thing out for twenty minutes. So there I was, out on the street. Then I realised it must still be your lunch hour, so I called in the hope of sounding off and maybe getting some sympathy."

Jack marshalled the last mouthful of food from his plate on to his fork and raised it towards his mouth. "You must be really pissed off." The final forkful was delivered on the last syllable.

"Yes and no. It's obviously frustrating to have got myself all worked up for an interview that turned out to be a waste of time. On the other hand, if the woman had a domestic crisis that can't be helped. And I ended up feeling sorry for the young fellow who interviewed me. Would you believe, he actually asked me what grades I got at A-level." The recollection triggered a wry grin. "Anyway, it's done now. No point in crying over spilt milk. How long do we have before you've got to be back in the office?"

Jack took a final swig from the can, washing down the last of his lunch. "I'm not due back for half an hour, but I've got to make a detour via Leyden Street."

"I don't know it."

"Turn right down Bishopsgate, left on to Middlesex Street, and then off to the left again. I need to pick up a couple of camping knick-knacks from the outdoor supplies place there."

"I didn't know you had a camping trip planned."

"Not me. Ollie. He's off with Cubs tomorrow. They're not going very far at all, but they are camping overnight. I just need to get the last two things on the kit list."

"Sorry?"

"What is it? What do you mean?"

Ayesha pushed her seat backwards noisily and straightened her back. "You just said Ollie is camping overnight tomorrow."

"Yes. And?" Pause. "Oh shit!"

"Oh shit indeed. When I suggested we go out for a meal tomorrow night you told me you couldn't do it because you'd promised to take Ollie to the cinema. So which is it? Is Ollie going to see a movie with you or is he going camping with Cubs?"

Jack's mouth and throat were arid. He could feel his cheeks combusting. The change in atmosphere at their table was palpable to the extent that diners at other tables were stealing furtive glances. Jack's eyes caught theirs as he sought to avoid Ayesha's stare, causing them to look hurriedly away. Jack's eyes finally settled on the empty plate in front of him. "Ollie's going with Cubs."

"So why tell me you're taking him to the cinema?"

"Well …"

"Well? Oh that's just great, Jack. Look, if you don't want to go out with me then all you need to do is say so."

"No, it's not that. I agreed I'd go to the football with the lads, and we usually go on for a few jars afterwards."

"I'm sorry, now you're just confusing me. Are you saying you'd rather go out drinking with your mates than go for a meal with me? Not very flattering, but at least I know where I stand."

"No! No, that's not it at all. It's the complete opposite."

"Now I'm definitely confused. Keep working that spade, Jack. I'm intrigued to see how deep a hole you can dig."

Jack picked up the empty Fanta can and squeezed it into a bowtie between the fingers and thumb of his right hand. "The lads have been on at me about going back to the football for ages. I've not been since Debs died even though I've got a season ticket. Anyway I agreed a few weeks ago that I'd go to the game with them tomorrow."

"So why say you were going to a movie with Ollie?"

"Because I thought it sounded better. I thought you'd be more understanding if I told you that than if I said I was going out with the lads."

"You're talking to me, Jack. But you're not making any sense. Why would I be more understanding if you lied to me?"

"I'd much rather go for a meal with you than go drinking with the lads. But I'd promised them. When you suggested going for a meal, I thought you might be offended at the thought I'd rather be with them. I thought if I said I had to go out with Ollie it would sound better."

"Does it sound better now? For god's sake Jack! If you'd promised to go out with your mates, that's fine. That was all you needed to say."

"I know. I realise that now."

"But your first instinct was to lie to me?"

"No. Well no, not exactly. Well yes. It was a lie. A really stupid lie. I said it because I thought it sounded better than the truth. I'm a complete arse. I'm really, really sorry."

A century elapsed before sentence was passed. "For god's sake put that can down before you completely destroy it. I believe you. And I accept your apology. Jack, I don't own you. You don't need to pretend for me. I don't want you to feel awkward, or that you have to feel the need to present things in a way you imagine I'd prefer."

"Thank you. I know. And I am sorry."

"I said your apology was accepted. No need to keep repeating it."

"Yes. Sorry."

"Jack!" A smile erupted, signalling an immediate thaw in their sudden cold war. "Look, I'm sorry too."

"You've nothing to be sorry about."

"No. I do. I'm sorry for coming all over a bit bunny boiler. I've got this hang up with honesty. Maybe it's a good thing this came up now. At least we both know where we stand. I suggest we learn the lessons, forget the incident and move on. Okay?"

"Sounds like a plan."

"That's settled then."

"Talking of settling, you don't happen to have any cash on you?"

"About sixty quid in notes, plus some loose change. Why?"

"This place is cash only, and I was relying on Bob to pay."

"Cash only? Really?" Another smile. "Well that really is old school. But you don't need to worry about paying."

"What do you mean?"

"When Bob fetched me my latte, I saw him pay with two tenners and get just coins in change. Given the prices in here he obviously paid for your meals at the same time."

"Nothing gets past you, eh Clouseau?" Ayesha's eyes narrowed and he reproached himself silently for the clumsiness that threatened the fragility of his recovered position. He knew that she was making a calculation in that fraction of a second. Despite the speed with which she delivered a *Don't push it* smile that both forgave and admonished, his head was swimming.

"I'll walk with you as far as Liverpool Street."

"You sure?"

"Yeah. I'll catch the tube from there." They made their way along Worship Street and right on to Norton Folgate, past the rank of largely unused Boris bikes and on to Bishopsgate. The distant Gherkin provided a beacon as they passed obliviously between glass and concrete cathedrals of commerce, each focused only on chat with the other. Humming traffic, people queuing at traffic lights and bus stops, piles of Evening Standards at an unmanned kiosk, widening pavements pounded by purposeful pedestrians. All were mere wallpaper on the corridor leading to the entrance to the station. Once they arrived, the Victorian architecture and variety of retailers and food outlets provided a more human scale. The pair stopped at the corner of the flight of three shallow stairs that, somewhat perversely, took passengers up to the escalators and more stairs, which then allowed downwards access to the station concourse.

"Guess this is it then. What will you do with your afternoon?" Jack was unsure if his attempt at being casual seemed forced.

"I'm going to call into the agency that lined up today's interview and give them an update. Then I might call in on a couple of others I'm registered with just to make sure that I'm still on their radar. After that I plan to catch up with an old colleague who's in town for dinner."

"Sounds good." Jack wondered if he looked as lame as his response.

"Come here, you!" Ayesha stepped forward and pulled him into a hug, planting a firm kiss on his lips. "Tell Ollie to enjoy himself camping. You enjoy yourself at the football and with your friends. You can give me a call on Sunday to let me know how it all goes." She eased backwards slightly, but still with her arms around him, beaming as generously as ever.

He pulled her back towards him and returned the kiss, holding it for a second longer. "Thanks," he whispered intimately in the midst of the throng.

Ayesha stepped back, smile intact. "I'd better be going. And so should you! Speak to you on Sunday," nodding. "Byeee."

She turned and strode towards the escalators, left hand raised with fingers waving adieu. Jack's own goodbye was silent as he realised she wouldn't hear it. He watched until she disappeared before turning and continuing his journey to Leyden Street. Later he would wonder whether Ayesha's old colleague was male or female, but not now. His relaxed gait belied the emotional maelstrom within. Unequal measures of self-recrimination, relief, embarrassment, happiness, guilt, regret and hope flowed and eddied as he replayed the previous half-hour in his mind. But the most powerful feeling was of gratitude. Grateful to Ayesha, and *for* Ayesha. He knew he was a lucky man.

## Chapter 18

Incredulity transformed instantly into outrage and, in less than a heartbeat, morphed further into full-blown anger. Jack's face contorted with ire, he threw his right hand forward pointing at the cause of his enmity, and bellowed his fury. He was consumed by the injustice of the moment and, despite the sincerity and ferocity of his displeasure, there was an unconscious sweetness in being completely diverted from the bigger realities of a life that had been so badly vandalised. The roaring and baying all around, and his spontaneous participation in it, was an echo of a more complete and happier past time. He was like a junkie who had just had a hit, transferred to a place of comforting immediacy, insulated from the pain and grief visited on him by bereavement and the loss he'd suffered since he last went to the football.

"Can you believe that?" Pete was roaring in his right ear, "I mean, can you believe that? The dirty bastard!" Jack turned to see a face that mirrored his own passionate fury at the injustice that had unfolded before them. Pete answered his own rhetorical question, "It's unbelievable. Unbelievable!" Immediately behind them an enormously tall, skinny, denim-clad man missing his two front teeth machine-gun fired spittle as he screamed, "Bastard! Bastard! Bastard! Off! Off! Off!" Other much greater profanities filled the air all around in a hosanna of violent, resentful acrimony. Just in front of Jack a very small boy turned to gaze back at the toothless giant, gawping at him in a mixture of bewilderment, fear and awe. The kid couldn't be more than six years old and his demeanour gave Jack a sense of vindication that he had thus far resisted Ollie's entreaties to accompany him and be properly initiated into the tribe. The feeling was amplified when the youngster turned forward, mimicking Gap-Tooth in a high-pitched squeal and receiving an approving pat on the head from the adult accompanying him, who Jack took to be his father. His sense of distaste evaporated as the tumult around him mutated into a cacophony of jeering and whistling, and his entire focus returned to see what punishment the referee would regard as appropriate.

Far below, the black clad villain extended his arms, pointlessly pleading innocence, then feigning surprise when a yellow card was brandished in his direction. The jeering reached a crescendo as the coliseum of over fifty thousand claret and blue clad onlookers bayed their displeasure at what they regarded as leniency, while the splash of white clad visitors at the far end reciprocated by howling down the injustice. The match continued and, despite the fare on offer being insipid, Jack remained transfixed by the action unfolding far below. As the clock approached the ninetieth minute one West Ham substitute crossed from the left to another, who drove the ball into the net. Pandemonium erupted around the vast stadium as Irons fans leapt, danced, embraced and punched the air, exulting in the glory of a narrow victory over their opponents. Thronged around both tiers of the vast bowl of the London Stadium, their focus then settled on those sections of the amphitheatre housing followers of their "guests". Scorn and derision reverberated off the massive cantilevered roof, cascading towards the targets of the mass expression of triumphalism and schadenfreude. "Bubbles," blasted from the tannoy system as the DJ correctly judged that it would enhance the jubilant pandemonium.

Behind Jack, Gap-Tooth's previous apoplexy inducing rage had transformed into a malignant joy. Gesticulating aggressively at the distant Spurs supporters, almost incoherent with glee, he sprayed his judgement, "You faaaaacking Wankaaaaaaahs!"

The small boy in front dutifully mimicked his new mentor in falsetto. Pete was again in his ear, "Can you believe it? Can you believe it? One – nil and we've pissed on their chips!" The reprise was delivered with exhilaration, in total contrast to earlier exasperation.

Within moments, three sharp blasts of the referee's whistle signalled an end to the contest. Players in the drama below were variously shaking hands with one another and applauding the spectators, reciprocating the support they had received for their efforts throughout the afternoon. White, claret and blue plastic seating appeared amongst the throng, spreading like a rash as their former occupants vacated and moved towards the exit gangways.

Jack turned to Pete smiling, "What a bloody finish. I honestly thought we could've played till Christmas and not scored."

"I'm just pleased to get the win." Pete beamed back, "That lot haven't conceded a goal in their last five away matches. And that's the first time they've lost away this season."

Jack's grin widened. He regarded himself as a proper fan, but Pete's encyclopaedic knowledge about the club and ability to summon up obscure facts marked him out as a borderline fanatic. "You need to get a girlfriend, mate," he scolded affectionately.

Pete took it in good part. "Nah mate. I'm not two timing this old girl for any woman."

"So what's the drill now then?"

"We meet Rob and Bazza outside, then head for The Langthorne for a couple of jars. Gives the crowds time to disperse. No point in going straight to the station just now – it'll be heaving." Pete started making his way right along the now empty row of white plastic tip-up seats to the gangway where fellow supporters were ascending steadily towards the exit. Jack looked back around the stadium, absorbing a final impression of the new home ground on his first visit there. He was surprised to see how quickly it was emptying. Then, realising that Pete was moving at pace, he set off in brisk pursuit. In just moments the pair had rendezvoused with Rob and Bazza on the concourse outside and were moving with the throng through Pool Street towards Stratford High Street.

They proceeded four abreast, Jack on the outside with Rob on his left. "So what do you make of the place, Jack?"

"It's certainly different from Upton Park! I don't know. The colours, the fans, the songs – they're all familiar. But the place is so big, so open. I really don't know. It really is *so* different, but I can see how I could begin to think of it as home after a bit of time."

"I know what you mean. First few times I went I felt a bit like I did when we moved house when I was a kid. My parents were really excited, but I'd been happy at the old place and didn't want to go. But after a while I started to get used to it. Having my own bedroom instead of sharing with our James certainly helped."

"I can see that, just like I can see myself getting used to this place. I loved the old ground and it'll always hold special memories for me. But I can see how I could get used to the new place."

"So you're glad you kept your season ticket?"

"Definitely. There were times when imagined that I'd never go to the football – in fact never do anything – again. But that was in my worst days. That was what I felt, but not what I thought – if that makes sense?"

"Kind of. It's that time when all your experience and knowledge tells you something you know is true, but your heart doesn't agree."

"Yes, that's exactly it." Jack cast a quick sideways glance to catch Rob's eye, affirming one of those moments when men actually share feelings, rare as a unicorn sighting.

The rest of the walk towards the pub saw the conversation focus on the match, with a consensus that it had been a shit game on its own but that the win was the most important thing given the poor start the team had made to the season. The good mood continued as they approached the modern concrete Westfield retail centre where the Langthorne was located. The pub was busy, and a large number of drinkers had spilled out on to the wide pavement between the pub and the railing that marked the boundary with the road. Pete led the four-man snake through the crowds and inside where, surprisingly, the density of bodies in the spacious interior was less than outside despite it still being busy. Although located in a modern building, attempts to create a traditional pub interior had been largely successful with plenty of dark wood, ceiling cornicing, a large mirror and exotically styled cut glass shades on the pendant lights hanging above the bar. The floor adjacent to the bar was tiled, with the rest wooden or covered with a red patterned carpet that matched the colour of the various pillars scattered throughout. Wooden tables and chairs were ubiquitous and all fully occupied, with even more patrons standing than sitting. The air was thick with the perfume of beer and body heat and any sounds from the four television screens or fruit machines were inaudible above the hubbub of a high-spirited brigade of the claret and blue army celebrating a particularly sweet victory. Pete and Bazza made their way to the bar where the latter was served very quickly by one of the many staff adorned in West Ham tops, and soon they were back at the pillar Jack and Rob had secured a position beside. Bazza carried two lagers, one of which he handed to Rob, while Pete handed one of his two IPA's to Jack. A ritual "cheers' all round and the conversation was soon flowing. Initially the chat focused on analysis of the match, dissecting particular incidents, debating the merits of individual players and assessing managerial tactics, before the subject matter became broader. By the third pint the discussion was alternating between good-natured complaints from Bazza about being hen pecked and Pete bemoaning the latest romance to crash and burn after three weeks, an enduring relationship by his standards.

"What about you Jack? I bumped into young Harry Evans the other day and he said he'd seen you out with a real looker."

Perhaps if he hadn't already had a couple of pints Jack might have been wrong-footed by Bazza's unexpected question, but the mildly anaesthetising effect of the ale afforded him a relaxed response. "Rely on Harry to broadcast your deepest, darkest secrets," he smiled. "It's true, he saw me out with a girl called Ayesha. We were at school together – Ayesha Alfarsi. Does that ring any bells Pete?"

"The name kind of sounds like I should remember it, mate, but in all honesty I don't. Surprising, as I'm sure I'd remember anyone who was a looker."

"I think she's probably changed in the past twenty years. Anyway the story is that I bumped into her unexpectedly and we got chatting. She'd not long arrived back in London looking for work after being abroad for a few years. Her family all live up north and she was at a bit of a loose end. We agreed to go out for a meal and catch up on old times and just hit it off. I've seen her a few times since."

"Any pics on your phone? Like I said, young Harry says she

was a real bit of all right. I'd like a butchers." Baz's follow up broke the respectful silence with which the others were digesting the surprising news that Jack was seeing a woman.

"Fuck sake Baz. Have you got no dignity at all? We've got Jack spilling his guts here and you go lowering the tone by asking for pictures of his new bird to leer at." Rob's reproach was light heartedly delivered, rather than chiding. He turned to Jack, struggling to maintain his expression of faux concern, "But, seeing as he's asked, *do* you have any photos?"

The company dissolved in mirth, with Jack's laugh loudest.

"Better be careful guys." Pete had taken up the baton. "You know Jack's like cheap toilet paper."

"What? Go on then."

"He doesn't take shit off anyone."

The laughter was ramped up a further notch and the tone was set. They were men in their thirties, but today they were lads together. And they were having fun. Jack was having fun. He hadn't realised that his friends not knowing about Ayesha was a burden. The sense of liberation, of being unshackled from an unnecessary secret, turbocharged his joy. Later, as the crowd in the pub thinned, awareness of a song being sung on the televisions intruded on Jack's consciousness. The distinctive strains of the one-hit-wonders eighties indie band Department S connected. *Is Vic there? Is Vic there? Is Vic there? Is Vic there? Is Vic there?* Jack made a mental note to chase Rachel.

## Chapter 19

Jack pressed his phone hard against his ear as he swiftly negotiated the stairs to the first floor, where mobile reception was significantly better than at ground level. "Hello? Rachel? Can you hear me now?

"Yes, that's much better. You've gone upstairs, haven't you? I remember having to do that to get decent reception at your place."

"That's right. I can hear you much more clearly too."

"I hope you don't mind me ringing you on a Sunday?"

"Not at all. Thanks for ringing back. So, do you have any news?"

"I'm afraid that the headline is that there is no news."

"What do you mean?"

"In simple terms, we've drawn a blank. We don't know who Vic is and we can't trace the number."

"So you're telling me that the resources of the entire Met can't trace one poxy phone? And it's been weeks, when you said it would only take days!"

"I know Jack, and I'm sorry. I should have got back to you sooner and you shouldn't have had to chase me."

"Okay, apology noted. But surely to God you must have found out something?"

"You might think so, but it's not the case. If someone wants an untraceable phone it's not that hard to achieve. Buy a pay-as-you-go cheap basic mobile from a shop, and give them a false name and address if they ask. Buy a SIM card from another shop. Use cash for each transaction and take care to avoid any surveillance cameras. Then you're pretty much fixed."

"There's got to be more to it than that. What happened when you rang the number? I'm sure I've read that you can physically locate a mobile phone with a precision of a couple of metres. Have you tried that? It just doesn't seem credible that this can't be traced."

"Jack, I've got the report here in front of me. It runs to nearly four pages, but I can talk you through it if you want."

"Too bloody right I do."

"All right. First of all, the number *was* checked out as part of the original investigation."

"I'm listening."

"The number, as you know, was shown against the name Vic. That name didn't figure amongst any of Debs' known acquaintances. There had been seven calls from Debs number to this number in the last three months of her life. They all took place on Tuesdays at lunchtime, and they never lasted more than a minute each time. Shortest was 32 seconds and longest was 54 seconds."

"I know all this. I told it to you!"

"Sorry, I'm just skim reading the report for you. So, because it wasn't an easily identified acquaintance and because of the pattern of calls, the number was flagged for investigation."

"And?"

"The number was dialled on two separate occasions. Each time we got nothing – it appears it was switched off. It was probably just a basic device rather than a smart phone. We identified the carrier and made contact, but they had nothing useful in terms of a contract because it was a pay as you go phone and a pre-paid SIM. The decision was taken not to bother trying to trace its location as it was switched off. There was no opportunity to try and get a fix on where it was."

"And that was it?"

"That was it at the time. After you came in and told me about the call you'd made we tried it again. There have been another four calls to the number since your report, but it still doesn't ring out. Two of the calls were from a police landline and two were made using a piece of technology that emulates another caller, in this case Debs' number. We can only conclude that the battery has been removed, or that the handset has been destroyed. Whatever the case, this line of investigation has drawn a blank."

"Don't you think this stinks? First time round you called it, it was dead. Then I call. Then you guys call again and it's dead again. Doesn't that strike you as suspicious?"

"It certainly raises questions, Jack. But the simple reality is that we are not able to pursue this any further."

"Hang on a minute. When those original calls were made, were they made on a Tuesday lunchtime? Were any of them using this emulator thing?"

"No they weren't Jack. Both were made on a Friday morning from the same police landline."

"Bloody hell, Rachel! Don't you think they missed a trick then?"

"Perhaps. Look, I don't mean to sound defensive, but they tried the number twice and got absolutely nothing. They probably didn't even consider using the emulator. Imagine if you are someone who does know Debs – and the fact that she's dead – and then you get a call from her number? If it had occurred to them to do it, they'd probably have dismissed it as too insensitive."

A pause. "Maybe. But can you understand my frustration? The whole thing just doesn't add up. Somebody is hiding something."

"I do understand how you feel, and I sympathise. But …" Rachel's voice stalled the way voices often do on that word.

"But what?"

"Jack, I don't know how to say this." Another pause, and an uncomfortable clearing of the throat. "When you first reported this stuff about Vic you asked me if I thought Debs had been having an affair."

"Yes. And you said it wasn't remotely likely. You said that there was no way she could have been having an affair and you lot not finding out about it."

"Yes, I did say that. And it was what I thought at the time."

"But it's not what you think now?"

"No. I mean I don't know. Look Jack, this is really uncomfortable for me. I know how awful losing Debs has been for you and your family. I don't want to add any more to your suffering. But look at the facts. Debs had the number for someone called Vic on her phone. She called him frequently. You knew nothing about his existence. When you found out you called him and introduced yourself as Jack Laidlaw. If he did know Debs then he probably knew you were her husband. He blanked you, and now he can't be contacted on that number any more. What conclusion would you come to?"

"I know how it looks." He did know how it looked, but he still couldn't bring himself to believe it. "I'm not naïve, Rachel. Of course I was suspicious, but I was confident you'd find an explanation. Maybe confident is the wrong word. Hopeful, perhaps. Now you're virtually telling me Debs was having an affair…"

"I didn't say that."

"No, but it's what you meant. And I can see why you would think that. I can even see why *I* should think that. But I don't. I just don't believe it. If Debs was having an affair I'd have known. But she *never* would."

"I'm sorry Jack. I don't mean to upset you or to cast aspersions about Debs. I don't know that Debs was having an affair, and I'm not saying that she was. All I'm doing is reporting the facts to you and saying how it looks."

"Look Rachel, I know you're a good person, and that you're just doing your job and calling it as you see it. But I know in my bones that it's not how it looks." Noises from downstairs alerted him that his presence was required. "I have to go."

"Okay Jack, I'll let you go. You know that you can always call if you think I can help. 'Bye."

"Thanks, Rachel. It's important that you know Debs simply wouldn't have had an affair. Really must go. 'Bye." The question of whether he was trying to convince Rachel or himself ghosted into his mind, before being immediately banished by the sound of voices from downstairs.

## Chapter 20

Ayesha leaned back into the large black leather sofa and tried to relax. She had been surprised, first by the early Sunday morning call, and second by the invitation to come to his place – her first visit there, with the suggestion that she could revisit old haunts. *Make yourself at home* he'd said. *Take a seat. I'll just get rid of this call and I'll be right back with you.* She inhaled slowly and deeply. The sitting room and dining room had been knocked through, probably in the nineteen seventies or eighties when it was fashionable to do so, to form one much larger room. Fortunately the large bay window at the front was south facing, so there was sufficient natural light for even the furthest corners. The concave arched coving and the six-inch chamfered skirting boards were the only details that betrayed the room's nineteen thirties origins. Ayesha noted that care had been taken to ensure both appeared seamless after the internal wall had been taken out. There were no fireplaces or chimney breasts, and she speculated to herself that any coving and skirting rendered spare by their removal might have been cannibalised for the making good process. The two original four panel doors leading to the hallway corridor, one at each end of the left-hand wall, were made modern by their brushed aluminium handles. The colour scheme was what she thought of as classic contemporary. Silvers, black, white, greys and occasional accents of soft, muted pink harmonised elegantly with the modern styling of the dining suite at the far end of the room, the angular leather sofas and chair, and the ebonised furniture and shelving placed against the right-hand wall. A large rectangular mirror adorned the far wall, strategically positioned to give the illusion of even more space whilst also reflecting back maximum natural light. The overall effect was a successful fusion of style with comfort and functionality. Jack had mentioned that Debs had a talent for design, a fact Ayesha was now able to appreciate for herself. She liked this room. She approved.

Closer inspection revealed battle scars wrought on a room striving valiantly to maintain a chic veneer in the face of intermittent assaults by kids engaged in the business of being growing children. The nasty gash in the dining room chair leg from its collision with the wing of a Spitfire launched with more force than intended. The traces of blackcurrant juice splashed at shin height by the farthest away door wiped clean, but not to the point of invisibility. The stain on the carpet not entirely disguised by the strategically placed rug. The garish yellow of The Beano Annual 2017 and green of Diary of a Wimpy Kid: The Last Straw, incongruous on a black shelf. The imperfections made the room real, lived in, part of a home. Ayesha smiled her approval unconsciously.

Debs was everywhere. There were four pictures of or including her. She was fair haired and pretty, and smiling in all of them. Smiling naturally, rather than just for the camera. Whoever had taken the photographs had done so with skill and love. And a reciprocal love, or at least a hint of its essence, was also there in the room. Ayesha knew that she would have liked Debs.

The faraway door exploded open and a noisy frantic cartoon chase erupted into the room with a yelling girl pursuing a smaller boy who was struggling to run as he convulsed with laughter. "Give me that back right now you…" The words stopped as suddenly as the movement, awareness of Ayesha's presence coming suddenly to the children.

"Who are you?" demanded the boy.

"I'm Ayesha." His gaze told her clearly that this was insufficient. "I'm a friend of your Dad's."

"Where is he?"

'He's just stepped outside to take a 'phone call."

"Why?"

"I'm sorry?"

"Why has he stepped outside to take it? Why didn't he take it in here?"

"I don't know, to be honest with you. I think maybe it might have been something to do with his work."

"Oh. Okay. He gets loads of calls to do with work. He always tries to go somewhere quiet to answer them. And he says that mobile reception is much better upstairs." She seemed to have satisfied her interrogator.

"I'm Fi," the girl took a small step forward. She was fair-haired like her brother, but otherwise her features marked her out as definitely being Jack's daughter, right down to the cleft chin. Her face was red from exertion and Ayesha guessed that she had been chasing her brother for some distance.

"Pleased to meet you."

"It's very nice to meet you too. Do you know, I think we have something in common."

"Oh, what?"

"Well, my brother is two years younger than me and he has spent his whole life just being annoying."

Fi's puzzled expression broke into a wide grin, uncannily like her father's, "His whole life? Don't tell me that!"

"I am not annoying!" Ollie interrupted. He stepped between the others and looked straight into Ayesha's eyes. "Are you my Dad's girlfriend?"

Ayesha hesitated briefly, "Well, I am a girl and I am your Dad's friend. So I suppose you could call me that."

"You are not a girl. You are a woman, a grown up woman. Fi is a girl, but you're a woman. I mean are you his girlfriend like in kissing him and stuff?"

"Ollie Laidlaw! You do not ask a lady questions like that! Now, say that you're sorry immediately." A petite woman of about seventy stood in the farthest doorway; her voice was soft with a Caledonian brogue, but firm and authoritative. A stern frown in Ollie's direction was sufficient to extract a begrudged, "I'm sorry."

"I do hope you'll forgive my grandson. I'm Fiona Laidlaw, Jack's mum." She crossed the room with a slightly laboured gait, her frown transforming into what Ayesha was now beginning to recognise as the Laidlaw smile, with her right hand extended.

Ayesha rose from the sofa, accepting the soft but firm handshake, "I'm Ayesha Alfarsi, a friend of Jack's."

"I'm very pleased to meet you. Now, please do sit back

down." Fiona sat at the opposite end of the same sofa, at an angle that meant she was facing Ayesha. "I really am sorry about Ollie."

"Honestly, it's no problem. I think he's quite funny actually." She looked at Ollie, winked, flashed him a quick smile and was gratified to receive a grin in return.

"Well, we'll say no more about it then. But Ollie will help his sister make us a cup of tea. Won't you, Ollie?" The tone and accompanying ominous glare ensured that Ollie understood the question was rhetorical. "How do you take yours, Ayesha?"

"Oh, white with no sugar please. Thank you." The children exited through the faraway door towards where Ayesha presumed the kitchen to be.

"So how do you know Jack? Do you work together?"

"Well, no. Actually we were at school together almost twenty years ago and then bumped into each other – literally – just recently."

"Ah. You said your surname is Alfarsi. Was your mother the Head at Redbridge Primary School?"

"Why yes, yes she was. Did you know my Mum?"

"I didn't know her personally, only by her excellent reputation. I was a teacher at Christchurch Primary and had some colleagues who left to join your mother's school. I knew when Jack went to Valentines High School that Mrs. Alfarsi had a daughter going into the same year group. So when you said you'd been at school with Jack I made the link."

"Of course. Very Miss Marple of you," Ayesha smiled warmly. "I didn't know that you were a teacher."

"I taught for over thirty years. The first few years were in Lanark but then we moved south and I spent the bulk of my career at various schools in Redbridge. All ancient history now – I've been retired these past twelve years."

"Twelve years? You don't look old enough."

"That's very gracious of you, but I think we both know that I look every day of my seventy-two years, and more." It was true. Fiona's hair was white and thin, her face lined and the pallor of her skin did nothing to suggest that she was anything other than at least as old as her years. She had swollen feet, suggestive of peripheral edema, and small yellow xanthomas bumped the skin of both hands. Ayesha didn't respond to the comment and the exchange moved on.

Fiona continued to extract information skilfully as she weighed up this new woman her son had never mentioned. As she gathered data, sometimes almost forensically, the acuity with which she did so demonstrated that time had wrought no damage on her mental faculties. For each biographical nugget she mined she traded some Laidlaw family knowledge. Ayesha understood what was happening and was an enthusiastic participant. She liked the charming and polite way that Fiona was assessing her, gauging whether or not she was a threat to her vulnerable son and grandchildren. She liked Fiona. She hoped Fiona liked her.

The conversation was interrupted by the reappearance of Fi and Ollie, each carrying a circular yellow plastic coaster and a mug of tea. Fi placed her coaster and mug on the table at her grandmother's end of the sofa. Ollie proceeded haltingly towards the side table at Ayesha's end, the slightly too full mug in his right hand, left hand using the coaster to support it from below, eyes concentrated on the untrustworthy tea, and the tip of his tongue just protruding between tight lips.

"Ollie! Surely you could have found a better mug than that for our guest?" Fiona's tone made her irritation clear.

Ayesha glanced at the maroon and blue mug adorned with a golden motif of crossed hammers over a three turreted castle. It had a large chip out of the rim near the handle. Her eyes flicked to Ollie's crestfallen face, "It's absolutely perfect. Ollie can spot a fellow Hammer a mile off. I've got one with this very same pattern at home. Thank you very much." She took the mug and coaster from him carefully and placed them on the side table. They exchanged grins and this time it was Ollie who winked. Fiona smiled at the small kindness shown to her grandson.

Jack reappeared at the nearest door. "Ayesha, I'm really sorry. That took much longer than I thought."

"Don't worry about it. As you can see, I've been very well entertained and waited upon." Ayesha rotated her upturned palm with a flourish to showcase her mug, while at the same time throwing him an *are you all right?* look.

"So I see." Jack responded to her comment but not her look. He turned to Fiona, brow creased. "Mum, you're home much earlier than usual. Is everything okay?"

"Yes, everything's fine. There's a gala on at the pool later today so the public session had to end an hour and a half earlier than usual. There were signs up last week to tell us, but I completely forgot about it and so did the kids. But they did still get an hour in the water, and the pool was much less crowded than usual."

"Ah, okay. I see." Jack paused and so did everything else as a collective awkwardness suddenly descended like a mist threatening to chill the easy conversation.

"I used to go to the same school as your dad," Ayesha beamed at Fi and Ollie. "But I had to move away, let me think, nineteen years ago. When we bumped into each other recently we got talking about old times and I explained that I hadn't been back to Ilford since I left. We ended up deciding that it might be fun for me to come back and visit – see what's new and what's stayed the same. That's why he invited me across this morning. So what would you two recommend I should see – the number one, top of the list, must-see thing?"

"The Idol! The Idol! You've gotta see The Idol!" Ollie was bouncing up and down with excitement.

"Yeah, the Idol is pretty cool," echoed Fi.

"Hang on kids. Ayesha was keen to come back and visit places she remembers from her childhood. You know, take a walk in Valentine's park – that sort of thing. The Idol isn't even in Ilford, it's in Barking." Jack's voice was calm and even, but his face betrayed incipient panic at the turn which events seemed to be taking.

"I did say I was interested in seeing new things too," Ayesha reminded him. "And this Idol thing seems to be a big favourite with Fi and Ollie. What exactly is it?"

"It's fantastic, brilliant," enthused Ollie. "It's like a big play area that's a cyborg that you climb through the inside of and crawl about in and it's kind of spooky fun and adults go in it as well as kids and the drop slide is amazing." The torrent abated as Ollie paused to catch his breath. Fi took over, "It's a play area on two different floors. But it is for adults as well as kids and the whole place is like being in an old black and white movie. It really is pretty cool for a play area."

Ayesha smiled at the cloak of sophistication Fi used to legitimise her own enthusiasm. "Right, that settles it. This is something that I have to see for myself. Are you guys busy today, or do you think that you could make time to show me around this Idol? That's if it's okay with your dad, of course?"

Four pairs of eyes focused on Jack. He made an *Are You Sure?* face at Ayesha and took his cue from her barely perceptible nod, "Sure, The Idol it is."

Ollie let out a yelp of excitement and the delight on Fi's face was unmistakable.

"If we head off now and manage to get parked there, we should have time for some fun before grabbing a late lunch." Jack turned to Fiona, "Do you want to came along too Mum?"

"I've had quite enough fun and excitement this morning already, thanks. You go and enjoy yourselves and I'll have a nice quiet lunch here by myself."


Less than five minutes later, Jack and his three passengers were in his 3-series BMW, en route for The Idol. He was pleasantly surprised at how light the traffic was on both the A12 and the North Circular Road, reflecting the fact that it was Sunday morning. He was even more pleased after fifteen minutes when they arrived at Bobby Moore Way in Barking, the street named after the borough's most celebrated son. They pulled into the Abbey Leisure Centre just as someone was leaving, freeing up one of the very limited parking spaces. The centre had a gym that had developed a good reputation, as well as boasting two pools, a martial arts studio and a luxury spa that included a hydrotherapy pool, a rock sauna and three separate steam rooms. All of this was in addition to The Idol play area and meant that there were always plenty of people around, which helped visits there with the kids feel like an occasion.

As they got out of the car Ayesha paused, appraising the two-storey structure – a rectangle of dark brick, glass and white concrete colonnades. "It certainly looks very modern."

"Yes, it's pretty functional as a structure. Built for a purpose, you see." Jack smiled at her, "Having said that, I think they managed to pull off a pretty decent building for the budget. It's right opposite the Abbey Green with the remains of the old Barking Abbey and St. Margarette's Church, which is Grade 1 listed."

"Really?" Ayesha teased, eyebrows raised and *ooh fancy that* grinning.

"I am such a nerd! I blame the job. Ten years in facilities management means I can't help myself. I actually read up on this stuff when there are new buildings going up. Confession time – and this is truly shameful – but I genuinely find this kind of stuff interesting." He was grinning too now. "And, just so you know, the original Barking Abbey was once a strict Benedictine nunnery and was known as the greatest in the whole country. And," he paused for effect, "and, it was the only Saxon monastic foundation in Essex to survive until the Dissolution. So there!"

"I doff my cap to you, learned sir!" She held his gaze, beaming. "Now, shall we follow these children before they decide to abandon us completely?"

Fi and Ollie had raced ahead and were now waiting by the entrance, looking back impatiently. Ollie made his hand into a gun and pretended to shoot them. Fi folded her arms, looked skywards and mimed an exaggerated sigh. Ayesha didn't wait for a reply, "Race you!" She dashed off towards the kids at a pace Jack struggled to match and reached them with a comfortable two-metre lead. Jack pretended to be dismayed that both kids had cheered Ayesha to victory.

They were quickly inside and paid their entry fees. Once again Fi and Ollie tore ahead, eager to get on with the fun. "Well this is certainly interesting." Ayesha looked around, appraising the unusual surroundings, "Does your encyclopaedic knowledge extend to the interior of this place?"

Jack cocked his left eye in her direction, "Are you just taking the mickey now?"

"No, honestly. This place really is quite different. If you do know anything about it, I really would be keen to learn more."

"Okay, but don't blame me for being Mr. Geek here. Remember that you asked!"

"I promise." Innocent eyes and a closed mouth smile. The exchanges between them were an evenly matched game of tennis. Words were serves. Smiles, glances, laughter and impromptu touches were the forehand, volley, backhand and smashes of their rallies.

"Well then. First thing is that the idea for this is inspired by the Dagenham Idol. Does that ring any bells?"

A gentle but firm shake of the head.

"Right. The Dagenham Idol is a wooden carving of a human figure that's well over two thousand years old. It's about eighteen inches long and doesn't have any arms. Nobody knows whether it's meant to be a man or a woman. They found it back in nineteen twenty-two when they were excavating for sewer pipes where the Ford plant is now." Jack paused, checking for signs of genuine interest. Checking to ensure he wasn't just being wound up.

Ayesha nodded encouragement, "Go on."

"So that was the original inspiration, as far as I understand it. Anyway, when it came time to design the play area here, they commissioned an artist called Marvin Gaye Chetwynd to design it."

"Really?" There was a note of recognition in Ayesha's voice.

"What, do you know her?"

"I think I read an article about her somewhere. Really interesting woman. She was called Spartacus Chetwynd before she changed to Marvin Gaye Chetwynd. I think she might have been given a more conventional birth name before she got into changing, but I can't remember. Quite avant-garde."

"I never knew she was called Spartacus – fascinating. Any idea why she changes her name?"

"I'm sure it was explained in the article I read, but I don't remember."

"Doesn't really matter – I was just curious. I'll maybe Google it later. Anyway, she got the commission and came up with this." Jack extended both arms and rotated them in an outward semi-circle, "Behold."

The Idol was unlike anything Ayesha had seen before. What could have been a fairly run of the mill soft play area in yet another anonymous "community asset" was actually a unique and inspiring tribute to the artist's vision. The walls and floors were covered with huge black and white prints portraying a riot of unexpected images from Greek mythology, science fiction cyborgs and ancient Egyptian statues. Despite the restrictions of wipe clean vinyl, minimal sharp edges and other safety restrictions mandated by the purpose of the place, the anarchy of the imagery blended with the subtlety of the monochrome tones to produce a genuinely distinctive environment. At the centre of the space was The Idol itself, a two-storey high climbing frame formed into a huge cage-like robot figure, dominating everything around it.

"Come on you two. It's great, and there's not too many other people in here just now." They looked up to see Ollie beckoning them from inside one of the cyborg's eyes.

Jack and Ayesha entered the glossy black world of the cyborg. After about twenty minutes they became separated as Jack teamed up with Fi and Ayesha climbed upwards in pursuit of a hide-and-seek playing Ollie. As Ayesha navigated the labyrinth of ramps, nets, chambers and various levels she realised that despite there having been relatively few people inside when they first entered, there were now actually quite a few other people crowding the space. She wondered how busy the place could get. "You can't see me," Ollie's singsong voice teased above the general hubbub.

"But I can hear you."

"Doesn't matter if you can hear me. Not if you can't catch me."

Ollie was clearly quite familiar with the layout and was leading her a merry dance, barely able to contain his laughter at her pantomime attempts to locate him. Eventually she rounded a corner to find him sitting, grinning at her, on the edge of a frighteningly high and steep drop slide. "Found you!"

"Yes, but you've not caught me."

"Ollie, I think perhaps you should come back from the edge there. I think that maybe this slide is meant for older children." She leaned forward as if to move towards him. Ollie smiled and edged slightly away from her. From nowhere another boy, maybe ten or eleven years old, brushed past Ayesha, past Ollie, and disappeared down the slide. In the same instant Ollie was suddenly gone and a split second later there was a yelp of pain. Ayesha bolted forward to the edge, where she could see a tearful Ollie at the bottom of the drop slide cradling his left elbow in his right hand. There was no sign of the older boy. In an instant she had followed him down and was by his side, softly cradling the painful joint in both of her hands. "Oh Ollie, that was quite a bump. Let me have a look."

"That boy knocked me off," he sniffed, already beginning to regain his composure. "I came down funny. Landed on this," nodding at his elbow.

Ayesha gently felt around the elbow with both hands, peering at it intently for any signs of serious damage and finding none, as Ollie fought to contain his tears. Jack appeared round the corner, followed closely by Fi. "What's happened? We heard Ollie scream."

Seated on the floor beside Ollie, Ayesha looked up and fixed Jack with reassuring eyes, "Ollie's just come down rather awkwardly and bumped his elbow. Nothing serious, thank goodness. Just a bit sore for a while." As Jack inhaled a deep sigh of relief she turned back to the patient. "And you are being very brave about it, aren't you?"

Ollie was no longer crying, although his eyes were still watery as he looked up at her, "Still a bit sore though."

Ayesha leaned slightly closer to him, "Do you want me to kiss it better?"

The words had barely left her and she was immediately aware that the atmosphere had transformed in that instant. Ollie was staring into her face with an expression that she couldn't label. She turned and saw that Fi had edged close to Jack and had grasped his hand with hers. They were both looking at her with the same expression as Ollie, the one she couldn't identify. After an aeon long second, she broke the silence, "What? What is it?"

Fi's voice was tiny, "That's what Mummy said."

"Sorry?"

Ollie spoke quietly, "It's what Mummy said."

Realisation rapidly metamorphosed to acute embarrassment as Ayesha felt her cheeks and neck begin to burn. Flustered, she looked to Jack in search of rescue, or even just a cue.

It was Ollie who spoke, "Yes, I do."

"I'm sorry, what?"

"Yes I do. I do want you to kiss it better."

Now it was her eyes that were moist as she bent her head down to place a butterfly kiss.

"No. Not like that. Harder!"

She pressed her lips more firmly against the still soft skin of his young elbow.

"And go Mmmmmmmmmmwah!"

She kept pressing firmly with her lips, rotating them slightly from side to side and emitted a loud, nasal, "Mmmmmmmmmmmmmmmwah!"

"That's it!" Ollie grinned, withdrew his elbow, leapt to his feet and sprinted off in search of more adventure. Fi dropped Jack's hand and chased after him. Ayesha still sat on the floor. She had summoned a ghost. And the ghost had smiled. She looked up at Jack, "Sorry."

"What for? What are you talking about?"

"The whole kissing it better thing. I didn't realise."

"Don't worry about it. It's fine. I think it just kind of threw all of us when we heard you say it."

"Are you sure? Really?"

"Yes, honestly. It's fine."

"And sorry for not stopping Ollie from falling."

"Stop apologising. You've nothing to be sorry about. Ollie is forever bumping his head, grazing his knee or bashing some other part of his anatomy. He gets a bump, behaves like he's in need of the last rites and seconds later he's climbing Everest or wrestling an alligator or scoring at Wembley."

She threw her arms around his waist and pressed her cheek against his chest, squeezing her relief and gratitude into him.

"Woohoo!" Ollie was hurtling down the drop slide once more, although in a much more controlled manner than before. Fi was just a second behind him and shrieked with pleasure on her way down. Jack and Ayesha had to be light on their feet to avoid being bowled over.

"Right you two, I think that's probably enough for now. You must have worked up an appetite by now." Jack's tone made it evident that this was the start of a negotiation rather than a statement of fact. Following three more goes each on the drop slide the children were happy to settle for the prospect of chicken nuggets and fries, and the promise of a return to The Idol at some skilfully unspecified date in the future.

The journey back was interrupted by a brief stopover at a drive-thru to honour the promise of junk food for the children. Ayesha had a chicken salad and Jack a chicken sandwich, their perfunctory consumption a contrast to the relish with which the nuggets were devoured. The rubbish was stuffed in one of the many bins around the car park and the rest of the brief journey home played out to a symphony of battle sounds from the back seats as Fi and Ollie engaged the plastic action figures that had accompanied their meal in mortal combat.

"How was it?" Fiona's enquiry as their re-entry shattered her stillness seemed aimed at no one in particular. Fi and Ollie were oblivious to the question as their conflict skirmished through the living room, back out to the hallway and upstairs.

"Yeah, it was okay Mum."

"It was fun Fiona. And educational. I hadn't really known what to expect from the description beforehand. But now that I've been I can see why it's quite hard to describe. Have you been?"

"Yes, once. It was interesting, but these old bones weren't suited to doing much there. I could see the attraction for the children but my overwhelming impression was that it was just noisy."

"I suspect we were lucky today because it didn't seem too busy. I can imagine it could be absolute bedlam when the place is full of even more excited kids. There was a brief drama when Ollie took a tumble and hurt his elbow."

"Oh?" The kind of *Oh* that says *Are you telling me that you, a stranger, were careless enough to put my grandson at risk of injury*?

"He was fine Mum. You know what he's like; a quick tumble and it's Armageddon, then reassurance that he's fine and the whole thing never happened. Anyway, are you all right if we leave the kids here with you? The idea was that Ayesha should get the chance to visit a few old haunts, and I thought that she and I could go for a walk."

"Of course. I'll let the kids run about like crazy until the E numbers wear off and then take them to the playground later. You two head off and have your walk. I can take care of things here."

## Chapter 21

Gants Hill roundabout was its usual festival of fumes and engine noise, amplified by the brightness of the Autumn afternoon sun. The relative cool and quiet of the underpass was a starkly contrasting interlude as they used it to cross under Eastern Avenue. Their voices and footsteps echoed off the low ceiling and tiled floor and walls. "So, how long since you last saw Valentine's Park?"

"Now you're asking, Jack. It's got to be the best part of twenty years ago. Any particular reason for asking?"

"Just checking that you hadn't been back since the Mansion was restored. If you've not seen it it's well worth a look."

"Mansion?" Ayesha's voice had a quizzical note that harmonised with the beat of their footsteps echoing off the tiled walls.

"Yes, Valentine's Mansion. I'm not surprised if you don't remember it. I don't think it was something I was really conscious of when I was a kid either. It was pretty sad and neglected. Anyway, they got council money and lottery funding about ten or so years ago and set about restoring it. It's absolutely lovely now – three hundred years old and Grade II listed. They've done a really good job."

"Jack, are you at the wind up? I think I'd remember a three hundred-year-old listed mansion in Valentines Park!"

"I'm serious". He smiled as he tried to gauge whether her narrowed eyes signalled scepticism, or merely a reaction to being reacquainted with the sunlight as they emerged from the underpass. "It's at the Cranbrook Road end of the park."

"Oh, okay. That probably explains it. I used to hang out at the cricket pitch and boating lake end when I was there."

"Same as most folks in those days. I really think you might be surprised at how much has changed. Let's go down Cranbrook Road and in at the Emerson Road entrance."

It took less than five minutes until they were standing in front of a substantial three-storey house. The facing bricks were yellow brown stocks with red dressings to the sash windows and returns. The southern elevation was clearly the face of the property – nine bays symmetrically arranged two-plus-five-plus-two – characteristically late-Georgian pared-down Palladianism. Cantilevered iron brackets from the wall supported a first-floor stone balcony, adorned by a Regency style cast iron guardrail. An elegant, understated building, lacking in ostentation. "I told you it was lovely, didn't I?" There was a child-like eagerness in Jack's tone.

"Can we go inside?"

"Yes, but ideally not today. It's part of my cunning plan. They're setting up an exhibition of wildlife photographs that opens this evening. I was hoping to invite you back another time to view that and see the inside then. Another excuse to see you again." Jack smiled hope. Ayesha continued to look at the mansion, hands clasped loosely together in front of her chest almost in prayer, her head tilted contemplatively to the right. She didn't speak. "You've gone quiet. What are you thinking?"

She turned to him, cheeks ember tinted. "I can't tell you what's going through my mind. It's too cheesy for words." Her smile intimated shyness and encouragement simultaneously.

"Oh come on now. You can't tease me like that!"

"Handsome and understated." Cheeks aflame, eyes to the ground.

"What?"

"You toad! What I was thinking was that I was being shown a handsome and understated building by a handsome and understated man. And now you've made me say it out loud!"

The mock stricture in her tone wasn't enough to save Jack, and he could feel his own skin blaze. "Oh god, sorry."

"At least you've got the good grace to share my humiliation." A pause and a smile.

"I am so, so sorry."

"Don't be. If anyone should be sorry it's me, for coming out with a line like that. Look, I feel embarrassed and you feel embarrassed. Shall we just call it a draw and forget it?"

"I suppose so. Except …"

"Except what?"

"Except I can't forget that you called me handsome!"

"I'm sorry, but I don't remember that. What I actually think I called you was a toad."

"Okay. Okay. It's a draw." Mutual laughter, relieved and sincere rather than awkward, sealed their treaty. "Shall we grab a tea or a coffee? The Gardener's Cottage Café is just over there."

They were soon seated in metal-framed chairs at a matching table on the patio outside the café. A large white pyramid-shaped umbrella afforded blessed shade from the still powerful sun. Jack extolled the virtues of seeing the inside of the mansion, with its twenty odd different rooms and imposing principal staircase, as well as eulogising the photography listed for the exhibition until she promised she would accompany him on a return visit. The conversation continued to flow effortlessly, until Ayesha reprised their earlier exchange. "Jack, I really am sorry for causing any embarrassment earlier."

"Forget about it. It's really not a problem. Forgotten. A draw – remember?"

"I remember. Are you sure you're okay with it?"

"I just said so, didn't I? And when Mr. Toad says he's okay with something he means it."

She returned his smile. "Okay. Thank you. But I'm afraid there's something else that I wanted to ask you."

"Go on, I'm all ears." Jack's attempt to feign exasperation dissolved into a smile.

"I hope you don't think I'm being nosey. It's just that sometimes I get a sense that there's something I don't know, or that I'm not being told. It's kind of an instinct. And that's when it can get awkward, because my curiosity can sometimes get the better of me. Not being able just to say nothing can land me in uncomfortable situations"

"I see. Why do I get the feeling that this is leading somewhere?" The smile still there, but the note in his voice betraying its thinness.

'Oh god, Jack. I really don't want to screw things up again. But earlier today I just got the sense that something wasn't right."

"What? When we were out with the kids? When we were talking to Mum? I don't remember anything particularly out of place."

"Before that. Before we went out with the kids. I was talking to them and your Mum when you came back into the room after you'd taken a 'phone call. I got the sense that something was wrong. I put it down to the awkwardness of you discovering your Mum and the kids had come home unexpectedly. But somehow, I think it might be more than that. It's been niggling away at the back of my mind." She could see his body tense. The absence of a reply sounded the alarm. "Sorry. Ignore me. I've just done exactly what I didn't want to do. I've said something inappropriate. Just ignore me. Please."

Jack stretched to put his cup and saucer on the table and turned to face her. He inhaled slowly and sighed quietly, before leaning in closely towards her. He paused, breaking eye contact briefly, as if pondering whether to continue. Eye contact reinstated. "Don't apologise. You're right. That phone call threw me."

"You don't need to talk about it. Honestly you don't."

The briefest of pauses. "But I am going to. I don't mind." Jack explained the whole story. Debs voice. The phone. Vic. The call to Vic. The report to the police. And finally, the call to Rachel. He spared no detail. Ayesha listened without saying a word, leaning in towards him, eyes always on his, his left hand held gently in both of hers. He stopped, cleared his throat, "It's the doubt. That's what gnaws. The doubt."

"Oh god, Jack." She rose from her chair, rounded the table and knelt towards him, pressing her left temple against his right, each feeling the other's breath on their cheek. After forever she eased back slightly and focussed until he responded in kind. Taking his left hand in her right, she pulled her chair round with her free hand and effortlessly eased herself back into it, all without breaking eye contact. Softly, "Do you honestly believe Debs was having an affair?"

"No. Not really. Not in my heart. Despite everything, I just don't believe it."

"Then it isn't true. If you don't believe it, it isn't true. When Charlie was cheating on me, I had no idea. But after I caught him, I was able to look back and see that there were signs everywhere. And that wasn't just hindsight. There were plenty of clues. I simply hadn't been looking for them before. This feels really different from when it happened to me. With Debs it's just not like that. You're right not to believe it." She squeezed his hand tighter and he saw the moistness in her eyes. "Me with Gaston was like you with Debs. We were made for each other. Two sides of the same quilt. Separate spirits with a shared soul. If someone told me after he died that he'd been having an affair I would just know it was a crock of shit. I would know here," touching her left hand to her breast, then to her cheek, to divert the tear that had finally broken cover. A brief pause for breath, "Jack, I have no idea what the story with this Vic character is, but it's certainly not that there was anything going on between him and Debs. And you know that. You know it."

He leaned forward and hugged her to within an inch of her life. "Thank you. Thank you."

## Chapter 22

"This channel is 91% secure. Adopt the appropriate protocol."

"Understood."

"Report please."

"Steady progress. My integration with the mark is evolving and deepening. As I reported before, the research has paid off big time."

"And Alpha and Beta?"

"Fully on board. They remain circumspect, but I have their confidence. I sense that my deeper integration with the mark is helping them shape their plans."

"Any details?"

"Nothing yet. As I say, they're still circumspect. I have the feeling that when things crystallise there will be very short lead times."

"Evidence for that?"

"Nothing. Just a feeling."

"Your instincts are usually good. And it wouldn't be a surprise if things suddenly moved fast. Keep us posted."

"Will do."

"Goodbye and good luck."

"Thanks. Goodbye."

## Chapter 23

The sounds were indistinct and irregular, but sufficiently insistent to interrupt his dalliance with the world of Hypnos. Wakefulness, unwelcome having so recently departed, sneaked back despite his valiant rear-guard action. Head pushed further into the pillow and duvet pulled tightly over his head proved insufficient to prevent conscious realisation that the noise was coming from below, and that it was the children. He could also make out his Mum's voice, scolding and shushing with some effect. The damage was done and he was awake, if not alert. Slowly he lowered the duvet and squinted with one reluctant eye. The curtains were closed but recalcitrant sunshine poured its fifth columnists through the gaps above, below and between the badly drawn drapery.

Frying bacon and burnt toast blended to form a heady and seductive incense, calling irresistibly and promising alternative nourishment for his sleep deprivation. It was Sunday. Mum was in the habit of doing a proper cooked breakfast on Sunday mornings before she took the kids swimming. And she always burned the toast, no matter how well she executed the rest of the meal. Jack started to slowly ease himself up the bed, knowing that failure to appear in time would mean missing out on bacon, eggs, sausage, mushroom and fried scotch pancake. And burnt toast. He liked burnt toast, but only when liberally spread with salted butter whilst still hot enough for it to melt in. Pleasant contemplation was interrupted when his left elbow hit something solid. Puzzled, he reached back awkwardly to try to identify the interloper in his comfortable sanctuary. Metal. Cold. Smooth. Laptop. Laptop! He must have fallen asleep whilst still on his laptop. He sighed long and slow, satisfied that the conundrum was explained.

Jack sat bolt upright. The recollection of what he had been doing on the laptop exploded and he felt adrenalin rush through his body. The memory of the previous night's insight – the realisation that he was in love with Ayesha - removed every trace of weariness. The joyful news needed to be shared. He reached for his 'phone from the bedside table – five to ten. He dialled Pete. Three rings then Pete's voice, "Hello."

"Pete, it's Jack. Are you free? I really need to talk to you."

"Okay then – go ahead."

"No like talk, speak properly. Face to face."

"Okay, when?"

"ASAP. As soon as you like. What are you doing now?"

"Aside from talking to you, nothing. Just thinking about getting out of bed."

"So, are you free?"
"Listen mate, I'm still in my scratcher. And I've not had any breakfast."

"Yes, yes sure. Same this end. Look, why don't you grab a shower and I'll do the same. I'll jump the Tube and meet you at your local – what's it called?"

"The Red Cow."

"Yes, The Red Cow. I'll see you there at opening. Breakfast on me – yes?"

"Sounds good to me. Jack …"

"What?"

"Is there something wrong?"

"No. No. Nothing wrong. Nothing wrong in the whole world. See you at the Red Cow at eleven."

"Right. See you then." Jack swung himself round, sitting with legs off the side of the bed.

As he stood up to head for the ensuite his Mum's voice drifted up the stairway, "Jack, is that you up? Are you coming down for breakfast?"

Jack stepped over to the door, opened it a fraction so his voice would carry better, "No thanks Mum. I'm heading out shortly to meet Pete for brunch."

Fifteen minutes later, shaved, showered and freshly dressed, he checked his hair in the still steamed up mirror as he ran a comb through it. The smell of his deodorant was heavy in the moist air and clashed with the toothpaste's mint aftertaste. But he felt good.

He skipped down the stairs, taking them two at a time. He

quickly stuck his head round the door to the kitchen-diner and smiled at his Mum, Fi and Ollie. "Just off to meet Pete for a bit of brunch and a catch-up. Shouldn't be back any later than two, maybe sooner. Might even be back before you get back from swimming." And, without waiting for any reply or acknowledgement he turned and was gone from the house. A short tube ride as smooth as Miles Davis playing *Summertime*, followed by a brisk five-minute walk, found him on Whiteladies Street. He could see Pete in the distance coming towards him and exchanged waves. Pete arrived at the pub first by a matter of only a second, "Fancy bumping into you here!"

"Amazing. Fancy grabbing a bite to eat?" The sound of the pub door being emphatically unbolted from inside confirmed the almost impossible perfection of their joint timing, and Pete led the way inside.

It was a crap boozer but Jack knew better than to voice any criticism. Pete was the fourth generation of his family to regard it as his local and was fiercely defensive of it, despite the fact that it had obviously declined over many years to become the shithole that it was today. Inside, although it had just opened, the sour smell of the previous night's stale ale hung heavily in the air. The bandit's plaintive siren song battled forlornly against the Sky commentator's overhyped build up to a boxing match so unappealing that it's re-run had been relegated to a morning slot on a Sunday. The barman, eyes as glassy as the optics, gazed up at the screen, bored senseless just a moment into his shift and glad of any distraction that involved no effort. Pete interrupted his contemplation of the sporting oracle by signalling their desire for service. He took their order – two full Englishes and two pints of Best – ungrudgingly but unenthusiastically. He was neither welcoming nor hostile. Neutral like Switzerland, but with less personality. He spoke only to confirm their order, ask for payment and state that the food would take ten minutes. Jack and Pete took their glasses and contemplated where to sit, as the drudge pulled another pint of Best and poured a large vodka into an almost clean tumbler. He then presented them to a small, elderly man – shabby grey raincoat, checked flat cap and folded Sunday tabloid – who had materialised at the bar. The old man paid exactly the right money, took his drinks and shuffled to a small round wooden table. The entire transaction was conducted wordlessly.

Pete listened as Jack confided in him. He put his glass down, clasped both hands lightly together and rested them on the table. There was no artifice in his expression, his bewilderment genuine. "I don't believe it, Jack. I simply don't believe it. You have got to be kidding me, mate."

"Yeah, yeah. Okay. Keep it down. It's not something I want broadcast." Jack's eyes and demeanour were even more imploring than his words. Pete hadn't been particularly loud, but Jack's embarrassment had heightened his sensitivity to his surroundings, and despite the fact the pub was virtually deserted he really didn't want any eavesdroppers savouring his discomfiture.

Pete's response was in a lower register, but the tone was unchanged, "Okay, but really Jack? A spreadsheet? A bloody spreadsheet? Nobody analyses their emotional state on a spreadsheet!"

"I know, I know, I know. But bear with me. It's not the spreadsheet itself. It's what it tells me. No. No, that's wrong. It's what it's helped me realise. It's how it's helped me to clarify my thinking."

"Go on then. This will be good." Pete's smile was expectant rather than encouraging.

"Two columns. The first listing all the negatives and the second all the positives. Then I put a minus value against each negative and a plus value against each positive."

Pete gave a tiny, almost imperceptible shake of his head. Then, realising Jack had caught him, nodded, "Go on then."

"Not if you're going to take the piss."

"No, no I won't. Go on."

"First was this feeling that it's disloyal to Debs. I know she's dead and that life moves on. But it's like we were forever, and that this is wrong somehow. That's a biggie for me. I scored it minus five."

Mention of Debs transformed Pete's demeanour. "Okay mate, I can understand that. How does your scoring scale work?"

"It's zero to plus or minus five. Zero means that, when I actually think about it, it doesn't really matter. Five, plus or minus, is the maximum. This sense of disloyalty, of guilt I suppose, really matters to me. It keeps coming back into my mind. Not all the time, and maybe less frequently than before, but it is still there."

"Yes, I can see that. But I think that's just natural given what's happened to Debs. You need to remember that it's not your fault. And you know that Debs would want you to be happy. She wouldn't want you to sacrifice your happiness because you feel guilty about something that's not your fault."

"I know that, and I keep telling myself that. But I also think if it was the other way round, if it was me that was killed, and Debs met someone else, I'd be jealous."

"But you wouldn't be jealous. Look, I'm not trying to be funny, or insensitive, but you wouldn't be 'feeling' anything."

"I know that too. And I'm not trying to say that any of this is logical, or even sensible. It's just what's going on in my mind."

"I get that. What else is on your list then?"

"The second thing I put down was 'Too soon/what will people think?' Looking at it now I wonder if they're actually two different things. Debs has been dead less than a year. Am I really over that? No. Does seeing someone else sound right? No. Will other people think I don't care about what happened to Debs, that I've got over it, forgotten her so soon?"

"Nobody would think that. And anyway, it doesn't matter what other people think."

"I know both those things. I know it isn't meant to matter about what other people think. But it's there in my mind and I'd be kidding myself if I pretended it wasn't. I put it at minus two and a half."

"You can have halves?"

"I know. I'm not pretending this is some precise scientific measure. Not like two point five zero. I just couldn't decide between two and three."

"It should be a two then."

"Probably. Possibly. It doesn't matter. Next thing I have is 'Is Ayesha too good to be true?' What I mean is that I've known her for ten minutes, yet I'm contemplating betting my whole world on her. I don't even know if this is a negative, and I'm certainly not explaining it very well. Not even to myself. I've put minus one against it."

"Not too big a concern then?"

"Oh Pete, I just don't know," Jack sighed. "It's either minus a thousand or it's a zero. And I think it's a zero because I don't honestly think she is too good to be true. But you can't ever be certain, can you? See – I'm going round in circles again. Can we just leave that one too?"

"Whatever you want mate. I'm just here to listen."

"Last one is the kids. How will they react? She's been over three weekends in a row now. They like her. Really like her. She really likes them. But I don't know how they would react if it got more serious. Whether they'd think I was forgetting their Mum. I wouldn't want to do anything that would hurt them. That's obviously a minus five too."

"Of course you wouldn't. So that's four negatives, yeah?"

"Yes. There were about a dozen things in each column, but I boiled them down, combined some, deleted others – trying to get a focus on what really matters."

"So, the positives then?"

"Number one is the kids. They like Ayesha and she likes them, as I said before. They're happy around her. Also, I'm happy when she's around and that rubs off on the kids too. That's a plus five. The next thing is me. Sounds selfish, and it probably is, but she makes me feel good about myself and about the future. I put that as a plus two, but if I'm being honest it's more than that."

"Surely that's another five?"

"Maybe. Whatever. Next I put my Mum at plus one. Mum takes her time to make her mind up about people. She doesn't rush to judgement, but she reads people brilliantly and – apart from you – I've never known her to be wrong about anyone. She is definitely warming to Ayesha."

"Just to be clear Jack, your Mum has an unblemished 100% record. Her very high opinion of me is completely justified."

"Yes, okay idiot. Whatever makes you happy. Then the last

one on the list." Jack paused.

Pete looked him in the eye expectantly, "And?"

"Ayesha. I just wrote Ayesha. Then I put in a hundred. Then I deleted it and put in a hundred billion. I'd have gone bigger, but that's all that would fit in the cell."

Pete grinned, "You've got your answer then, haven't you?"

"Yes." Smiling. Sheepish. Confessional. Relieved. Happy. Above all, happy.

"I'm delighted for you mate. Chuffed. But really – a spreadsheet? That's just sad. Crazy."

Jack smiled and shrugged. "Just trying my best to make sense of things."

"Don't try to justify using a spreadsheet to work out how you feel about someone. You're the only tosser in the whole world who would even think about doing something that pathetic."

"This conversation never took place, obviously."

"Obviously. That spreadsheet is between you, me and only my closest friends on Facebook."

The arrival of two full English breakfasts perfectly punctuated the discussion like a full stop and allowed the conversation to move seamlessly on to other subject matter.

## Chapter 24

The phone rang just as Jack realised there must be a mistake in the spreadsheet he'd spent the last forty-five minutes working on. Irritation and distraction soured his tone as he answered. "Jack Laidlaw."

"Jack, is this a bad time? If it is just say and I'll call back."

The husky voice fractured his focus on the numbers as he defaulted to mental red alert. An unexpected call from Hannah Hamilton normally presaged bad news. "No, not at all, Hannah. It's fine. How can I help you?"

"I just wondered if you could spare me a few minutes?"

"Sure, fire away."

"Actually, I meant could you spare me a few minutes in person?"

"Of course. Would now be convenient?"

"Thank you, Jack. That would be helpful."

"I'll be with you in five minutes." He replaced the phone as his mind ran through an inventory of possible causes for Hannah to want to see him - nothing. The words hadn't been spoken but the clear message was that there was a problem. Jack rose to his feet and strode towards the main office door, pausing by Martha's desk. She looked up as he leaned slightly forward. "I'm just off to see Hannah Hamilton," his voice low to avoid disturbing others. A flicker of concern crossed Martha's face. She'd been at the bank long enough to understand the implications of a meeting with the Infosec Director. "I'm sure it won't be anything to worry about." He flashed a reassuring smile that he hoped would be more convincing than it felt. "I'll give you an update when I get back."

Two minutes later Jack was following the tall, slim figure of Hannah Hamilton into the meeting room adjacent to her desk – another unhappy portent. He took a seat at a small rectangular beech and chrome table opposite Hannah. He studied her as she sat down, hoping for some clue about the reason for the meeting. She placed the orange cardboard folder she had been carrying on to the surface between them. Hannah Hamilton was a handsome woman. Thick straight black hair just reached the shoulders of her navy jacket and framed a symmetrical face where large eyes, wide mouth and Roman nose were pleasingly in proportion. She looked at him, radiating a smile that elevated her face a division to the rank of almost beautiful. "Thank you for coming up so promptly, Jack. You didn't want a tea or coffee, did you?" Jack shook his head in response to the rhetorical question. "Good, let's get down to business then. I'm sure you've got plenty of other things that you'd like to be getting on with." She beamed at him again as she opened the folder between them.

Jack avoided her glance and concentrated on the folder. Hannah didn't intimidate him the way she did some others, but he was wary of her. She had reached the highest echelons within the bank before the age of forty based on her widely acknowledged capability and a ferocious appetite for hard work. She was an undeniably attractive woman that Jack had never found himself attracted to, despite a vague sense that she might feel differently towards him. Nor was he switched off to her because she was a rival to his great friend Bob – he had a number of friends who didn't get on particularly well with each other. His aversion flowed from his awareness that she was a profoundly political animal, skilled in deploying whatever combination of expertise, effort, looks and charm would best help achieve her agenda. "What's this about, Hannah?"

"Just some questions about one of your team, Jack. Martha Mulraney."

"Martha?"

"Yes, Martha. I already know what there is that can be learned about her from her personnel file – don't worry, I've squared this conversation with HR. What I wanted to know from you was whether you've noticed anything different about her recently."

"What do you mean different?"

"If I knew that I wouldn't need to be asking you."

Jack ignored the barb. "I've not noticed anything different about Martha at all. What the hell is this about?"

Hannah held her right hand up, palm towards him. "Just stop there, Jack, and let me explain." She turned the open file and the papers it contained through a right angle so that they could both tilt their heads to see the contents. "This is a print out of Martha Mulraney's web browsing history over the past three months. There are some entries that I need to point out to you. Do you see here, here and here again?" Her index finger skipped down the page. Jack's eyes narrowed as he followed, trying to make sense of the rows and columns of small, tightly printed text and numbers. He could see the rows that Hannah was indicating were marked with fluorescent yellow highlighter. "These are the entries that are of particular interest."

"Sorry Hannah, you're going to have to explain this to me."

"The left-hand column shows the date, the next columns the start and end time that a particular site was browsed, and the long line to the right of each is the web address and particular page visited. The rest of the stuff is all technical data that I can take you through if you want, but isn't really material to this discussion."

"Okay, I understand. So what's the problem?"

"Well, the good news is that Miss Mulraney is very conscientious and seems only ever to browse the web outside of official working hours. You can see that her entries are all before eight-thirty, after five-thirty, or within a forty-five-minute window between noon and two on any given day. The majority of cases caught by this check are normally wastrels who are simply web surfing or chatting online with friends when they should be working."

"So that's not the problem then, is it?"

"No Jack. The problem is some of what she's been looking at. There's the usual visits to the BBC news site, online grocery shopping, holiday research and even some searches that seem work related. However, there have also been frequent visits to sites that give us real cause for concern. Those are the ones that are highlighted. As you can see, there are multiple entries over the period."

"I'm not clairvoyant, Hannah. What kind of sites are we talking about?"

"Terrorist sites." She paused to let the words sink in. "Specifically Islamist terrorist sites and sites designed to promote Islamist ideology."

Jack hesitated as he struggled to process what he was hearing. "That makes no sense whatsoever. Are you sure this is right?"

Hannah's disdain gave the lie to the cliché that there is no such thing as a stupid question. "Yes."

"It just doesn't add up at all."

"The first instance is exactly three months ago yesterday. There was a flurry for three or four weeks – multiple sites visited in the same session, looking more than once a day. Since then it has been less frequent, but at least once each week, and sometimes more. Eleven different sites visited on a total of more than sixty occasions across thirteen weeks. If you want to look at this report online, we can click on the hyperlinks so that you can see the sites visited yourself. But I need to warn you that a couple of them are quite gruesome."

"I'll take your word for it, Hannah. If I'm honest I'm struggling to get my head round this. What do we do next?"

"We speak to her. Ask her to explain herself."

"What, here? Now?"

"No time like the present. It will be an 'informal discussion.' As I said, I've okayed this with Jane in HR. She has agreed to give us the chance to learn more before triggering formal procedures. I presume that you're all right with it too?" Her tone signalled benevolent concern, but her eyes dared him to challenge.

Jack weighed up whether to test Hannah further, but decided against it, "I'll give her a call now, shall I?" Hannah nodded assent as she rose and moved to close the blind, obscuring the meeting room from the rest of the open plan office beyond the glass partition. "Martha, it's Jack. I wonder of you can spare a few minutes to join me with Hannah Hamilton?" A pause. "In the meeting room adjacent to her desk in Infosec. Thanks."

"She's on her way then?" Hannah noted Jack's nod. "Do your best to put her at ease when she gets here, but don't interrupt if it looks like she's avoiding answering my questions." A second silent nod acknowledged the pecking order in the room.

Martha entered apologetically, head slightly bowed with dinner plate eyes fixed on Jack for any sign of encouragement or explanation. "Where would you like me?" Jack indicated the empty chair at the end of the table. Martha sat down awkwardly and then shuffled position. "How can I help you? I'm not really sure what this is about." She cast a hopeful smile, fishing for reassurance.

"I'm sure there will be nothing to worry about, Martha." Jack knew his anaemic grin would be unlikely to provide consolation. "Infosec run a series of routine checks on various systems and one of those has flagged up an issue that we hoped you might be able to help us with." He thought he detected a barely perceptible stiffening of Martha's posture, a subtle switch of expression from vulnerable to defensive blankness. "Do you think you might know what I'm talking about?"

"Am I under some sort of investigation, Jack? Shouldn't I be given some sort of notice if that's the case?" A pause. "Don't I have the right to be accompanied? Shouldn't there be someone here from HR?"

Jack knew Martha well enough to recognise that she was afraid. He surprised himself by wondering whether the fear was simply because of the situation she found herself in, or whether there was some other reason. He also knew her well enough to sense that she knew what the discussion was about. "Relax, Martha. The reason for this meeting is that we hope it will prevent the need for anything more formal. Now, *do* you have an idea of what I'm talking about?"

Martha's hands were clasped in her lap, head bowed like a penitent in church. There was no attempt to make eye contact. "I feel like I'm on trial here." Her voice was quiet, half an octave lower than normal.

"No one's on trial here, Martha."

"Then what's this bloody kangaroo court all about?" She stared hard into Jack's eyes. Her face was flushed and she was blinking to prevent tears from spilling. The sudden vehemence of the outburst wrong-footed Jack, who was struggling to think of how to retrieve matters when the familiar low, throaty voice cut across him, signalling that his failure in the supposedly simple task of putting Martha at ease had led to demotion.

"If you will take a moment to compose yourself, I will explain exactly what this is all about. Here!" Hannah pushed a box of tissues that seemed to have appeared from nowhere across the table. "One of my teams run routine tests to review the online activity of randomly selected staff members. Occasionally those tests identify individuals who are web surfing when they should be working, or attempting to access porn or gambling sites, or other sites that are proscribed by bank policy. When that happens HR normally get involved and the disciplinary procedure is invoked." She paused to gauge the impact of her words. Martha dabbed her eyes and blew her nose heavily into two tissues, then returned Hannah's gaze. "Over the past three months we have observed that you have visited almost a dozen sites that promote or condone Islamic fundamentalism and terrorism. You have done so on sixty-eight separate occasions. Given the nature of the bank's business and its profile as a potential target for terrorist activity, we are naturally concerned." She paused again, studying Martha's reaction.

"I've never done any private web browsing on bank time."

"We can see that from your record."

"And I've never used my work pc to browse the web."

"Using your phone rather than your pc made no difference as you were still using the bank's wi-fi. But those points are not the issue. The concern is the nature of the sites that you have been visiting so frequently. This is your opportunity to explain yourself and pre-empt a more formal process."

Martha placed her hands on the table, slowly strangle-twisting the used tissues between them. She bowed her head, inhaled slowly and deeply, and then raised her eyes to meet those of her inquisitors. "My boyfriend Pete, Pjeter, and I have been going out for almost nine months. About three months ago he told me he was becoming very concerned about his brother Vik."

"Vic?" Jack's interjection was involuntary.

"Yes, Vik. Short for Vikram. He's just twenty – six years younger than Pete. Pete was worried that Vik was becoming radicalised by a group that he'd fallen in with at university. He'd started becoming much more devout, more fastidious in his observance of religious teachings, and increasingly isolated from his non-Muslim friends. The real alarm bell for Pete was when he found out that Vik had spent five days away at a camp in Iran. We were both massively worried and I was doing research both here and at home to see what I could find out."

A silence descended. Martha looked first to Hannah, and then Jack. There was no more sign of tears. She seemed composed, almost expectant as she awaited a response.

It was Jack who spoke first. "Pete and Vic don't sound like particularly Muslim names to me."

For the first time in the half dozen years he had known her, Jack was on the receiving end of a withering response from Martha. "Short for Pjeter and Vikram – *as I've already explained.*" She had displayed a range of emotions in the short time since she entered the room, and now there was cold fury as she glared at him. "Their father was Albanian and the family is Muslim. Pete and Vik were born and brought up here, and were never particularly religious. That seemed to change for Vik when their father died last year – he seemed to find it a source of comfort."

"Thank you, Martha." Hannah spoke slowly, the rhythm of her voice damping the tension in the room. "What conclusions have you arrived at about Vik? Has he been radicalised? Does he pose a threat to anyone?"

"I don't know. We don't want to believe it. Certainly Pete doesn't. And his mother certainly doesn't."

"And what about you?"

"As I say, I just don't know. I don't want it to be the case. But the more reading and research I do, the more I think there is a risk that his head could have been turned."

"And this reading and research – why were you doing it at work?"

"Not just at work. I've been doing it at home too. But it was easy and convenient to do it here as well."

"All right. And given your suspicions about Vik, have you flagged those concerns to anyone in authority?"

"No. We are hoping it's just a phase."

"I see. What is Vik's surname?"

"Leka. Why?"

"Because I need to have your story checked out and I have a responsibility to liaise with the appropriate agencies. I'm sure you understand that, and that you are not going to say anything to Vik or anyone in his family."

Martha looked thoughtful. "What will happen?"

"I've just explained. I expect that you may need to be interviewed by some other people about this. But for now we are done. You can go."

"What? Just like that? What happens now?"

"You go back to work, Martha. Jack will update you on what happens next when we know the next steps." Hannah smiled emptily and indicated the door with her eyes. Martha rose to her feet, fired an icy glare at Jack, and made her way to the door, closing it behind her. Hannah waited until Martha would be out of earshot. "Well, Jack, you know her. What do you make of that?"

"Honestly, I'm still trying to process it. I'm also a bit emotional about it because she clearly feels that I've somehow betrayed her."

"That's understandable, Jack. But I am keen to know whether or not you believe her."

"I've never seen her like that before. So many emotions. So much anger. She's normally a very private person. I suppose that she's embarrassed, and maybe that might explain some of it."

"That's all very well. But do you *believe* her? Has she mentioned this Pete or Vik to you before?"

"As I say, she's very private. Don't get me wrong – she's very good socially and interacts well with people. She just doesn't say that much about herself. I did know that she had a boyfriend, but I don't know if I'd heard his name. I'm certain I've never heard her mention Vik."

"And do you think she's telling the truth?"

"I think so. She seemed completely genuine. Why would she lie?"

"Why indeed?"

"So what happens now?"

"I'll close the loop with HR. I'll need to tell the boss what's going on and then I'll give my contact in the security services a call. Once I've been round those houses, I'll catch up with you and let you know where we go next." Hannah smiled as she rose to her feet and once more indicated the door with the slightest nod of her head. "Are you okay, Jack?"

"Yes, fine. I'll wait to hear from you."

## Chapter 25

"Come on then. Spill!"

"Huh?" Jack looked at his untouched lager on the table. Completely intact, no overflow. "What spill? I don't understand."

"Don't be such a dork, Jack. I mean spill the beans. What is it that's on your mind?"

"What do you mean?" His eyes betrayed the fact the question wasn't really *'what's on your mind?'* Rather it should be *'where is your mind?'* as it clearly wasn't in the here and now.

Ayesha leaned across the small, circular mahogany table and placed her right hand on top of Jack's left. Her eyes searched his until there was a flicker of acknowledgement. "First, you call and ask if we can meet earlier than planned for lunch. Then you suggest we come to this pub instead of meeting at Sandro's. When we get here you order a lager to have with your baguette – when you've told me before that you never have alcohol during working hours. And, most tellingly of all, you've taken two ant-sized nibbles of that baguette and not eaten a single chip in the five minutes since we sat down." There was a light, almost jocular note to her voice, but her eyes and posture betrayed concern. She leaned a few degrees closer. "So, Jack Laidlaw, I don't exactly need to be Miss Marple to work out that something is bothering you."

Jack exhaled, long and slow. He lowered his baguette on to its plate before using his freed hand to sandwich hers. "A really shitty thing happened at work this morning." Ayesha gave a *do tell* tilt of her head and widened her eyes expectantly. Jack leaned back slightly and checked their surroundings. They were tucked into one of half a dozen intimate little booths that might each accommodate four people at a pinch, which ran the length of the back wall of the Victorian pub. The booths were sufficiently high-backed to ensure as much privacy as the occupants desired. The place was filling rapidly with the clock approaching midday, and bodies were already doubling up at the bar as the staff behind struggled to keep up with the rush of food orders. The lunchtime hum was building nicely. Jack leaned back in and quietly explained the events of the morning involving him, Hannah and Martha. Ayesha interrupted a few times to clarify things or express a view, but largely remained silent. A casual observer would have known that theirs was a discussion about something that really mattered. "Then when I got back down to my desk Martha looked at me in a way that made me feel like I'd actually been punched."

"So the atmosphere was a bit frosty then?"

"More like Ice Station Zebra. I couldn't wait to get out of there. That's when I called you." Jack's right hand reached for his baguette and he bit off an enormous mouthful. He chewed with relish, before swallowing. "So what do you think?" Another bite reduced the baguette to just over half its original size.

"Where to start? It's a hell of a lot to take in. From what you say it's an open and shut case that Martha has been on these sites. No-one's disputing that, are they?" She received an affirmatory nod from Jack, whose enthusiastic masticating prohibited speech. "So the real question is motivation then. Do we believe Martha's story, or do we think that there's something more sinister to it?"

The tomato in Jack's ham baguette didn't provide sufficient moisture. "Do you mind if I have a mouthful of your orange juice?"

"Go ahead." Ayesha pushed her glass in his direction. "Don't want your lager then?"

"Thanks. No. I must have been on autopilot at the bar. As you say, I don't mix work and drink. And today's probably a really bad time to start."

"So, do you believe Martha's story?"

"As I said to Hannah, why would she lie?" He paused and looked at her as he returned her orange juice across the table. "What do you think?"

"How am I meant to know? I've never even met the girl. From the things you've said previously when you've mentioned her, I have to say it sounds a bit far-fetched to imagine she's involved in anything sinister." A pause and the merest hint of a shrug. "But then again, who knows?"

"I'm pretty sure. I've worked beside her for years. She's just not that sort of person."

"And what sort of person is that, Jack? How do any of us really know what's going on in someone else's life? What's *really* going on in their head? Unless you live with them, or you've known them their entire life, you can't really know them for certain."

The earnestness of Ayesha's tone caused Jack to withdraw his baguette just as he was on the cusp of tearing off another almost-too-big mouthful. His expression was a hybrid of thoughtful and quizzical. "I suppose you're right to an extent. But you get a sense of people. You kind of just know in your gut when people are being straight and when they're not. Certainly if you spend any length of time with them."

"Even if they they are deliberately trying to create a false impression? To mislead you?"

"I reckon so." Jack paused as the sudden recollection of how Ayesha had been the victim of infidelity speared him with guilt at his insensitivity. "No. That's wrong. Of course it's possible for people to deceive and be deceived. It's just that in this case I can't bring myself to believe Martha is lying." He hoped his partial volte-face wasn't too clumsy or obvious.

"Jack, you know Martha well, and I'm sure you're right. But at least you acknowledge the possibility that she might not be everything she seems?"

"I suppose it's possible, but the idea just doesn't sit right."

"Fair enough. Am I right in assuming that you think there's a chance she'll be in Sandro's for lunch today, and that's why you brought us here instead?"

"Got it in one."

"You do realise that you have to work together and that you can't avoid her?"

"I know. And I also know that it'll be fine once we get over this initial upset and work our way through things. It's my job to make it work, and I will. It was just that it was so raw when I came back down into the office. I felt the need to get out, get some space and thinking time. You understand?"

"Definitely. I can just imagine how awkward it must have been. Are you okay with it now?"

"Yes, I'm feeling better. It's Martha that I feel sorry for. She must be all over the place – embarrassed, worried, and insecure – the lot. I'll take the temperature when I get back and judge when to have a quiet word with her."

"That sounds good. I imagine you'll need to handle that sensitively. Getting the balance between being supportive to her and not prejudicing the investigation might be tricky." Ayesha had to wait for a response as Jack concentrated on grinding another mighty mouthful of chips, bread, ham and tomato.

"You're right, but I'm sure it'll all be okay. Anyway, mentioning Sandro's reminds me. On a completely different topic, there might be an opportunity for you to meet up with someone you know."

"I'm all ears. Do tell."

"Well, you know I've been looking for someone to work alongside Alex. We'd seen four people and none of them were right, for various reasons. Anyway, yesterday afternoon Alex and I interviewed a woman who was absolutely perfect for the role.HR saw her separately and they rated her too. Long and short of it is that they got an offer out to her last night and she's verbally accepted."

"All sounds good. But who is it I'm meant to know?" Ayesha's voice carried a note pitched between curiosity and irritation.

"Just coming to that. This woman, Donna, would be relocating from Leicester to take our job. I asked what the attraction of moving to London was and she explained she was moving in with her boyfriend. They've been in a long-distance relationship for over two years since they met on holiday in Barbados. Her boyfriend is a chap called Henry Kingswood." Jack paused expectantly, smiling a nod of encouragement that was swallowed by the black hole of Ayesha's blank expression. "Henry Kingswood! Apparently, he's worked at Chartered Municipal for about the last eight years. You must know him."

Ayesha stiffened slightly, and seemed momentarily thrown.

"Yes. I know that name. Did you mention me to Donna?"

"I told her that I knew someone that had worked at CM for a number of years and that would probably know her boyfriend."

"Did you mention my name?"

"I don't think so." Jack furrowed his brow. "No, I'm pretty sure that I didn't. Definitely not. Is there a problem?"

Ayesha eased visibly and the tension that had appeared on her face vanished as suddenly as it had arrived. "No, not a problem, as such. It's just that I haven't heard the name for a number of years. And…"

"And?"

"And he was a good friend of Charlie's. I got on perfectly well with him, but he was very much one of Charlie's close buddies."

"Oh! I simply didn't even think about that. Look, I don't think there's a problem. As I say, I mentioned that I knew someone that worked there, but nothing more."
"Relax, Jack. It's no big deal. You did throw me a bit by mentioning CM and then Henry, but it's not a problem."
"Are you sure?"

"I'm absolutely sure. But you mentioned me meeting someone?"

"Oh yes. It's a kind of induction thing we offer to new starters. At the end of their first week the team like to take the newbie out on the Friday evening for dinner, usually at Sandro's. Partners are invited along and the department budget picks up the tab. We usually get a really good turnout that way and we find it's a useful way to help new starters to begin to integrate more quickly."

"And you thought you might invite me, and that I'd be able to meet my old colleague Henry Kingswood."

"Bingo! But I guess that's perhaps not such a good idea now?"

"I don't know. When would it be likely to take place?"

"Donna is on two months' notice with her current employer. By the time she formally accepts, resigns, works her notice and relocates down here I reckon we're looking at the thick end of three months away."

"Oh, okay. Well let's not rule me in or out right now. There's plenty of time to decide. But maybe avoid mentioning my name to Donna. No point in setting any hares running with Henry for now."

Jack swallowed the last mouthful of baguette and chips and wiped his mouth with the paper napkin. "Of course. I won't even see Donna until she starts, and I'd be surprised if she remembers me mentioning it by then." He glanced at the half-drunk glass of orange juice and made his eyes huge, in a passable impersonation of Puss in Boots from Shrek.

"Oh for god's sake, just finish it!" Ayesha giggled. "And about the 'newbie' dinner at Sandro's. You said that bank staff's partners are invited."

"Thank you." Jack gulped the entire contents of the glass in one go. "Yes, that's right."

"So I'm your 'partner' then, am I?" She made quotation marks in the air with her fingers.

"If you play your cards right, maybe."

Ayesha leaned across the table and cuffed his shoulder with a loose fist. "You cheeky pig!"

Jack grabbed her wrist and pulled her towards him, leaned in and planted a delicate kiss on her lips. "An irresistible cheeky pig."

Ayesha leaned back smiling. "Maybe. Now haven't you got more important things to be doing?"

He acknowledged the reality check with a wry grin and a nod. "You're right, I'd better get back. I'll give you a call this evening to let you know how I get on."

## Chapter 26

The lighting was muted, and cool jazz playing quietly over the sound system provided a pleasing counterpoint to the melody of a dozen different hushed conversations. Ayesha perched on the leather and chrome barstool, right leg crossed over her left, skirt ridden up just above her knees. Her toes were in place in her court shoe, but the stiletto end hung loose, freeing her heel and ankle to breathe. Her foot swayed, ever so slightly, ever so gently. Jack had seen her do this before on more than one occasion and the effect was always the same. The slim, beautifully sculpted ankle acted like a hypnotist's dangling watch and he became mesmerised. He had always joked to anyone who would listen that he had the ankles of a Greek god. Now he was in the company of a genuine goddess, the perfection of her elegantly swaying tarsus casting its spell on an ardent disciple.

"Am I that boring?"

"Sorry, I was miles away."

"Well that's hardly very flattering. What's a girl to think when her date would rather stare at the floor than talk to her?" Her tone was amused, teasing.

"Actually, I wasn't staring at the floor."

"I saw you, you Muppet. Don't try to deny it."

"I was looking at your shoe, if you must know."

"Surely you can do better than that?"

"Okay, if you must know. I was watching your ankle."

"Oh yeah?"

"Yes I was. Watching rather than staring by the way."

"And my ankle is that interesting, is it?"

"Well, since you ask, yes, it is. That ankle is beyond mere beauty. It is the most aesthetically pleasing creation that has ever been in existence. The only drawback is that if I want to appreciate it, I have to pretend to be interested in its owner."

"Jack Laidlaw! You are more full of shit than I have the words to describe." The words admonished, but the tone encouraged.

She looked at him over the rim of her cocktail glass; chin tilted slightly downwards, the attempt to disguise her smile failing miserably.

He couldn't maintain the charade as her smile infected him. "Just trying to confess to my ankle fetish, and wishing I hadn't."

"You don't get off that easily. Before you decided to stare at the floor …"

"Worship your ankle!"

"Before you decided to stare at the floor you were desperately trying to avoid telling me more about Martha. Which is strange, given that you're so keen to sing her praises any other time."

"What *are* you talking about?"

"Oh come on Jack! *Martha said this today. Martha sorted that out for me. Martha always seems to know the right thing to say. I don't know how we'd manage without Martha.* You know – ***that*** Martha!"

"You're jealous!"

"Don't flatter yourself. I'm just curious, that's all."

"If you say so. What is it you want to know about her?"

"Oh, I don't know. What age she is? What she looks like? I just don't have a picture of her in my mind."

"Okay then. She's younger than us; I'd say late twenties. She's always impeccably dressed – she takes real care about her appearance. And I believe that she's single."

"You *believe* that she's single?"

"That's what I said."

"You work all day beside this woman – this girl – and you're not sure whether she's single or not?"

Jack couldn't keep it up. "Martha is lovely and she's a really important part of the team at work. I've got all the time in the world for her. But you have nothing to worry about. Really, nothing. Hang on a minute." He fished his phone from his pocket and started to scroll. "Here." He handed the phone to Ayesha.

"What am I looking at?"

"Our office Christmas party from last year. That's me with my arm round Martha's shoulder."

"Oh," Ayesha paused as she contemplated the image. Then

her thumb and forefinger enlarged it. "She looks ... nice. Really nice. Reliable. Friendly ..."

"She's all of those things." Jack was struggling to avoid his smile becoming a smirk. Their eyes were level, but he was enjoying looking down on the view from the moral high ground. "She's lovely, but her ankles are nothing to write home about."

"You beast, Jack!" Ayesha lent forward and punched him in the shoulder with his phone, her smile a beguiling marriage of embarrassment and delight. "You led me into that deliberately."

"I only led you where you were willing to go." He took back the phone and pocketed it, then took her free hand in his. "And talking about going, we'd better make a move soon or we'll never find anywhere with a free table. Our 'one quick cocktail before dinner', has turned into four!"

"Wow, you're right! I hadn't noticed the time. We'll never find anywhere decent with a table at this time on a Friday night." Her left hand stroked her chin.

"What's on your mind?"

"I was just thinking ..."

"Yes?"

"I was just thinking that there's a really decent Chinese takeaway on my street. We could jump a cab there and then take it back to my flat to eat."

"Are you sure?"

"Only if you think it's a good idea."

"I'm all for it. As you say, we're not going to get a table anywhere decent. Shall we?" Ayesha nodded and they each slid down from their barstools. Jack took her left hand in his right and led her to the door. They exited on to the busy street and Ayesha let his hand go, instead wrapping her arm round his waist and pulling him close. The aroma of half a dozen different cuisines competed on the warm night air, the traffic was cacophonous and people – singles, couples, groups – zigzagged and chit-chatted towards their various rendezvous. The unseasonal late evening sun was still bright and both Jack and Ayesha squinted as they struggled to cope with the sudden assault on their senses. Any temptation to simply retreat back into the comforting calm of the wine bar was banished when serendipity and a red traffic light delivered a black cab, taxi sign illuminated, to the pavement's edge in front of them. Jack stepped forward, tapped the window and exchanged a nod with the driver, then opened the door for Ayesha and followed her in before closing it firmly behind him.

"Where to?"

"Denbigh Street in Pimlico." The traffic light turned to green and the cab accelerated fiercely in acknowledgement that the destination was recognised. Traffic was surprisingly light and the journey was negotiated in barely ten minutes, almost to the disappointment of two passengers engaged in passionate embraces and caresses. Jack paid the driver, tipping him heavily, and contemplated his surroundings, keen to drink in the street that was Ayesha's home. It was elegant and oozed prosperity, like virtually every SW1 address. Each side of the short street consisted of three, four or even five storey Georgian terraces, some complete townhouses, others with retail or commercial premises on the ground floor. Various styles of balcony at first floor level, elegant black and gold painted street lights and a scattering of trees along one pavement underlined affluence. His evaluation of the location was cut short by Ayesha's insistent tug on his arm and in moments the pair had soon ordered and collected the set meal for two, chosen in the accurate expectation that it would be ready quickly.

A further ninety seconds and Ayesha was unlocking the door to her first floor flat. Jack followed along the corridor past two doors, the second open to reveal a bathroom, and through into a galley kitchen that opened into a reception room still made bright by fading late evening sun shimmering through two generous sash windows. "Put the food on the table and I'll get some plates." Jack put the brown paper carrier bag down absent-mindedly as he surveyed the arctic interior. Walls and ceilings were white. Pure, brilliant absolute white. The floor bleached oak. The blinds on the windows were unpatterned solid white and even the radiators, rectangular with length vertical, were colour coded to match the walls. The square table he had placed the bag on was a high quality white melamine, with two matching chairs, thankfully with integral white leather cushions. The rest of the reception area had a white leather two-seater sofa against one wall, facing a white-framed wall mounted television, with a low glass table between. A TV remote rested on its surface. In the kitchen, the stainless steel cooker hood and the taps over the sink provided the only relief from the snowscape. "Come on Dozy, get the food out of the bag!" Ayesha put two plates, knives, forks and a selection of spoons on the table and planted a kiss on his cheek. "I've got a nice Riesling chilling, let me just get some glasses."

"It's really white. Really, really white."

"Riesling? It certainly is!" She grinned in response to his mock stern frown at the tease. "Tell me about it! It's all a bit sparse and antiseptic here." Ayesha placed two large glasses down and turned to the fridge for the wine. "The area is great and the rent is just about reasonable for where it is, but I can't wait to find my own place and move my furniture from storage. Here!" She handed him the wine and a waiter's friend retrieved from the cutlery drawer. "You do the honours."

Jack took the bottle and corkscrew as Ayesha emptied the cartons of food from the bag and removed the lids. "So how long a lease have you got on this place?"

"I've got it on a monthly rolling contract, which means I'm really flexible if I see somewhere else that I'd prefer." Looking up, "Sit down and join me. Do you want to serve yourself or shall I dish up for both of us?"

"Please do dish up for both of us, thanks." He removed the cork from the bottle with a flourish, "Here you go! Shall I pour?"

"Yes, please. I knew that there must be some use in having a man around the flat."

"Let me tell you, madam, that I am a man of considerable hidden talents."

"Are you? Really?" The conversation was punctuated as they each tried the wine, eyes locked over the rims of their respective glasses.

"The wine is lovely. It goes particularly well with the prawns and ginger."

"Mmmm, yes. I love it when you combine two things and find

that they really go well together. It can be a discovery of delight." The meal and the small talk continued for a further few minutes, Ayesha's coquettishness stirring Jack's other appetites as effectively as the food was satisfying his hunger. "At this rate, it will still be quite early by the time we've finished eating." She took another sip from her glass, inviting his response with an arched left eyebrow.

"You're right. Are there any decent pubs nearby?'

"I wasn't really thinking about going out. How would you feel about watching some breakfast telly?"

"Breakfast telly?"

"That's what I said," Ayesha got up from her chair and circled round the table, before easing herself on to his lap and draping her right arm around his neck. "Of course, we'd need to think of something else to do to fill the time before the first programme starts." Her left hand cradled the back of his head, pulling it gently forward until their mouths locked. She eased back slowly, slid off his lap and took his hand in hers and pulled him softly to his feet. They continued to hold hands as she led him back down the corridor to what he already knew must be the bedroom.

## Chapter 27

Jack closed the fridge door and turned to see if the pickings on the table were any less sparse. He surveyed last night's Marie Celeste meal. It brought an unwelcome recollection, of waking up as a student to find a half-eaten Chinese take-away by his bed and actually finishing it. He picked a prawn cracker to sample. It was still crisp and snapped with a satisfying crunch as he bit into it. The oiliness inside his mouth was not the ideal way to start the morning, but beggars couldn't be choosers. He leaned forward and picked out another two crackers, then straightened with a jolt as two arms pincered and squeezed his waist from behind, and a body pressed against his back. "Are you really *that* hungry?"

"A little bit peckish." Jack rotated a hundred and eighty degrees, bent forward and placed a kiss on the lips of his captor.

"Yeuch! You taste of those prawn crackers!" Ayesha pushed him backwards gently, smiling broadly despite her protestation of disgust.

"Well, I checked the fridge and half a pint of milk, some Jarlsberg and half a pound of butter – oh, and another bottle of Riesling – hardly constitute the ingredients for an appetising breakfast."

"How do some pains au chocolat and coffee sound then?"

"Fantastic. But where …" Jack's protest question died half-born. He watched Ayesha go to a previously invisible white ceramic bread bin on the kitchen worktop, and retrieve an unopened pack bearing the legend *Freshly Baked For You*.

"You're in luck. There are four of these, they're huge and the use by date is tomorrow. How do you want your coffee?" She retrieved two large mugs and a pair of matching side plates from one of the head-height cupboards.

"Strong, milky and one sugar please."

"Coming right up." She filled the kettle, switched it on and spooned coffee granules and sugar into the mugs. As an afterthought, "Instant okay?"

"Absolutely fine." Jack leaned forward to accept the proffered plate of two precariously balanced rolls. "Yum. Thanks." He took one of them, biting off over a quarter and chewing with undisguised relish.

"So you don't want me to warm yours up?" Ayesha's grin was as wide as Jack's eyes as he gestured no, unable to speak. "So that's just further confirmation of your status as a barbarian then." Jack's eyebrows protested. "What else am I to think? A man who devours a breakfast pain au chocolat cold like a wild animal. Who thinks it's acceptable to get up at twenty to seven on a Saturday morning? You have to agree your behaviour hardly epitomises the pinnacle of human civilisation." She turned to pour the freshly boiled water into the mugs and fetch the milk from the fridge.

"I tried not to wake you."

"But you did, didn't you? You great noisy beast!" She placed the two cups of coffee on the table and turned away to fetch the other pair of rolls from the heating rack over the toaster. Their delicious aroma made Jack wish he'd waited and had his heated too.

Jack cleared the remains of the chocolaty delight with his first swig of coffee. "I really am sorry." Ayesha took the seat at ninety degrees to his left, raised her mug to her mouth, eyes twinkling impishly over the gently tilted rim. Realisation dawned. "You're at it! You're winding me up!"

"So how do **you** like it then?"

"What? What are you on about?"

"Last night? In the wine bar? *Martha's young, single, always really smartly turned out.* I think you remember."

"Ah, yes. Fair enough – let's call it quits." Jack smiled and half-bit, half tore a huge piece from his second pain au chocolat, using his pinkie to prod it into his mouth. He signalled he had more to say, but his mouth was full. Ayesha indulged him with a smile as she waited, nibbling at the corner of her own roll. Jack swigged some more coffee and continued. "So what do you survive on? There's not enough food in that fridge to feed a flea."

"To be honest, I eat out most of the time. I usually go to a little place round the corner that does lovely breakfasts. I keep a few ready meals in the freezer and a few tins in the cupboard, and I pick up essentials like bread and milk as and when."

"Fair enough, although I have to say that this place barely feels lived in."

"What makes you say that?" Ayesha followed another nibble of her roll with a mouthful of coffee and fixed him with *a what do you mean?* look.

"Well for a start, the whole place is spotless. There's virtually nothing to eat. And in the bathroom this morning I couldn't help but notice that there was barely a fraction of the toiletries that I'd expect a woman to have."

"So now it's your turn to play Clouseau?" Ayesha put her mug down and sighed lightly. "In a way you're right. No one lives here. I mean really *lives* here." His arched eyebrow demanded an explanation. "When I said last night that the rent was reasonable, that's because I get the place at mates rates. An old colleague from Chartered Municipal, Chloe, was assigned to Tampa for six months the week before I was due back in London. So it all sort of fell into place and now I'm kind of house-sitting the place for her while she's away and I'm looking for something more permanent. It's a nice flat in a great area, but I feel like a lodger. I don't want to mess up anything of Chloe's and I only brought two suitcases with me – plus what I've bought since I got back, so I haven't got enough of my own stuff to put my stamp on the place. So you see, I don't feel like I properly live here – it's just too transient. Does that make sense?"

"Absolutely, that makes sense." Jack's eye wandered towards Ayesha's plate.

"Do you want that one too?" Ayesha indicated the last pastry by waving its quarter eaten sibling towards it."

"Only if you're sure." Jack was already reaching for it.

"I'll struggle to finish this one. I don't know where you put it all. It's amazing you don't pile on the pounds."

Jack swallowed a mouthful. "I'm a mesomorph. It's genetic. You've seen my mum. My dad was the same. Both used to joke they could eat for Britain if it was an Olympic sport, and not a pick on either of them." He bit off another huge chunk and followed it with a swill of coffee.

"So what's with getting up this early on a Saturday morning then?"

"Nothing. To be honest, it's completely out of character. I usually have a long lie on a Saturday. It can be ten or half past before I get up."

"And wandering round a girl's flat, measuring her toiletries against those of your daughter?" The tone a gentle tease.

"Oh no, I wasn't thinking of Fi. It was more the sheer volume of stuff Debs used to keep in the bathroom." Jack's voice trailed off and there was a sudden hush, almost tangible rather than audible. Ayesha's hand reached over the table and took his. They both sat unspeaking until eventually Jack adjusted his stare into the middle distance and returned her gaze.

"Are you all right?" The compassion in her eyes in perfect harmony with her tone.

"Yes."

"Sure?"

"Yes. And you?"

"I'm fine. I think."

Jack tightened his hold on her hand slightly. "How do you … how do you feel?"

"I don't know. Not bad. But not quite normal either. Does that sound mad?"

"Not at all. I think that's how I feel. I'm not sure I've got the words. I wanted last night to happen. And I'm glad it did. Really glad. But now – no, that's wrong. I don't mean but. And now … oh God, I can't think of a word."

Ayesha's grip tightened more than his had done. Her eyes were moist. "I know. I understand. I feel it too. I don't think there is a word. It's not rational, I don't think. It's not guilt and it's not regret because I don't feel guilty or regretful about last night. It's not feeling disloyal either. But it is like I've underlined the fact that Gaston is gone. That somehow he's even further away." Her blink arrested a tear.

"It's all right. I get it. Really, I do. I feel the same. Like maybe I need approval somehow, to be told it's okay. I imagined before how I might feel if this happened. I thought about how I would feel if it was the other way round – if I were dead and Debs met someone else. I would be a bit jealous in my heart, but my head would want her to be happy." A pause. "Huh. Sounds like I think she's up there right now watching and listening. I don't even know if I believe in any sort of afterlife. But I know how I feel right now." Ayesha moved silently round the table and sat gently on Jack's lap. She placed a light, tender kiss on his lips, slid her arms around him and rested her head on his shoulder. He cuddled her softly, in a prolonged silence.

Eventually Ayesha straightened her back and looked him in the eye. "Okay?"

Jack smiled and nodded. "Yes, fine thanks. You?"

"I'm fine too." Another light caress of his lips with hers, and a smile. "More coffee?"

"Actually yes, that would hit the spot."

Ayesha stood up, gathered their mugs and stepped over to the counter to make another round of drinks. "So, Jack Laidlaw, you normally lie in till half past ten on a Saturday? What happens to Fi and Ollie while you abandon your paternal responsibilities in such a cavalier fashion?"

Jack's face exploded into a grin at the return to teasing banter. "My mum takes them both swimming, if you must know. Almost every Saturday and Sunday morning. Brings them back around lunchtime with huge appetites, which – on Saturdays - are satisfied by the consumption of a fantastically nourishing lunch prepared with fatherly love."

"A fantastically nourishing lunch? Unexpected cordon bleu talent! Do tell." Ayesha put the two fresh mugs of coffee down on the table and returned to her seat.

"Generously buttered fresh rolls. Sausages fried so they're crispy on the outside but still juicy on the inside. And..." Jack's two forefingers drum rolled on the table top. "And ... tons of brown sauce. Absolutely unbeatable!"

"Further proof that you really are an absolute barbarian!"

"What?"

"You force those poor children to eat brown sauce! I have no choice but to report you to the authorities."

"You don't mean …"

"Yes, Jack. I'm a ketchup girl. One hundred per cent. And to be honest, if I'd known about this vile aspect of your character …" Ayesha liquefied into giggles, unable to maintain the nonsense. She leaned over the table, put both her hands behind his head and planted a firm kiss on his lips.

"I'm sorry. There can be no rapprochement. You can try and kiss me, seduce me with your charms. But the simple reality is that the divide between red and brown tribes is simply unbridgeable. I'm afraid I'll have to go."

"I know you're right. You are Montague and I'm Capulet. You can use my toothbrush before you go."

"Actually I've got a toothbrush of my own in my jacket pocket."

Ayesha's surprise was genuine, "What?"

"I've been carrying it for the last few weeks. Just in case." The smile of a cheeky schoolboy.

"You presumptuous arse!" She cuffed his chest gently with the heel of her hand. "And have you been bragging to your friends about your evil designs on me?"

The light-hearted joshing persuaded Jack to go for broke. "Of course not! Only my mum."

"What!"

"Only my mum." The schoolboy cheek had vanished, replaced by an adolescent shiftiness.

"Only your mum? *Only* your mum! You told your *mum*! God Almighty!"

"I just texted her to let her know I wouldn't be home last night."

"You *texted* her! Good God. This just gets worse. What were you thinking of? What will she have thought? What will she think of *me*? Oh for God's sake!"

Jack reached across the table and took her hand in his, slightly surprised and relieved at the absence of any resistance. "Look, if I didn't get back last night, she would have been worried. That's the deal when you're a grown adult who lives with his mum. By texting to say I wouldn't be home she could go to bed and sleep, rather than fret about me."

"I suppose I can see that."

"I told her a few weeks ago that I'd text if I wasn't coming home."

"What?"

"I said I told her a few ..."

"Yes! Yes, I heard what you said! What do you mean? You and your mum were talking about our non-existent sex life? Oh God! Really, Jack? Really?"

"Relax. Mum was interested in how serious I was about you. The conversation just progressed ..."

"Lalalalalalalalalalala." Ayesha's hands were over her ears, eyes tight shut and head shaking rapidly from side to side.

Jack waited, smiling, for the denial to abate. "The conversation – which I found bloody uncomfortable, if that makes you feel better – just progressed."

"Progressed how?" Still now, looking him in the eye.

"She asked if we were 'intimate'."

"Aaaaargh!" Ayesha's elbows were on the table, head bowed forward into her hands.

"You should think yourself lucky you weren't there! If this is horrible for you to hear, can you imagine how awkward it was for me?"

Her eyes rose to engage his. Her lips toyed with a smile. "I honestly can't imagine. How did you handle it? What did you say?"

"I stumbled and stuttered, as you'd imagine. I told her that it really wasn't any of her business and she countered by saying it was her business if it meant I wasn't going to be around for the kids."

"She had a point."

"I know. I could hardly disagree. I told her that we were taking things steadily, but that if the time came when I might be – I think I used the word 'delayed' – then I'd let her know by phone or text."

"And she was okay with that?"

"She said something like 'that'll be by text then', and changed the subject. Very much to my relief."

Ayesha got up and moved round to sit on his lap. She put her arms round his shoulders and pulled him into a lingering kiss. "I can't imagine ever having a conversation like that with either of my parents. And I can't imagine I'll be able to look your mum in the eye next time I see her."

"I'm just going to avoid eye contact with her for the next few weeks."

Ayesha half-laughed, half-smiled and leant in for another kiss. "You'll be seeing her later – might as well just face up to it and get it over with."

"I know. You're right. But can I just pretend that it's not something I need to worry about?"

"Whatever. When do you need to be back?"

"As long as I'm there in time to cook lunch. Say, half eleven or so."

"That's still more than four hours away." She slipped off his lap, straightened up and took his hand in hers. "What was that weird saying you came out with the other day? 'Might as well be hung for a sheep as a lamb'? Well, Jack Laidlaw, it looks like I have plenty of time to delay you for a little longer." She tugged him to his feet and, for the second time in less than twelve hours, led him towards the increasingly familiar corridor.

## Chapter 28

"This channel is 90% secure. Adopt the appropriate protocol."
"Understood."
"Report please."
"Things are moving very fast."
"Go on."
"The party is definitely next Sunday week."
"Definitely? Can you confirm the venue and time?"
"Yes. The venue is as we anticipated and it will be a lunchtime party."
"Lunchtime?"
"Yes. Some preparation before midday – I have to deliver some collateral beforehand. I'll transmit the postcode to you when I have it. Then after twelve the main event gets under way."
"Do we know what that involves?"
"Not yet. Alpha and Beta continue to play their cards close to their chests. I can confirm that we will be taking presents to the party, and that I will be delivering the collateral to Gamma and Delta beforehand."
"Let me check that. Each guest is taking a separate present?"
"Yes."
"And you are delivering collateral to Gamma and Delta beforehand. Where precisely?"
"As I said, I'll transmit the postcode when I have it."
"And have you met Gamma and Delta?"
"No. The first time will be when I deliver the collateral."
"Understood. Anything more?"
"Not just now. I'll keep you posted."
"Thanks. Good luck."
"Thanks."

## Chapter 29

"Mirza? Hi, I'm Ayesha. Thank you so much for agreeing to help us out like this."

She shook his hand warmly and returned his smile. He was tall, six foot three, probably in his late twenties and high-cheekboned handsome. His thick black hair was Number Four short all over and his neat beard was sufficiently trimmed that it only just qualified as more than mere stubble.

"Think nothing of it. Any friend of Simon is a friend of ours. Delighted to help." His voice was rich, mellifluous, baritone and warm. "And these, I presume, must be our stars", switching his glance and turning towards Fiona, Fi and Ollie.

Ayesha took his cue and effected introductions. "Yes indeed. This is Fiona, Jack's mother, and these are Fi and Ollie, his children."

Fi and Ollie both smiled shyly as Fiona stepped forward to accept the proffered handshake. "It really is very kind of you Mirza. The children are rather excited about this whole adventure and, if I'm being honest, so am I."

"Good. I'm sure that you'll find the whole thing is a lot of fun." Mirza turned back towards Ayesha, "And will you be joining us too?"

"No. I'm actually going to have lunch with Jack to ensure he's kept occupied and doesn't suspect anything. Fiona's got my number, so if someone gives me a ring to let me know when everything is finished, I can pop back later and collect them. Do you have any idea how long this will take?"

"I can't imagine that this will be a very complicated shoot. Of course it depends how long you want the finished product to be, but I can't see this taking more than three or four hours."

Ayesha and Fiona exchanged nods. "Sounds good to me. Ayesha, could you pass the shopping bag with the sandwiches and drinks in it from the car, otherwise we'll forget and end up starving here while you're enjoying a nice Sunday lunch with my son! Also, you might want to put the children's swimming things in the boot so Jack doesn't see them and get suspicious."

Ayesha retrieved the bag and handed it to Fiona with a smile. "I'll park my car out of sight when I rendezvous with Jack, so there's no chance he'll see the swimming gear. I'd better be off now – I don't want to keep Jack waiting. Remember to give me a ring to let me know when you want picked up." The others variously smiled or shouted or waved their goodbyes to her as she got back into the car before driving off.

"Well, shall we go inside and let you see the place that the magic happens?" Mirza's beaming smile was infectious as he held open the door by its large stainless-steel T Bar handle. He beckoned them inside into a surprisingly spacious foyer area. Two low slung, wide black leather chairs adorned with plush red cushions sat at right angles against the left-hand wall, either side of a funky square glass and gun metal coffee table upon which rested a couple of magazines and that morning's newspaper. The walls were predominantly light grey and the floor a very dark grey wood effect laminate. Two large framed posters advertising television shows that Fiona recognised adorned the wall above the table and chairs. A spectacularly colourful collage of photographs and DVD case inserts covered the far wall. Ceiling mounted strip lighting that might have been considered harsh actually complemented the natural light admitted by the external glass door and brightened an area that was both professional and welcoming.

"This is very nice." Fiona surveyed their environs with an appreciative eye.

"Thank you. This place has only been operating for about nine or ten months, so everything is still quite fresh. The owners have spent well on this reception area but have really invested quite a bit on equipping the actual studio itself. There's a make-up room, a screening room, an editing suite, a small office and a couple of large store rooms as well as the studio. The studio is soundproof and has all the works – full lighting grid, blue/green screen, dry and wet – and there's post production capacity including live capture and data storage too."

"Well that all sounds very impressive, although I'm sure I don't understand most of it." Fiona's thoughts were also those of Fi and Ollie.

"Of course. I'm sorry – I sometimes get carried away. Let's not delay another moment." Mirza smiled, leaned down and picked up the newspaper then turned through ninety degrees, "Follow me please folks."

The three of them followed him round the corner and along a corridor to a door marked 'Studio'. Mirza turned the brushed aluminium handle, pushed the door inward and then held it open. "On you go folks!"

Ollie took the lead, closely followed by Fi and Fiona, all three of them slightly surprised at the starkly different environment. The floor was the same as outside, but everything else was black – the soundproofed walls and ceiling, the overhead rail mounted lights and the freestanding camera. Everything that is, except the bright green screen that filled the entire wall at the far end of the room.

As their eyes adjusted to the lower light levels, they became aware of another presence in the room. A tall man wearing headphones and crouched behind a camera in the corner introduced himself in a voice very similar to that of Mirza, "Hi, I'm Eshan." He straightened up, smiled and gave a little wave. The resemblance to Mirza was striking. Eshan's hair was slightly longer, he was clean-shaven and perhaps half an inch taller, but otherwise virtually indistinguishable from Mirza. He nodded his acknowledgement of their waves back to him and then crouched back behind the camera.

Fiona turned to Mirza, "Well, there's no mistaking you pair for anything other than brothers."

"Everyone says that. But actually we're not related at all."

"Well, I must say that does surprise me."

"Actually, when we stand side by side, you'll see that I'm considerably better looking than he is."

"I couldn't possibly comment on that!" Fiona's smile danced between coy and shy.

Mirza grinned in return then looked over towards the camera. "Eshan! Are you ready to take a quick tester of these three good people?"

"Yo!"

Mirza turned to the Laidlaw trio. "Before we begin properly, Eshan will just take a quick shot of the three of you together. We're currently using a working title of 'Jack Laidlaw Surprise Birthday Video', which is hardly striking in its originality. I'm sure you will come up with something much better. Now, if you stand in front of the green screen and just introduce yourselves and say today's date, that would be great. Fiona, if you could go first and perhaps hold up this newspaper as you're speaking. Then pass the paper to Fi who does the same thing and then on to Ollie. It just lets Eshan get a feel for your voices, see you handle a prop and get a measure on sound levels, and lets us see how your clothes and skin tone look against the background. I think they'll be fine and that we won't need any make up, but it's just sensible to check all this stuff before we start on the real work. Everyone okay with that?"

Fiona, Fi and Ollie all nodded assent and moved towards the green screen where they took up positions three abreast, facing the camera operated by Eshan. Fiona, somewhat self-consciously held the Sunday Times in front of her, one hand on each of the top corners, and announced, "My name is Fiona Laidlaw, and today is Sunday the fifth of November." There was a blinding flash as Mirza captured the scene on his camera 'phone.

Fiona was discombobulated. "I wasn't expecting that." She blinked heavily as she waited for the dazzling galaxies bleaching her retinas to subside.

"I'm sorry. I should have warned you," Mirza's rich baritone soothed. "The flash helps Eshan measure light levels at the console. Also, if I'm being honest, I like to take stills of people we film for my own personal library. I won't make the same mistake again. If you could pass the newspaper to Fi, Eshan will keep the camera rolling and I'll give a warning when I'm about to take a flash picture with my 'phone. If that's okay, can you pass over the paper?"

Fiona's vision had recovered sufficiently and she turned to hand the broadsheet to her granddaughter. "Here you are Fi. Can you hold it up for the camera the same way that I did?"

"That's great Fi. Eshan's filming you now and I'm just about to take another still photograph on my camera 'phone. Just keep smiling like that and try not to screw up your eyes." Mirza seemed to be struggling to still himself sufficiently to take the picture. His entire body exuded excess energy and it took a clear effort to control his propensity to shift he weight from one foot to the other. A second flash illuminated the studio, but this time Fiona screwed her eyes tight and tilted her head slightly to the side.

"Excellent. Well done Fi. Now if you could pass the paper to Ollie, we'll go through the same routine again." Mirza was in full director mode. "Exactly the same as with your Grandma and your sister now Ollie. That's it – hold it up just there. Perfect. Now, everyone ready for another flash in three, two, one. Bingo! Got it – well done."

Fiona had protected her eyes in the same way as for the photo of Fi, thus avoiding the temporary impairment to her vision that she had suffered when her own picture was taken. She was able to observe the same silent exchange between the filmmakers after the third photo as she had noticed after Fi's picture was snapped. Mirza glanced at his 'phone and then nodded confirmation towards Eshan, who tipped his head in soundless acknowledgement.

Despite having been retired for twelve years, over three decades of managing classrooms meant that Fiona had developed still sharp radar for detecting when something was afoot. She smiled at Mirza, "If I didn't know better, I'd think those photos reminded me of pictures one sees of people who've been taken hostage." Mirza's pupils widened only to an extent that could be perceived subliminally, but the double blink of his eyes alerted Fiona's instincts and an adrenalin surge dried her throat. Mirza was immediately aware of a reciprocal change in Fiona's eyes and the smile that previously had played so easily on his face tightened as his lips thinned, taut over his teeth. He cleared his throat, "Fi, Ollie! Why don't you go over and join Eshan at the console? He can talk you through what each of the controls do." He nodded, smiling encouragement, and the children followed his cue, eagerly dashing over towards the exciting technology.

Fiona fought to suppress the grimace brought on by the sudden, sharp arthritic pain in her left knee as she stepped towards Mirza. She stopped just twelve conspiratorial inches from him and thirty degrees clockwise of full face-to-face. He was easily nine or ten inches taller than her, the discrepancy exaggerated by their proximity. Each of them lowered their chins, their heads tilted almost imperceptibly to the right, and eyes locked. Fiona's peripheral vision detected a vein twitch in his temple. "I think that it's time you explained to me what is really going on, Mirza," the aridity of her throat affording a voice that hovered between hoarse and husky.

Mirza leaned an inch closer, appraising his inquisitor, eyes narrowing, lips still pursed tight and inhaling deeply through his nose. She was small, slight and quietly fierce, holding his gaze with her own. Her teeth were clenched inside her closed mouth, giving her jaw particularly precise definition as she raised her face, cleft chin leading in mute defiance.

His lean forward was barely discernible, the voice emanating from his ventriloquist's rictus just above a whisper, "What on earth do you mean, Fiona?"

She stretched her neck, pushed her chin slightly further forward as her left eyebrow arched. Eyes locked, the exchange was wordless for an aeon-long second until Fiona's hushed acknowledgement of the balance of power. "You won't hurt the children, will you?"

His lips loosened over strong, pearlescent teeth as a faint hint of a smile skipped briefly over his face. His head eased backwards as he continued to appraise her eyes with his own, "It's true what they say about age and wisdom. You are an old woman Fiona, and that was a wise decision. If the children are harmed by Eshan or I it would only be as a consequence of you prompting it by not doing exactly as you are told."

"I would never do anything that would put my grandchildren in harm's way, you bastard." Narrowed eyes blazed ferociously, her whisper harsh as she edged to the side, placing herself directly between him and the console where Fi and Ollie were engaged in animated discussion with Eshan.

"I'm very pleased to hear it." His smile was broad now and he raised himself to his full height as his left leg took a quarter pace backwards. "If you and the children play along nicely then this will soon be over and all of us can leave here in one piece. Now, please can you hand me your mobile 'phone?"

Fiona reached into her bag to retrieve her 'phone. She brought it out in her right hand, paused briefly as her eyes darted between the device and Mirza, then thrust it aggressively into his proffered hand.

## Chapter 30

Jack turned into Bartholomew Lane and was pleased to see that a slot in one of the two disabled parking bays was free. As he brought the car to a halt, he recognised the Range Rover – also without a disabled badge on display. "Looks like Bob had the same idea and has got here before us."

"Bob?"

"Yes Bob Malcolm, our IT head honcho. I've mentioned him before."

"Of course, the CIO. Your friend."

Jack waited for Ayesha to slam her door shut then locked the car with his remote. He turned and strode purposefully in the direction of Lothbury, Ayesha close by his side. "Bob will have had the same call as I've had. Jalal is simply following protocol. He's the on-call person for Facilities and he's decided to escalate the call to me because he feels we need my access privileges. I presume that the IT person on call has done the same and asked Bob to come in."

"Does this sort of thing happen often?"

"Not at all. Only the second time since I've been here."

"What happened the last time?"

"It was five or six years ago now. The on-call guys had responded to an alert from the security guards who reported the alarm had gone off. The guys checked it out and couldn't find anything. They tried to re-set the alarm, but it kept going off again and they couldn't figure out why. Turned out a squirrel – of all things – had chewed through some cables and caused a short circuit."

"A squirrel? How on earth did it get into the Bank?"

"No idea whatsoever. We found the poor things body. It had been electrocuted. To be honest I found it quite upsetting."

"Really? Why?"

"I love nature – not that I get much time to enjoy it. And it just seemed so sad that that poor creature had come to its end that way. I really hope it's not something like that again."

"Let's hope not. So we're heading for Lothbury rather than Threadneedle Street?"

"Yes, that's where the back door is. It's where the cash and bullion gets in and out and where staff enter on their bikes. It's also where the chauffeurs drive in when we have dignitaries visiting."

They covered the short distance to the end of Bartholomew Lane and turned left into Lothbury, all the time with the windowless and doorless Portland stone ground floor of the Bank building on their left. Jack took out his 'phone and pressed to dial a pre-installed number. "Andy? It's Jack Laidlaw. I'm just coming to the back door now. Responding to the call to come in from Jalal Yetka. It's all completely clear here. I'm accompanied by one female. I can vouch for her. Okay. Thanks."

They made their way the short distance along Lothbury to the tall, metal double doors that constituted the rear entrance to the bank just as the one on the left swung slowly and heavily open. Jack beckoned Ayesha through and followed her quickly as the door closed again, much faster than it had opened. "Thanks Andy," Jack smiled at the burly security guard bedecked in pink frock coat and top hat. "I take it I'm the last to arrive?"

"That's correct Mr. Laidlaw. The two Mr. Yetka's have been in for a couple of hours, maybe slightly longer, and Mr. Malcolm got here about five minutes ago."

"Right. And what's your take on what's going on?"

"Honestly Mr. Laidlaw, I'm not sure. The security control system started playing up shortly after nine this morning. Alerts flashing from various different locations inside the bank intermittently, that when we investigate them appear to be false alarms. Further intermittent power downs of surveillance equipment – specifically CCTV – that then come back online randomly."

"Very odd. Okay Andy, could you take us to the others please?"

"Of course sir. They're waiting for you at the smaller office adjacent to the parlours. Follow me." Andy nodded to the gatekeeper, who ushered the three of them through the internal gate before securing it behind them, and set off at a brisk pace.

Ayesha seemed slightly overawed by the unfamiliar surroundings as she whispered to Jack. "It's just so big. Much, much bigger and grander than I would have imagined."

"You're right. There are over four hundred thousand square feet spread over seven floors, and another three hundred thousand square feet across the three floors underground. That's where we've got the library, the dentist, the doctor and the gym as well as the vaults and other offices. People who have worked here for years can still get confused by all of the corridors and secret stairways." Jack's pride in the Bank was evident in his tone.

Ayesha was considering asking him about the secret stairways when they turned a corner and Andy stopped outside a door that was slightly ajar, "Mr. Malcolm and the two Mr. Yetka's are inside, sir."

"Okay Andy, thanks. I'll give a you a shout if we have any problems or, with any luck, I'll let you know that we've got this sorted."

"Thanks Mr. Laidlaw. I'll wait to hear. You know where to find me."

Jack pushed the door open and stepped inside, Ayesha right behind him. Bob, Jalal and Idris were sitting on functional cloth and chrome chairs at a rectangular white melamine table, examining a laptop screen. All three rose to their feet as Jack and Ayesha entered.

"Bob, Jalal, Idris hi. Sorry I'm late. This is Ayesha. She was with me when I got the call. I hope you don't mind …"

"Not at all, not at all," Bob strode towards Ayesha and took her hand in his. "Jack has told me all about you and I'm delighted to meet you. Mind you, he didn't tell me just how stunning you are."

"I'm very pleased to meet you," Ayesha's head was bowed slightly as she sought to shrug off the compliment. She turned and shook the hand of Jalal and Idris in turn, repeating, "I'm very pleased to meet you."

Introductions over, Jack looked to Bob. "So, what's the score here?"

"I was literally just starting to get an update from Jalal and Idris when you came in. Jalal, would you mind starting again, please?"

Jalal's eyes switched between those of Jack and Bob. "Sure Bob – no problem. As I was just saying, Idris and I both got calls shortly before nine o' clock this morning, saying that the security systems seemed to be going crazy. It was lucky we were both on call together as we could share a taxi in, so we were both here just before half past nine. Andy briefed us on what had been happening. We followed all of the established protocols as soon as we arrived and ran all of the diagnostic checks. Absolutely nothing showed up. So we ran them all again and still got zippo. There are clear physical manifestations of the problem – CCTV not working, for example. And the metal detectors."

"The metal detectors?" Jack looked at him quizzically.

"Yes, although that problem doesn't seem to be intermittent. They were off when we arrived and still seem to be. It was Idris who noticed that we'd both come straight through the detectors carrying our laptop bags and not triggered the alarm."

"Same with me," reported Bob. "I had my laptop bag over my shoulder, and my keys and 'phone in my pocket and I sailed through without a cheep."

Jack realised he had done exactly the same thing and that Ayesha has also come through with her handbag, which undoubtedly had keys and a 'phone inside too. "You're absolutely right. I never even noticed on the way in. Good spot by Idris. Do go on."

"Since we got here the frequency of different alerts on the main console has definitely diminished, although we haven't been able to identify any pattern. We haven't found any evidence that the problem is electrical or electronic. We are coming to the conclusion that this issue must be software related."

"Is that your view Idris?" Bob interrupted. Idris nodded. "I can see why you would think that. Do we need to involve Hannah Hamilton's Infosec team?"

"Possibly, but not yet." Idris spoke slowly and calmly. "It's certain that it is not a regular software failure and there is some risk that it is a cyber-attack, although I suspect that, if so, it's not a full-on assault."

"What makes you say that?"

"The nature of what's happening. If it is an attack, it seems to me that whoever's responsible is just prodding and testing us. Assessing our defences, working out what our vulnerabilities might be. There's also a chance that some hacker has bypassed security and is having some fun at our expense. Equally, I think there's just as good a chance that some form of malware has been uploaded, or downloaded inadvertently, and that's the source of the problems we're seeing."

Bob studied Idris's expressionless face. "Idris, you spent enough time working with the Infosec boys to understand that we have to call them in if we think there is any risk at all that this is a cyber-attack. Do we need to call them in?"

All eyes were now focussed on Idris, although he seemed oblivious of the fact as he addressed himself towards Bob. "Possibly Bob, but not yet. I've used the threat assessment template and, whilst there is some suggestion of a possible threat, the data is far from definitive. I think there's just as good a chance that it's a hacker or malware as a cyber-attack. If we can access the secure rooms, I can run a couple of checks and be sure. I'd hate for us to escalate to those guys unnecessarily and then get all the stick that would come our way."

Bob's expression was sceptical but seemed to relax slightly after a pause for consideration. "Okay Idris, but if it was anyone other than you, I'd already have escalated this to Infosec."

"Thanks boss. We will be able to tell in less than half an hour. Can we go to the central processing rooms to run the checks?"

Bob nodded assent, his familiar smile returning. "All right dear colleagues and honoured guest, please accompany me down to my palace." He exited the door first, the Yekta brothers in close attendance, with Jack and Ayesha right behind.

Ayesha tossed Jack a quizzical glance, arching her eyebrows briefly.

He smiled back reassuringly, "We're going to the first floor down, where all the tech is and the geeks live. Bob and his entire team have their offices there, and it's where we house all of the various kit and hardware that support the most critical applications."

All five took the lift the short ride down one level, where they exited into a different world from the mausoleum above with its high ceilings and floor mosaics. Now the environment was more akin to that of a nuclear bunker with endless identical claustrophobic corridors and thick security doors. An unexpected low rumbling sound caused Ayesha to flinch and she looked questioningly to Jack. "Just a tube train,' he reassured her with a smile.

At last they arrived at Bob's 'palace' – a vast open plan sea of desks separated into pods by four-foot-high lilac screens, flanked by ceiling high glass walls screening a series of meeting rooms at one end and two hardware suites at the other. The lights in the area flicked on as they entered, triggered by motion sensors.

Once inside, Idris closed the door behind them and then took a few paces to stand beside his brother. Ayesha left Jack's side and took a position on Jalal's other side. Jack and Bob both watched silently, instinct telling them that this was odd behaviour and their other senses heightened as a consequence.

Jalal and Idris reached simultaneously into the laptop bags each had slung over their shoulder, at the same time as Ayesha reached into her handbag. All three pulled out identical 9-millimetre Glock 17 Gen4 handguns. Jalal pointed his pistol at Jack and Bob, while Idris and Ayesha screwed titanium silencers to the ends of theirs.

Jack broke the silence. "What the hell is going on?"

Jalal's gun aimed directly at Jack's chest. "Shut it. Just shut your mouth!"

"Ayesha? For god's sake! What the hell is going on?"

"I told you to shut it! Don't imagine I'm bluffing, Jack. These guns are real and if we need to use them, we will." Jalal stared straight into Jack's eyes. "Do exactly what I say or, I swear, I will not hesitate to shoot."

"And if you shoot me, then what? If I don't do what you want and you shoot me, what do you do then?"

The broad smile spreading across Jalal's face was not the response Jack had expected. The gun in his right hand continued to point directly at Jack while Jalal retrieved his 'phone from his left-hand jacket pocket. The briefest of glances at the screen as his thumb traced a madcap dance across it reminded Jack that Jalal was left-handed, and now demonstrating how truly sinister he was. Another flicked glance at the screen and the smiled evolved towards a grin. Jalal took a single stride forward towards Jack, left hand outstretched, phone between his index finger and thumb. Wordlessly he nodded to Jack to take the proffered device.

Jack matched Jalal's pace forward and took the phone. He peered at the screen, his eyes narrowing. The entire exchange took mere seconds, but had a *Matrix* like quality for Jack, the rest of the world frozen motionless around him as his thumb scrolled forwards and backwards through the pictures on the screen. The surreal scene that he was part of was rendered humdrum by the near hypnagogic images in front of him. His fear and horror grew simultaneously and proportionately with his understanding. He raised his eyes to meet Jalal's, returned the phone and stepped back. He felt Bob's hand land gently and supportively on his left shoulder as he bowed his head slowly. Jalal, Idris and Ayesha kept their pistols trained on the pair.

## Chapter 31

Jack inhaled slowly, although even the instinctive act of breathing no longer felt natural. Nothing was normal. Gradually he raised his head and addressed their eyes with his. He thought that his voice sounded as though someone else was speaking. "What the hell is going on?"

"Surely it's clear Jack. You've seen that we have your kids and your mother. They are our insurance policy." Jalal's voice was flat calm, his words deliberate.

"Insurance policy?"

"Yes Jack. You will do exactly what we want, and that way no harm will come to your family." He paused, observing Jack's eyes blaze and the barely perceptible, miniscule drop of the shoulders that signals preparation for a pounce forward. "Your anger is understandable, but attacking either Ayesha or me will ensure that retribution is taken against your family. You will do exactly what we tell you."

"A frail old woman and two kids, for God's sake! You wouldn't hurt them."

"Look at me Jack." They stared at each other. "We would have no hesitation in killing them. None. Unless Eshan receives a call from me every half an hour he has clear instructions to kill all three of them. And Eshan is very diligent in matters such as these."

Jack's head swum briefly as his nervous system pumped even more adrenaline and cortisol. His mouth was arid."You bastard. What if I simply refuse to grant you access? Are you going to shoot me too?"

"If you are obstructive, I will call Eshan and instruct him to kill your mother in front of your children. If you persist in hindering us, I will have him kill your daughter. Then your son, if necessary. Then I kill you. But it's not going to come to that Jack, because you *will* help us."

"You'd murder a sick old woman? You'd kill my mother, even though your own mother is so ill and I've done my best to support you?"

Jalal leaned forward, placing both hands on the highly polished table, looking down into Jack's eyes, their heads barely two feet apart. "My mother is already dead. Murdered. Murdered by you." The pitch of his voice was higher, his acid eyes furious.

"What the hell are you talking about?"

"Three years ago my mother went home to visit her sister. There was a drone strike. My mother, her sister and thirteen other members of our family were killed. Six of them were children."

"What has that got to do with me?"

"Everything Jack, everything. Actions carried out by your government and its allies are carried out in your name. You see the news. You see the killings. You choose to ignore them or to shrug them off as 'collateral damage'. Sometimes you launch 'investigations'. Seven months after you murdered my mother you issued a statement. The entire statement was redacted, except for the conclusion that blamed ISIS for using civilians as human shields."

"For God's sake Jalal, it's a war in a faraway land that's got nothing to do with me. I'm sorry for what happened to your mother, but it's nothing to do with me."

"You're really not listening Jack. You know what's going on and you do nothing to stop it. If you are not against what is happening then you are for it."

"And you're not listening to me. It has nothing to do with me, you mad bastard!"

"I'm mad, am I?" A thin smile danced briefly on Jalal's lips, quickly banished by a frown. "I'll tell you what is mad. Mad is when you see your family and your people being attacked and killed, and do nothing to try to stop it. Mad is when you condone the slaughter of innocent people by standing by and doing nothing. Mad is letting a murderer think it is okay to kill women and children and old people. Mad is letting them do it over and over and over again. That's what mad is Jack, and I'm not mad."

Jack studied him intently. The words cascaded fiercely. The zealous passion was patently genuine, but still controlled. This was the authentic Jalal, strong, inspired and on a mission – no longer the contained, prim colleague of before. He ***would*** have the kids and Mum killed if he believed he needed to. "Okay. I get it. You need to do something. But what? What is it you're going to do and why do you need me?"

"Do you know Jack, I think you ***do*** get it. And that's good. It means we can work together and get this thing done. Then you can get your family back safe." The smile was victorious, arctic and real.

"I do understand the stakes and you're right, I'm not going to do anything to put the kids and Mum at risk. I just don't know what it is you need me to do."

"Access. We need you to get us into the bank and then into the central computer suite. That's all we need. When you do that for us you will be free to go and your mother and children will be released."

"How do I know that? How can I be sure that they'll be safe?"

Ayesha cleared her throat and both men turned in her direction. She was still standing, holding the gun with both hands, pointing at Jack. "They will be safe Jack. We're not interested in harming them – unless we have to. You just need to do as Jalal says and it'll all be fine."

"And I'm to believe it because you say so? Like I believed everything else about you? You lying bitch!"

"You should believe me because it's the truth. By doing what you are told, you will guarantee their safety."

"Who the hell are you?" Jack's eyes filled and a tear collapsed down his right cheek, followed by a partner on the left. "Just who the hell are you – really?"

"I'm Ayesha Alfarsi, Jack. Most of what I told you about me is true, except for the last few years. Three years ago six of my relatives were amongst more than eighty killed. The wedding they were attending was bombed 'by mistake'. The Western alliance talking heads were apologetic, but no one was brought to trial and no one was ever punished or even blamed. Just six weeks after the wedding another 'error' led to seven children being killed in a primary school just two streets away. That's when it clicked for me. Jalal is right. It's mad to just stand by and let it continue without doing anything. Now I'm doing something about it. *That's* who I am." Her answer was delivered with an unnerving calmness.

Jalal smiled approval. Jack, tear streaks already almost dry, a barely perceptible shake of his head, realised that he did not know this woman at all. He stared glacially. His mind was soup and her little speech was the gas below it. The heat transformed the ingredients. Fear for the kids and Mum became self- pity. Bewilderment transformed into hideous comprehension.Disbelief mutated into a righteous, indignant sense of betrayal. The different constituents combined into a broth of bitter hatred. "You bitch."

"Shut it!" The bark from Jalal bayoneted Jack's focus on Ayesha and commanded his attention. "Plenty of time for name calling later on Jack, but first you have work to do."

"All right. You want into the bank and into the central computing suite. You do realise it's pointless and impossible?"

"It's far from impossible Jack, and even further from pointless."

"Come on Jalal, you've been at the bank long enough to know how things work. It might be a weekend, but security never relaxes. Even if we were able to get in, the computer suite has its own independent security. Anyway, there'd be no point in trying. Security for the gold bullion is physical, and the related IT systems operate separately and remotely from Threadneedle Street."

"Ah Jack, you really don't understand. You think we're stupid? We know how well the bullion is guarded. There's six thousand tonnes in there, about half a million bars. It's worth what? Easily over a hundred billion pounds." Jalal was smiling, enjoying superiority of knowledge and purpose. "It's typical that you should think it's all about the money, because that is what motivates you. It's why you and the Americans and the Russians bomb and kill our people. You fight your proxy wars, slaughtering innocents, because you want the money that comes from oil."

"So if it's not about the gold, what the hell is the point of all this?"

Jalal's smile blossomed into a grin. "It is about money Jack, but not in the way you're thinking. It is the pursuit of money that motivates you barbarians to slaughter our people. So we intend to use money to strike back at you. It will be poetic justice, and it will be delicious."

"You've lost me Jalal." Jack's confusion was genuine. He didn't want to be provocative and didn't voice his growing belief that Jalal was indeed mad.

"You think that we defenders are unsophisticated, naïve, brainwashed, mentally retarded, misfits or fanatics. You think we can only use suicide bombs, beheadings, car bombs, guns, massacres and guns. You call us medieval, primitive. We are an annoyance, but more to be despised and pitied than respected and feared."

"I'm none the wiser Jalal. What's your point?"

"My point, Jack, is this. My brother has a first from Imperial, as do Eshan and Mirza. I have a first from Leeds and Ayesha has a first from Oxford. We are not stupid people, manipulated by others. We have a plan to strike back at you using your own god – money."

Jack quickly glanced to his right to see Bob, sombre and alert, utterly focused on Jalal before turning back. "I don't understand, Jalal."

Jalal grinned superiority, "Then let me enlighten you. Every single day millions of financial transactions take place all over the world. All of those dollars and Euros and pounds and Yen have to be cleared through a relatively small number of clearinghouses and systems, each controlled by the Western powers or their regulated financial institutions. No single part of the global financial system is wholly independent. If there's a problem somewhere it's simply not possible to isolate it and shut it down. A crisis in any particular place spreads everywhere. You get panic. As soon as a particular part of the system is shut down human nature dictates that people immediately rush to a different part of the system to try to get their money back.

It becomes viral. The panic multiplies exponentially. Everyone sells shares, bonds, property – every saleable asset class that they have. They all want their money back immediately. All of them at the same time.

The money markets will close down, so people will rush to the banks to get at their money. But the banks are closed so they try to sell their shares, but the stock exchanges and bourses are all suspended. The minute one part of the system shuts down all the demand for liquidity flows to a different part that also quickly dries up and has to be shut down too. Sooner than you could imagine the entire system is in lockdown because the whole thing is interconnected.

Suddenly the world is reliant on hard cash to transact business, to lubricate the transactions that are part of everyday life. But there isn't actually that much cash around any more – particularly in the Western world. People use credit cards, debit cards, PayPal, Apple Pay, online banking, ATM's. It's nearly all digital, and when people try to use it, they will find that they can't.

And when people can't access their money everything breaks down. Everything. The rules don't work any more. There is confusion, fear, and anger. Civil society starts to fracture. Law and order quickly starts to fray under the pressure and you have turmoil and political chaos."

Jalal paused for both breath and effect. Jack couldn't help himself, "You *are* mad. Completely bloody mad."

"No. No he's not mad. He paints an entirely credible picture." Bob had found his voice and Jack's attention switched to his friend. "The entire financial system is incredibly complicated and sophisticated, but it is also exactly as Jalal describes – highly interconnected and fragile, and therefore also vulnerable." He nodded at Jalal, the gesture beckoning him to continue.

The irritation that had flared in his eyes at Jack's insult was gone, replaced by the return of the previous smirk, as Jalal resumed his pontification. "Thank you, Bob. The system is indeed fragile and vulnerable. And right here, in this building, we control the central computer suite that processes the Real Time Gross Settlement service, settling about £500 billion between banks most days.

What we are going to do is to access the systems that underpin that service with some of Idris's very smart software. Effectively we will make that money disappear, literally without any trace. It will be as if it had never existed. The accounts that it is coming from will still be debited, but there will be no record at all of where the money went to, or where it was meant to go, or why. The accounts that should have been credited will receive nothing and all records of where money should have been coming from – the amounts, sources and reasons for the transactions – will be wiped and completely unrecoverable. When the global economy realises what has happened the panic I have described will begin."

Bob turned to Jack as Jalal paused. "Well he isn't mad, but he's clearly stupid." Turning back, he held Jalal's eyes steadily with his own. "You need access to the central suite. That's why you've engineered it so that you have both Jack and me here. You need both of our biometrics to get through security. You think that you've been incredibly clever. You think that by taking hostages you'll ensure we co-operate. But you're wrong. You see you're really not that bright. You might be able to coerce Jack here by threatening his family, but I'm afraid that I will not play along in any way. You've made a stupid error of judgement. Really, really stupid. Did you honestly believe that you and your motley crew could breach Bank security? A woman, someone with a personality disorder, and you – a queer? You really are the most stupid little queer. You just …."

Bob's gamble that mentioning Jalal's secret sexuality might disorient their captor backfired on him spectacularly. The crack of Jalal's pistol cut him short and he recoiled in agony, a poppy crimson whorl flowering around the black bullet hole in the upper sleeve of his right arm. Despite the silencer, the sound of the muzzle blast, the bullet moving through the air and the action working within the pistol were still sufficiently loud to startle. Jack was the first to come out of the instinctive hunching crouch and stepped forward, reaching to support his stricken friend. Idris and Ayesha both turned towards Jalal, the former seemed to be trying to form some words, the latter tight-lipped.

"Idris! Ayesha! You two keep your guns on the pair of them."

Jalal waved his own weapon towards Jack and the grimacing Bob. He took a half pace forward on his left foot, squared his shoulders and drilled Jack's eyes with his own. "Stupid? STUPID? Who's fucking stupid now? AND I AM NOT QUEER!" He raised the Glock and pointed it unsteadily at Bob's forehead. Deep inhalation. Long, slow exhalation. Calmer. "I really am *not* stupid Bob. If you don't co-operate, I *will* just kill you. We don't need you alive for the biometrics. Your fingerprint will still be your fingerprint, alive or dead. Same goes for your irises. We can chop your finger off. Rip your eye out. It's up to you."

The air of defeat that settled on Bob was as sudden as the bullet had been, and as total as Jalal's control of the situation. His attempted shrug of resignation brought a grimace as the pain lanced him. He shook his head gently, dejection oozing from his every pore, more so even than the blood from his wound.

"We need to staunch that wound," Ayesha's voice was flat calm, matter-of-fact. She loosened her red and yellow silk neck scarf with her left hand and threw it to Jack, nodding the instruction that it should be applied to Bob's upper right arm. Jack turned to Bob, whose heavy-lidded eyes suggested that he might be slipping towards unconsciousness. "I need some help to get his jacket off!"

Jalal and Idris exchanged a silent glance and the latter lowered his gun and moved to help Jack.

"Here, you take his weight on that side while I get his other sleeve off. Hurry, before he bleeds any more!" The urgency in Jack's tone galvanised Idris, who leaned in to place his own left arm under Bob's wounded right arm, taking the weight on that side of his body and allowing Jack to move Bob's left arm sufficiently to ease it from his jacket sleeve.

Jack was surprised to realise that, in the midst of all the turmoil, he was aware that he could smell Bob's blood – an odd mixture of sweetness and metal. "That's it Bob, nice and easy. Now let's just transfer your weight to this side and we'll get the jacket completely off. Then we can get that wound bandaged. Stay strong – this will probably hurt a bit." Bob's eyes flared and in a single, hair-trigger pirouette his body swung free from

Jack's support and his left forearm and balled fist smashed into Idris's temple like a mace. The momentum carried both men off balance and they tumbled to the floor. As they fell the sound of a shot being fired, although more muffled than before, was unmistakable. Both men landed on their backs, the rapidly spreading redness on the shirt over his midriff irrefutably declaring the violence the bullet had wrought on Idris's body.

Jalal screamed, an incoherent, primeval sound, and aimed his pistol at the prone figure of Bob. The shot rang out, followed by a louder, rawer shriek of agony.

Jack was back in *Matrix* world, although this time it was he who was virtually frozen whilst everything else moved around him at multiples of normal speed. He surveyed the carnage in front of him, trying to interpret, to understand. Bob was on his back, breathing heavily and tentatively patting his wound with his left hand. Idris too was on his back, head tilted to the side, vacant staring eyes reflecting the departure of his soul. The red on his shirt was no longer spreading, the pump having fallen silent and blood flow now governed solely by gravity. Jalal was crouched on his hunkers, emitting a constant low groan that was barely mammalian. Tears and snot streaked his face like Martian canals as his bowed head stared down at his left hand cupping his shattered, bloody right. Ayesha was standing to Jalal's right, upright with a pistol in each hand, looking directly at Jack. Her mouth was moving. Forming words? The pistol in her left hand was Jalal's – Jack had watched her pick it up from the floor when he dropped it after she had shot him. She had shot Jalal. In the hand. She was shouting.

"Jack! Jack!"

Her urgency pierced the dream and he was transported from bemused observer to confused participant.

"Jack! Help Bob. Now!" The gun in her right hand was still trained on the wretched Jalal. She squeezed the other firearm inside her waistband and used her free hand to retrieve her phone. "Now Jack! Help Bob now."

The spell was broken, and he was suddenly back in the room, aware of everything, although still uncomprehending. In a single movement he was crouched beside Bob, cradling his head with his right arm. "It's okay Bob, it's okay. Everything's going to be fine."

Ayesha hit a number that she clearly had on speed dial on her phone and was answered immediately. She spoke swiftly in a register too low for Jack to make out what she was saying. A pause as she listened to a reply then a quick, "Yes. All right." The call was over. Her gun still aimed directly at him, she crouched over Jalal and reached into his right-hand pocket with her left hand. She fished out his phone, stood upright and stepped backwards. She tried to operate the phone using her thumb, then stared straight at Jalal. "The security number on your phone!" A command rather than a question. Her voice was clear and even.

Jalal returned her stare, "Fuck off bitch."

She stepped one pace forwards and kicked his shattered hand hard, eliciting a piercing, agonised shriek. "The security number on your phone. Now! Or I swear to God Jalal, I'll shoot your other hand right off."

If it was an idle bluff it fooled everyone in the room. Jalal glanced into her eyes, dropped his own to contemplate his smashed hand and whisper-sobbed, "Zero-nine, one-one, zero-one."

"You sick, pathetic animal." She tapped the number into the phone and, having found what she appeared to be looking for very quickly, proceeded to type in a brief text message. She switched it off and slipped it into her own pocket rather than return it to Jalal, whose absorption in his own suffering rendered him oblivious to his phone's fate,

"Ayesha, please. What the hell is going on?" Jack's tone towards the stranger-he-thought-he-knew was imploring.

"No time, Jack. Help, including medical assistance is on the way and will be here in a matter of minutes. We need to focus on your Mum, Fi and Ollie – that's the priority now."

## Chapter 32

Something was amiss. Even if Fiona's awareness of everything going on around her were not heightened, she would not have failed to observe Mirza's growing agitation. He had checked his wristwatch three times in the last five minutes, and consulted his mobile 'phone twice. She saw the silent eye semaphore exchange between him and Eshan that indicated a need for dialogue. "Fiona, I just want to have a quick chat with Mirza. If you just use these controls here you will be able to rewind and replay the last little sketch that you did with the children. If all three of you review it a couple of times, I'd be very interested to hear any suggestions for how we could improve it." Eshan demonstrated how to operate the simple controls – effectively the same as those on most television remote controls, just with larger chrome buttons set slightly proud of the sleek black console. Fiona marvelled at how sincere the smile he tossed her seemed. "Go ahead, have a play around with it but, and this is particularly for you Fi and Ollie, be careful not to break anything. I'll be back in just a couple of minutes." With that he headed to join his partner and the pair exited the studio door.

Outside, Eshan checked the door handle to ensure that it was properly closed and took a couple of steps away as if to ensure they were out of earshot of those still inside, despite knowing that the room was soundproofed.He turned to face Mirza, both with their eyes narrowed as they adjusted to the greater ambient light in the corridor. "So, what's going on?"

"No signal from Jalal."

Eshan knew Mirza better than Mirza himself. The note of concern in his voice was on the cusp of morphing into fear. And that was a very short step from panic. When Mirza panicked there was no reasoning with him.

"Stay calm big fellow. Deep breath, then tell me – slowly – exactly what the issue is."

"Every thirty minutes exactly, on the hour and half past the hour precisely, Jalal should text me the simple message 'All OK'. Six of those texts have come through precisely on time, but the last one should have come eight minutes ago, and it hasn't."

"Okay, let's just think this through. How long ago did Ayesha drop the old woman and the kids off?"

"Just under an hour and a half. Almost an hour and twenty-five minutes ago. She left them here at quarter past eleven – just as had been agreed."

"So, by the time she left here, met up with Jack, Jack got the 'phone call to go into the bank, they drove there, got through security, met up with the others – how long?"

"Between forty-five and forty-eight minutes. You know that. We've tested the journey time on six separate Sundays. We know how long it takes."

"I know, I know. Calm down. We're just thinking this through. So, she and Jack will have got there at least three quarters of an hour ago. By the time they've met up with the others, been appraised of what's going on and then made their way into the central computer suite, it could easily take another half hour. It would all depend on how long it took to persuade Jack and Bob to grant access. That was always a variable that we couldn't tie down in advance."

"That's irrelevant. The last text from Jalal was at midday. There should have been another at half past twelve – eight, no nine, minutes ago. It's not come. Something's wrong Eshan."

"Not necessarily. Let's just think this through. They've reached the stage where variables come into play. The timings were never going to be precise. It's hardly a surprise if the next message comes through a few minutes late."

"That's the whole point. The messages have to come through at precisely the right moment to provide reassurance that everything is still going to plan. Jalal had set a timer on his phone to remind him every half hour to send the 'All OK' message – assuming everything *is* okay. The fact that it hasn't come doesn't mean they've forgotten or are distracted. It means that everything is *not* okay." There was a tremor in Mirza's voice as he stared hard into the other's eyes. "I've texted Jalal and got no reply. I've texted Idris and got no reply either. Eshan, something has gone wrong. Something has gone *seriously* wrong."

"I wouldn't have thought someone with your education would need a lecture in false positives from me." Eshan's tone was as unconvincing as his smile.

"Cut the crap and get real Eshan! I know you think I'm a drama queen but try to engage your bloody brain. We have practised and rehearsed this whole operation time and time again. The planning has been meticulous. Now, for no good reason, one of our fail-safes has triggered and you seem to think we should just ignore it. You know Jalal just as well as I do. If he hasn't sent that text then there is a problem."

Eshan pored over the various data points with the intensity of a house clearer scrutinising the obituary notices. His brow furrowed. "You're right. Shit. Neither Jalal nor Idris are responding? Do you have Ayesha's number?"

"No. Need to know basis was what Jalal said."

The reminder of Jalal's obsessive concern about security underscored Mirza's apprehension and cemented Eshan's growing conviction that his brother-in-arms was right to be worried. "You know what we need to do," he said cheerlessly.

"Let me just check the flight times," Mirza tapped and swiped the screen of his smartphone. "Yes, the 5.15 pm flight from Stansted to Amsterdam is still on schedule and the onward connection to Oslo is also fine. We can set Fatboy for 5.45 as planned – half an hour is plenty of contingency with those flights."

"What about our guests?" Eshan nodded towards the studio doors.

"We should shoot them now. If we're blown and the security services get here, we don't need anyone telling them anything helpful. Particularly the old lady – she's sharp as a tack. She could have picked something up. I think she's some sort of witch."

"For God's sake Mirz!" Eshan often abbreviated his name. "There really isn't any point. Fatboy will take care of them."

"You're not listening to me Eshan. If the authorities get to them before Fatboy does his business they might be able to provide some sort of a clue. We shouldn't take the risk. Three bullets in the head. Pop. Pop. Pop. Risk eliminated. Don't tell me you've got cold feet?"

Eshan did have cold feet. Despite the certainty that Fatboy would extinguish Fiona and her grandchildren in a heartbeat anyway, the prospect of assassination by gunshot sat uncomfortably with his incoherent value set. He racked his brain for some bone to throw the increasingly rabid dog that Mirza was becoming.

"Let's be smarter than that, Mirz. We can actually use them to help with the diversion. If we let one of them overhear us discussing getting to City airport, they'd be bound to mention it if anyone gets to them before Fatboy."

Mirza inhaled slowly as he paused to consider Eshan's suggestion. There were tickets booked in their names on the 5.30 pm flight from London City to Istanbul. They had laid the red herring in order to divert any potential pursuers, while they exited the country with false identities and passports via Stansted. The Yekta brothers were booked on the same flight from City to Istanbul, but had been scheduled to leave incognito through Heathrow some twenty minutes earlier.

"Okay. There's some sense to that. If I ask you to let me see the tickets when we're back in there and we have a quick discussion about check-in times and flight times to Istanbul, that should be plenty. We don't want to be over elaborate or she'll sense that we're doing it for her benefit."

"Right. Our actual flights are at 5.15, with check-in two hours earlier. The best part of an hour to drive there, get parked and then checked in means leaving here at quarter past two."

"So, we've got just over an hour and a half to get Fatboy set and get out of here?"

"We would have had if we weren't blown. We need to act sooner now. They could be on their way here now." Eshan's voice tailed off as he watched his brother plunge his hand into his pocket to retrieve the phone that had just pinged its receipt of a message. "What is it?"

Mirza scrutinised the screen. *'Sorry. Minor distraction.*

*Sorted now. All OK.'* It's from Jalal. He's saying it's all okay. But I'm not so sure."

"Why? Why are you not so sure?"

"Because it says 'Sorry'. I've known Jalal for years. So have you. He wouldn't say he was sorry for anything. Would he?"

"Not normally, no. Having said that, this is hardly normal, is it? Look, I don't think it matters either way. We still move as quickly as possible. If everything is okay, then we've just cleared out of here quicker than we otherwise might have. If that is someone trying to fool us that everything's okay then we're out of here anyway. Agreed?"

"Agreed. We set Fatboy up, play out the flight conversation in front of the old woman, then lock them in the studio and get going. The suitcases are in the car and the tickets are in the glove compartment. Returns – so that we look like a couple of guys going out to business and returning three days later."

"Right. I'll go back in. You set up Fatboy and come back and join us once everything's set up. How long will it take you – an hour?"

"Maximum. Probably slightly less. But I've got to get it right."

"No argument from me on that score. Fine. I'll see you back here in the studio 0when you're done."

\*\*\*

Ayesha took her own phone out from her bag. She tapped the screen then stopped abruptly as the door they had entered by swung open. Five figures came through including the pink-coated Andy, who was clearly acting as a guide for the others.

"You okay?" The enquiry was directed to Ayesha by a short man, early thirties, with cropped dark red hair and neatly groomed beard. His canvas jacket, tee shirt, jeans and brogues were all slightly different shades of navy, and clearly expensive. He carried a Walther P99 semi-automatic pistol in his right hand in a manner that suggested it was a familiar tool.

"Fine. Civilian casualty with GSW to upper right arm – losing too much blood." Ayesha indicated Bob with a nod of her head. Then a glance at Idris's prone body, "Idris Yekta, dead." A further turn of her head to look back at Jalal. "Jalal

Yekta, GSW to his right hand." She then looked back to her inquisitor and, in the same surreally calm voice concluded her report, "No further casualties. No virus upload."

"Bit of a bloody shambles." It was unclear whether the newcomer's observation was directed towards anyone, or simply a summary for himself. A second man, fair-haired and clean-shaven, just shy of six feet, late twenties, light white bomber jacket over a lemon tee shirt, stonewashed jeans and black and white Vans took up position behind Jack and Bob, aiming another Walther P99 directly at Jalal. The two others, a man and a woman, both in their fifties and clad in green paramedic overalls, crouched either side of Bob, gently ushering Jack to one side. The female, short and slim with dark bobbed hair, pressed a swab hard against Bob's wound with her right hand whilst simultaneously raising his arm with her left. Her colleague, remaining sparse hair in full retreat from advanced male pattern baldness, explained softly to Bob that sucking gently on the fentanyl citrate 'lollipop' that he was offering to his lips would bring rapid pain relief. Bob's lips parted without hesitation.

"What's the situation elsewhere?" Ayesha's query was directed at her bearded interlocutor.

"As I said, bit of a bloody shambles." He paused, inhaled deeply, and addressed her question more informatively. "We think the device might be at the studio."

Ayesha's eyes narrowed briefly before understanding spread across her face like a bow wave of comprehension splitting a sea of confusion. "Tell me you're joking. Please." The veneer of calm was cracked, her tone betraying genuine concern. No such reassurance was forthcoming, merely a silent shrug of the shoulders. Ayesha turned and strode purposefully back to tower over the anarchy of blood, tears and mewling self-pity that was Jalal Yekta. "Is it true?"

"What?" No artifice. Bona fide puzzlement at the question that had interrupted his detached brooding.

"Is the device at the studio?"

"What are you talking about, you fucking shrew?"

"Don't test me Jalal. I told you already that I won't hesitate to shoot your other hand off."

"In front of all these witnesses? An unarmed man? A bleeding, wounded man? I don't think so."

She took the Glock from her waistband and pointed it steadily at his good hand. "I will shoot. Tell me now. Is the device at the studio?"

"Fuck off whore. You are the unbeliever's bitch. I damn you as a heretic."

"Last chance." Her finger tightened round the trigger.

He returned her gaze and his lips parted, but no words came forth. Instead, a thin gloat spread across his face, like a time-lapse movie of mould covering a Petrie dish. Embers of defiance glowed in his eyes, harbingers that the old, arrogant Jalal was preparing for his phoenix rebirth.

Ayesha lowered the gun slowly and slid it back into her waistband, all the time maintaining eye contact – hers polar, his smug. Other than a thinning of the lips, her face was expressionless as she shifted her weight on to her left foot. Her right foot flew forwards, toe connecting with the shattered palm of his hand, throwing both hand and arm into the air and causing crimson to spray in an upward arc from the wound. If anything, the screech of pain from Jalal was even more anguished than when she had kicked him previously. Turning to shambles man, composed and calm, there was quiet certainty in her voice, "The device is at the studio."

"You know this how?"

"I know *him* well enough," tilting her head backward towards Jalal, without turning to look at him. "What have we got at the studio?"

"Team of four. Lying low – observation only at the moment."

"Well we need to get the disposal team, the robot and the lab coat guys there *now*." The words had barely left her lips and the nameless beard was on his phone relaying instructions.

"Ayesha!" Jack had been confounded, rendered speechless by the bewildering events and the pace at which they unfolded. But now he found his voice, and his sense of purpose. "Ayesha! For God's sake! What is going on? Where are the kids and Mum? Are they safe? Can I see them?" He had stepped right in front of her, machine-gunning her with questions.

Ayesha waited until his magazine was empty then stretched her right arm out, hand up with the palm towards him. "Jack stop. Fiona, Fi and Ollie are not safe. They are with two men, two colleagues of Jalal and Idris. Time is not on our side. Every second that we stand here talking and explaining puts them deeper into danger. You have to trust me on this Jack. I am going to them now, and I don't have time to waste answering questions."

"Then I'm coming with you." He grabbed her by the raised wrist, pushing her hand down, and fixed her with a stare that brooked no debate.

"You can come Jack, but you do exactly what you are told. Exactly. At all times. If you do anything at all that you haven't been told to you will just be putting them at greater risk. Do you understand?"

Silent, nodded assent.

Ayesha exchanged glances with the beard, still with his phone to his ear, confirming that he was aware of what was happening. Another glance, this time to the younger, fair-haired gunman. "Can you ensure that the staff here are taken care of?"

"Already in hand."

"Good." She turned and stepped towards the door. "Come on Jack."

"Good luck, Mr. Laidlaw." Andy's stage whisper and small smile of encouragement registered with Jack as he followed Ayesha, matching her vigorous pace. They reached the lift in less than half the time they had taken when going in the opposite direction. Once inside she opened her bag and retrieved a discreetly small silver Bluetooth earpiece. "We'll take your car, but I'll drive."

The lift door slid open, affording Jack no opportunity to respond. Ayesha strode forward purposefully, before her sudden halt destroyed the illusion of familiarity with the environment. "What's the quickest way back to your car from here?"

Jack didn't pause as he passed her and took the lead through the familiar maze. They were quickly through the bank and out on to Bartholomew Lane, racing towards the car.

## Chapter 33

As they reached the car Jack grabbed her by the shoulder and spun her to face him. "What the fuck is happening?"

Ayesha placed her left hand on his right shoulder and slapped him hard with her free hand. "Stop wasting time! Stay focused! Give me the key."

Jack pulled the key from the right-hand pocket of his jacket, aimed it, pressed the remote unlock button and threw it to Ayesha. He raced around and entered the passenger door. As he sat down, she had already switched the engine on and was feeling below the front of her seat. He leaned across impatiently to guide her hand to the rail that slid the seat forwards. "The lever to the right adjusts the backrest."

"Okay."

Thirty seconds later she was belted in and had reversed the car out of the parking bay as part of a rapid three-point turn to leave them facing the opposite way on Bartholomew Lane, towards Threadneedle Street.

"It would have been quicker if you'd let me drive."

"It wouldn't."

"You've already wasted time faffing about with the bloody seat and mirrors."

Ayesha looked quickly to the right, checking for oncoming traffic, before rapidly turning left on to Threadneedle Street. Her right hand tapped the Bluetooth earpiece then returned to the wheel as her left handled the rapid switches up through the gears. "*Have you got me?*"

"What?"

"Quiet, I'm not talking to you. *Have you got me?*" A brief pause. "*Yes. Yes, that's right. Just making a left on to Bishopsgate. The A10. Have we got hold of the lights?*" Another pause. "*Good. Traffic's light here anyway just now, but I want a clear run the whole way.*" Catching a breath and listening. "*Good. Keep me updated on any news at all from the studio. Thanks.*"

"Ayesha, for God's sake. What is going on? Who are you talking to?"

"The deal was that you do as you're told and keep quiet. Not keep firing questions at me."

"I agreed to do as I'm told. There was never any mention of me staying schtum."

"Okay. I'm telling you to keep quiet now."

"That's simply not fair."

"I understand you've got questions, but I need to concentrate."

"Questions! My kids and my Mum are Christ knows where and in danger!"

"Calm down."

"Fuck's sake Ayesha! If you want me to calm down, bloody well tell me what's going on."

"I told you before. Fiona, Fi and Ollie are being held by two comrades of the Yekta brothers and they are in danger. That's where we're going now. Shit!"The car lurched violently to the right as Ayesha swerved to avoid a woman who had stepped off the pavement without noticing their rapid approach. An oncoming car lurched into the bus lane to avoid them; its driver's face a confusion of terror and anger.

"But who are they? Who are these men? What will they do to my kids, to my mum? Why is this allowed to happen?"

"I know you're upset. But talking about who, what and why isn't going to help get us there any faster. We just need to concentrate on that."

"Ayesha, please! Please explain what the hell is going on here. Where is it that we're going? Is it the studio that you were talking about?"

"Yes. They are at the studio. And that's where we're going now."

"And how do you know where it is?"

The car slowed perceptibly as Ayesha eased off the accelerator and took her eye off the road to glance across to him. "I know where the studio is, and I know that the children and your mother are there because I took them there."

For a moment there was silence inside the car. Since the second that Ayesha and the Yetka brothers had pulled out their guns at the bank, Jack's cosmos had been in a tumult. His unconscious had protected him by engaging an autopilot to help navigate the alien version of his world that he now found himself in, and to inure him against further shock. But his body's self-defence mechanism failed in the face of this latest revelation. Nonplussed, his mind strove to make sense of her simple words. His response was barely adequate. "What?"

"I know where the studio is, and that your mother and the children are there, because I took them."

The car was still moving at a slower pace and he sensed that she felt vulnerable, almost as though she was anticipating a physical assault. The urge to prove her correct was strong, but less powerful than his desperation to understand the madness that had engulfed him. He could hear his own voice as though it were another's, calm and disinterested. "And why would you have done that?"

"It was necessary Jack. It was all part of the plan to get them to show their hand."

"Who's 'them'? What the bloody hell is going on here? And how can you possibly justify putting my children and my mum into a situation like this?" He leaned towards her as he spoke, and the car slowed further as he sensed her flinch slightly.

"Getting angry isn't going to help. I *will* explain, but you need to let me concentrate on driving so we can get there as quickly as possible." Her lips were tight and thin over her teeth as she spoke, and Jack sensed a tension that had been absent before, even when guns had been going off.

"Drive then, damn you. But also explain to me exactly what is bloody well going on. And, so help me, Ayesha, if anything happens to any of my kids…"

"The quicker we get there the less likely anything will happen to them, or to anyone else."

"Fucking hell, woman, stop talking in bloody riddles and explain what in the name of Christ is going on."

The car had regained the speed it had before Ayesha's

revelation, and every light was again in their favour. "*Yes, we're back on track again. No, there won't be any more slowing down. Keep me updated. Yes, thanks.*"

"And who the hell are you speaking to?"

"Colleagues, Jack. They're monitoring our progress and controlling the traffic lights to ensure we get there as quickly as possible. They're also in a position to let us have any information that comes from the studio."

"Bloody hell. I do believe that you *can* actually control the traffic. My God Ayesha, I simply can't comprehend what's happening." A hackney cab travelling in the opposite direction suddenly executed a U-turn without signalling just a hundred yards ahead, causing Ayesha to slam on the brakes before pulling out to pass it, horn blaring. She didn't even glance in the rear-view mirror to witness the cab driver's single finger salute.

"Shut up and let me concentrate on driving." A quick glance to see what Jack was fumbling with. "What are you doing with your phone?"

"I'm going to ring my mum. Warn her what's going on."

"Don't be so fucking stupid!"

"What? Why's that stupid? Tell me what's going on or I swear I'll ring Mum, or maybe even a journalist." He paused and stared at her profile.

Both hands solidly on the steering wheel, eyes firmly on the road in front, a slow pregnant sigh. "You're a smart man, Jack. You heard Jalal's rant and you know that you're involved in a terrorist attack that the authorities are trying to stop. Your kids and mother are being held hostage by terrorists and those same authorities charged with protecting the public have facilitated the hostage taking."

It was the first time that she had acknowledged the nature of her own involvement, but Jack let it pass, eager to learn more. Frustratingly, Ayesha said nothing else. It was as if she had served and was waiting for him to return. He was irritated, "Go on."

"We believe that these particular individuals are intending to carry out the biggest terrorist atrocity the world has yet seen. The children and your mother are in no more danger in the hands of these men than if they were at home."

"That simply makes no sense, Ayesha. These are maniacs with guns. We've already seen that they're willing to use them. How can they be in no more danger than if they were at home?"

"Because of the scale of what's planned."

"I still don't get it. You said the biggest terrorist atrocity ever. Bigger than the Madrid train bombings? Bigger than Lockerbie? Bigger than 9/11? How big are we talking about?"

"We think that this is on a different scale entirely. We are looking at something that could devastate many square miles in terms of its impact. Potentially bigger than that."

This was a volley so powerful and unexpected that Jack was completely wrong footed. He had no answer, his cavernous silence barely adequate to accommodate the immensity of her statement. After a few seconds he found his voice, smaller than it had been before. "So, you think there's a nuke?"

"We believe there might be. We thought it might have been at or near the bank, but now we believe that it's at the studio."

"A nuke. Jesus. Why would anybody want to set off a nuke?"

"Why does anyone want to commit any terrorist act? Right now, why doesn't matter. It's what that matters, and how we stop it. We do that first and, if we're successful, we can philosophise about the whys and wherefores afterwards."

She was right, of course. Her simple summary helped Jack see through the bewildering broth and focus on the priority. "How long until we get there?"

"Not long now. Less than half an hour."

"And once we get there? What do we do?"

"We stop the bastards and we rescue Fiona and the kids."

"How?"

"I don't know."

Silence fell like snow, a blanket that chilled Jack's heart. Every new development had been more grotesque than the one before. People were not who they seemed to be. Guns had materialised at the bank. Bob had been shot. Idris had been killed. Jalal had been shot. Fi and Ollie and Mum were hostages. The crazed fanatics holding them had a nuclear weapon. He would have used the word surreal, but it was all too terrifyingly real.

He stared at Ayesha, fully concentrated on steering - and driving as fast as the surroundings and her invisible assistants would permit. Her physical beauty was more familiar to him than the backs of his own hands. On many mornings he had wakened early and lain studying her as she slept. The wide mouth and full lips. The high cheekbones and long, naturally thick eyelashes. The bearskin sheen of her hair. Translucent fine down on soft, perfect skin. Her features were the same, but not his reaction. The belief, the passion, the hope – the sense of being uplifted – had gone. He realised now that she had not changed. This is who she had always been but chosen not to show. Love and lust and loneliness had heightened some of his senses and unplugged others. She had set out to dupe him from the very start and it had been easy, because he so desperately wanted to buy what she was selling.

Such a realisation might normally trigger anger, but not right now. Any suggestion of fury was throttled in its infancy by the much more compelling fear for his kids and his Mum that dominated his consciousness. This woman was the agent of his despair and had put those dearest to him in mortal danger. But she might also be their best bet of surviving.

"Who or what are the disposal team, the robot and the lab coat guys?"

"What?"

"You mentioned them before we left the bank."

"So I did. It's the team that's needed to ensure we recover your family and the device safely."

"Go on."

"What else do you want me to tell you?" She made no attempt to disguise the note of irritation.

"How you intend to go about it. What the bloody hell a robot has to do with anything, far less guys in lab coats."

"The deal was that you would do exactly what you were told. So now I'm telling you to shut up and stop distracting me." She didn't even afford him a glance.

*I don't know her at all. I really, **really** don't know her at all.*

*She doesn't care about Fi and Ollie and Mum. She only cares about the bloody nuke. If Mum and the kids end up as 'collateral damage' it won't matter to her as long as the device is retrieved.*

"You don't give a shit about Mum or the kids, do you? If you cared about them, you wouldn't have delivered them to these bloody fanatics."

"For God's sake, Jack!" The exasperation in her voice was underscored by a lurch of the car as she clunked a gear change. "Of course I care about them. I couldn't have spent so much time with them and not ..." Her words trailed off as she reproached him with a baleful glance. "I've told you. They're ultimately in no more danger than if they were at home. Now please stop distracting me and let me concentrate on getting us there."

*Maybe she's right. If there is a nuke, then everyone in the city's in danger. Maybe she really does care about them. The way she responded there – it was real. She **does** care.*

*For God's sake, what am I thinking? I'm doing it again. I'm falling for it hook, line and sinker. I'm pretending to myself that I can tell when she's being sincere. Ha! I've got a great bloody track record there, haven't I?*

*But maybe this time she really **is** being honest. She's out in the open now, no need for any more pretence. And she's driving like a maniac – desperate to get there as soon as possible. There's already a team there, so she's just desperate to get there because she's worried about the kids and Mum.*

*And of course that's exactly what she wants me to think. She can manipulate me with just a look or a word. I love her. Loved her. And I believed she loved me. Everything she's ever told me is probably a lie. I can't trust a word she says.*

"The disposal team is a bad pun. There are bomb disposal experts and a team of agents whose task is to neutralise the bad guys – 'disposing' of them if necessary. The robot belongs to the explosive disarmament team. The lab coat guys are nuclear physicists associated with the military." Her voice was calm, her eyes locked on the road ahead.

"Thank you. Do you really not know how we're going to go about rescuing my family?"

"Not yet, no. But the guys on the scene will have evaluated everything and come up with options. We'll get a sit rep when we arrive."

"And if the kids and Mum need to be … to be sacrificed to secure the nuke?"

"That's not going to happen. And that kind of thinking isn't going to help anyone."

The admonishment signalled an abrupt end to the brief thaw. How much he could trust her was irrelevant. She was the only game in town. And he knew it.

"*Yes. Go ahead.*" Ayesha's eyes narrowed slightly as she listened for fully twenty seconds to the update. "*Understood. It doesn't change anything. Just confirms the urgency. Thanks.*"

Jack's expression was that of a well-trained Labrador sitting by the table, hoping for scraps.

"All four suspects – and me – are booked on the 5.30 flight from London City to Istanbul this afternoon. We were also booked on the same flights each of the last seven Sundays, and identical bookings exist for both one and two weeks from today. They booked three Sundays in a row initially. Then, after the first Sunday passed, they booked another one so that there was always a rolling three-week window with Sunday flights booked. We were unsure whether they were making the bookings as a red herring, or whether they were constantly having to postpone their plans. The only thing that we could be confident of was that they were most likely going to strike on a Sunday."

"You just said something about confirming the urgency?"

"Yes. Seems that we were blindsided by their tactics and became complacent.The block booking is a diversion, meant to distract anyone looking – like us. The two men are actually also booked on a 5.15 flight from Stansted to Amsterdam, and then connecting on to Oslo."

"And …?"

"It means that the journey time from the studio to the airport is about half an hour shorter, and the flight is leaving fifteen minutes earlier. The conclusion is that they will probably be on the move an hour earlier than we thought."

Jack checked his wristwatch, "It's nearly one o' clock now. When do you think they're planning to leave?"

"Shit!"

"What is it?"

Ayesha's left hand left the steering wheel and fumbled in her pocket. "Here!" She thrust Jalal's phone towards Jack. "Take it!"

Jack did as instructed. "What do you want me to do?"

"Type in the security code – zero nine, one one, zero one – and then go to texts and send the message *All OK* to the last number sent to as soon as it turns one o' clock. Got that?"

Jack nodded and again carried out her bidding. "Done!"

"Good. Thank you. Jalal is meant to send that message every half hour to reassure the others that things are going to plan. The twelve thirty message was late and we're probably blown, but it's worth sending anyway – just in case."

"Okay, I see. You did well to remember the security number."

"Not really – the sick bastard used the date of the nine-eleven attacks in the States. I wasn't likely to forget that. Anyway, getting back to your original question, I have no idea when they are intending to leave. It's …" Ayesha interrupted herself and her brow furrowed as she concentrated on the information flowing from her Bluetooth earpiece. "*Okay, yes – got that. What do your calcs show for my ETA?*" A brief pause. "*Right. Thanks.*" She glanced briefly in Jack's direction. "Scratch what I just said. We think they're planning to leave by 13.45."

"How do you know that? What's changed?"

"We're listening to them, Jack. We have mic's in there and we can pick up some of their conversation. The kids and your mum are fine. They haven't been harmed. The guys have been spooked by the 12.30 call being late and they've pulled things forward as a result."

"If you're listening to them and what's going on, then why couldn't you tell me that before now?"

"Our bugs were being jammed, which isn't that much of a surprise. They are incredibly cautious, and that includes taking precautions to ensure that they aren't being bugged. They've switched off their jamming device now though, which our guys think means they are arming the bomb. They are probably concerned that the jammer could interfere with it."

Jack paused to digest the latest revelation. "When are we expected to get there?"

"Just under twenty minutes. We'll be there at 13.22."

"And when do your colleagues at the studio intend to intervene?"

"No later than 13.30."

The discourse was clipped; reflecting that time was now too precious to be squandered on the exchange of unnecessary words. Ayesha's foot squeezed the accelerator pedal slightly harder as they accelerated through a landscape that had already morphed from urban to suburban. Very light traffic and the succession of benign green lights barely registered in Jack's consciousness as he silently contemplated what might await their arrival.

## Chapter 34

Ayesha steered the 325i off the main carriageway, through a wide open-gated entrance. The road ahead was broad with junctions off to both left and right. Her speed made no concession to the multiple turns she executed as she navigated through the mosaic of light industrial units, offices and building sites before pulling into the car park outside a single-storey warehouse.

"Is this it?" Jack's hand reached to open the door as he searched her face for confirmation.

"Nearly. Wait." Ayesha pulled her mobile phone from her pocket, hit a speed dial number, then pressed the speaker icon so that Jack could hear the ring tone calling. It was answered after a single ring. "We're here."

*"Where exactly?"*

Ayesha leaned forward to look at the warehouse. "Outside number 183, four hundred yards round the corner from the studio. Okay to approach?"

*"Come down the spine road past the turning to the studio. Take the next left into the car park to the rear of 189. That'll avoid any sight lines from the studio, and they'll be unlikely to hear the car engine."* Jack listened to the disembodied voice. Flat West Midlands accent, a combination of urgency and calm.

Ayesha didn't pause to ring off, simply dropping the phone on to her lap as she put the BMW into gear and sped away. Within seconds they were being beckoned by a rangy, bearded, thirty-something man to a parking bay beside three large pantechnicons, all bearing the legend *'Walton Delivery Services – Romford, Essex.'*

The car had barely stopped before Ayesha and Jack were out and following their guide up two fold down steps and through the doorway in the side of the furthermost van. Inside was what Jack imagined a scaled down version of mission control might look like for a manned spaceflight, save for the fact that it was dimly lit and with an incongruous but distinct smell of ammonia. Two banks of four screens, one above the other, were flanked on either side by a range of hi-tech equipment from floor to above head height. Four consoles, incorporating keyboards and a multiplicity of controls, aligned with the screens. Office-type swivel chairs were tucked below two desks while two others were occupied by individuals focused on the screens and controls in front of them. Jack gauged that one was female and the other male, but little more from his position in the entrance.

Ayesha placed her bag on the floor by the doorway beside Jack, stepped forwards and immediately addressed her audience in a commanding, authoritative voice. "I've had control in my ear the whole drive here, so I've got the big picture. Cut to the essentials of the sitrep. Talk to me."

"Cameras on all four aspects of the studio, with a separate one on the main front door and another on the fire exit to the rear. The mics are working fine and we've put heat sensors on the roof so we can track where people are in the building. They're less effective over the soundproofed area, but still sufficient to confirm warm bodies." Their guide was speaking, quickly and clearly, with the same flat vowels as before. "Slight problem though. Kris stumbled when he was placing one of the heat sensors. We think the guys inside might have heard him. He's still on top of the roof now, lying low."

"For fuck's sake, Josh!" Ayesha's tone underscored her annoyance. "Can somebody cut to the chase? The essentials, now!"

Josh's chastened expression made him look younger, somehow vulnerable. His mouth shaped to form words, but he was cut across by a precise female voice. "There's definitely a device of some sort and the arming process is underway. The targets estimated that task will be complete within the next ten or fifteen minutes. Their plan is to evacuate immediately that is the case." The factual summary, delivered earnestly in a calm Welsh accent commanded attention.

"Thanks, Izzy." Ayesha looked straight at her. "What else?"

"Everyone and everything needed for the device is here, in the other two mobile units. Aside from Kris on the roof, we've got

Tonyah out there covering the area between the front door and their car." She gestured towards the screen to the left of her console where the image of a black woman, crouched holding a pistol, was leaning with her back against the corner of a building. She waved to the camera to signal that she could hear their discussion.

"Okay, understood. Opinions?" Ayesha looked from Izzy to Josh, and then to the unnamed second man, then back once more to Izzy.

"We have to act now." Izzy was composed, although her tone was tinged with a dash of anxiety. "We only have minutes before they're on the move, or whatever they decide to do next. The Laidlaws are alive in there and we don't think the targets intend to kill them. But we can't know for sure. We must act while we still have the chance to take the initiative."

Jack's stomach convulsed at her words, almost as if he had been punched. Although his mouth was a desert, he could taste copper and had to fight to control the urge to retch.

"Right. What's the plan?" Ayesha directed her question to Josh.

"We have control of the security system. The targets believe that the front door and fire exits are both locked and can only be opened from inside, so we can surprise them. You and Tonyah will go in via the front entrance and disable target one while Kris and I will enter via the fire exit, disable target two and secure the device." Josh's composure had returned and his delivery was BBC newsreader matter-of-fact. He nodded in the direction of the seated man who had thus far been silent. "Jas?"

Jas jabbed his right index finger towards the large screen to the right above where he was sitting. "You can see the schematic of the internal layout of the building. I've overlaid the heat sensor data. You can also see four signatures together inside the big soundproof recording room, and another separately in this room over here. That signature has been there nearly forty minutes now, so we're confident he's in there arming the device. One of the other signatures has gone there twice, presumably his partner checking on progress. If we knew for certain that he was going to do so again we could go in then and disable them together at the same time, without any risk to the three others. The trouble is that we can't …"

## Chapter 35

"Fuck!" All eyes turned to Izzy and then to the furthest away screen indicated by her outstretched arm and pointing finger. There was the unmistakeable figure of Jack, Ayesha's gun in his right hand, racing towards the front entrance of the studio.

"Tonyah! Get after him!" A quick glance at her handbag on the floor confirmed her carelessness. Ayesha was composed, but shouting. "Kris! Jack's gone rogue! He's got my gun and he's heading for the front entrance to the studio. Meet Josh at the fire exit and await instructions. Tonyah, I'm right behind you." Josh had already jumped down the stairs from the van and was racing away. "Izzy, give me your weapon." Ayesha snatched it, turned out through the doorway, bounded down the steps and sprinted towards the entrance to the studio.

Jack pulled the brushed aluminium handle, noting gratefully the mechanism to the top that meant the door would soft close silently behind him. He inched into the spacious foyer and hunched instinctively, shortening his height by ten centimetres. He looked around; trying to orient himself to the floor plan and body heat signatures he had seen on Jas's screen.

His heart, already drumming, almost failed as he felt what he immediately recognised to be the barrel of a pistol tap him on the shoulder from behind. He turned to be confronted by a woman, all big hair and even bigger eyes, with her left index finger to her lips commanding him to remain mute. He recognised Tonyah from her image on the screen, but was surprised – even in these extreme circumstances - at her six-foot plus height. Behind her he could see a frowning Ayesha following through the doorway, gun in her right hand and left hand on her Bluetooth earpiece. A silent exchange of glances and a nod of the head directed them to follow her towards the corridor on the right and through the door marked 'Make up'. Despite the tension Jack still had time to direct an unspoken paean in thanks to the anonymous designer who had fitted the same soft close fittings to all the doors in the building.

As the door closed noiselessly behind them Ayesha grabbed Jack aggressively by the shoulder, hissing, "What the fuck are you playing at?

"No time for that now." Tonyah's low, quiet, incontrovertible observation had the desired effect.

"You're right. Look, Jack. We know what's at stake for you, but this is our situation. You *have* to let us deal with it. I'm here to save your children. Trust me." Ayesha squinted purposefully at Jack, then stepped back and touched her finger lightly to her earpiece, concentrating on the advice being relayed to her.

The same focused expression on Tonyah's face alerted Jack that they were both similarly wired and receiving the same transmission. "What's going on?" he asked in a voice both hushed and hoarse.

There was no response for a few more seconds as both women continued to listen to the update from Jas. Ayesha looked up at him. "Jack." Still whispering, and with no less intensity than a few seconds previously. "The sound proofing throughout the whole of this building is excellent and Mirza and Eshan are far enough from here that they can't hear us. But we still need to be really quiet. Understood?"

A small nod of confirmation. "So what's the plan?"

"Jas confirms that the single heat signature in the screening room is still there. We believe that is Mirza arming the device. There are four separate heat signatures coming from the recording room. We can hear multiple voices, but the soundproofing muffles them too much for us to distinguish what's being said. But we're confident it's your kids, your Mum and Eshan that are in there."

"And?" One word, a single note expressing as eloquently as a symphony relief that his kids were still alive, mixed with terror that they soon might not be.

"Kris and Josh are outside the fire exit. They will come in that way and go to the screening room. Tonyah and I will go to the recording room. When we are all in position, we enter both rooms simultaneously."

"And do what? What are you going to do in that recording room? How are you going to ensure they're safe?" Jack's throat was sandpaper, and each word he rasped hurt.

"The kids and Fiona will be fine. You just have to trust us." Ayesha looked at him with what might have been compassion, nodding her head slightly in search of reciprocal affirmation. Jack nodded understanding and assent. "Good. We do this in two stages. Kris? Josh?" She paused for acknowledgement as Jack realised they were all, literally, on the same wavelength. "Good. Stage one is you two come in through the fire exit. Jas, you are confirming it is unlocked. Right?" A pause. "Okay everyone, it looks like we're good to go. On my say so Kris and Josh go in and confirm access once inside. Ready? Go now!"


The siren was loud enough to cause physical pain.

Ayesha's left hand was pressed hard against her ear and she was screaming, presumably to Jas and Izzy about "the fucking alarm".

Tonyah had pulled the door open and was squatting against it, arms outstretched with her gun pointing into the corridor.

Jack sprang forward. Vaulted Tonyah. Sprinted in the direction of the recording room. The noise splitting his skull. In a corridor to his right faint awareness of Josh and another man. The sign above the door in front of him confirmed his destination. With all the force he could muster, barged it open with his shoulder. Too much force! Stumbled through the doorway. Fell forwards full length. Lost balance. Confronted by sudden extreme change of environment. A bright green background at the far end and the unmistakeable silhouettes of Mum and Fi. Silence, as sudden and unexpected as the siren. Ears adjusting. Fi screaming from the far end of the room. Stand up. A voice, Ollie's voice, shouting Dad! Dad! Dad! Turn to the right. Ollie, six feet away, being held off the ground by the arm of a huge man around his waist. Eshan? Yes, Eshan. He had a gun in his free hand.

"Gun!" Eshan barked and stared at Jack.

No comprehension. Confusion.

"Gun!" Eshan gestured with his own firearm.

Jack realised he was still carrying Ayesha's Glock. Slowly he reached out and placed it on the console to his right, as indicated by Eshan, and withdrew his hand. His eyes had adjusted to the darker surroundings, although white light from the corridor cascaded through the door wedged open by his brutish entry. The jangling in his ears had subsided. Fully alert now, one party to a Mexican stand-off.

Ollie sniffed back tears, eyes terrified and imploring. "It's okay, Ollie", Jack stepped half a pace forward and stopped sharply as Eshan pointed his gun at him. "It's going to be okay."

The sudden sound of gunfire popping like fireworks, as loud as it was unexpected, reverberated from elsewhere in the building. Eshan's eyes glanced towards the doorway for a fraction of a second. In that same infinitesimal moment Jack's brain processed more data than any super computer. Implications, timescales, options, risks, distance, speed – calculate, decide, execute. He launched himself through the air in a rugby dive, both arms outstretched towards Eshan's gun hand. The hit was harder than the one that had broken the door, causing Eshan to drop both the gun and Ollie as he fell backwards under the weight of the assault. Scrabbling on the floor, Jack managed to land a punch to the side of Eshan's nose, which broke with a crack and a splash of blood, before the bigger, stronger man threw him aside. In an instant Eshan had rolled to his gun and taken aim at Jack, the madness in his eyes brooking no debate about his intentions.

For the second time that day Jack heard the crack of a pistol up close. Much, much louder than previously. No silencer this time. The screech of pain was just as loud and the result identical – a hand about to pull the trigger interrupted by a bullet. Eshan's left hand cradled his right arm as he contemplated the damage to his shoulder. Jack looked to the doorway and nodded silent acknowledgement to Tonyah, frozen arms outstretched, her gun still trained on Eshan.

At the far end of the room Fi was screaming and Mum was cuddling her close. "Dad." Jack spun round. Ollie's eyes were huge and tear filled, and both nostrils were streaming. His whole frame was shaking. Jack scooped him up and held him tight enough that he could just breathe, squeezing gallons of love and

care and safety and reassurance into the pint-sized body.
"It's all right, son. It's all right."

## Chapter 36

"Everything under control?" Ayesha's voice was slightly breathless.

"Everything's cool." Tonyah's tone just-another-day-at-the-office. "The target has a sore shoulder – GSW – and will need a medic. The others are unharmed physically, but I think all four are suffering varying degrees of shock. Control will be listening to us now, so I expect the guys we need will be on their way as we speak. What about the others?"

"The other target is dead. Josh had no choice. The device hadn't been fully armed. Military are all over it. But it's not a nuke, thank fuck."

"So an RDD then? Plain old dirty bomb?"

"Yeah. Still nasty, but not as bad as we feared."

"Over there." Tonyah gestured towards Eshan with her pistol, directing the two military medics who had appeared at the door. "I'm going to baby-sit this pair while they patch him up. I'll catch you later," she said as she moved off towards the stricken Eshan.

Ayesha turned towards the brilliantly illuminated green screen at the far end of the room. Jack had made his way there, carrying Ollie, and was now crouched on one knee with his back to her. He still had Ollie in his left arm, head resting on his shoulder with little legs and feet dangling above the floor. Jack's other arm was around Fi, pulling her close to him and nuzzling heads together. Fiona stood to the side; part of the group, but not of its core. Her hand rested gently on Fi's back. She looked up as Ayesha approached, then downward at the gun she was carrying. Ayesha self-consciously pushed the weapon into her waistband as she stepped tentatively forward.

"Are all of you okay?" Four pairs of eyes fixed on hers.

Jack had no words. Confusion wrestled with contempt as he regarded the woman who had played fast and loose with the lives of his children. Fi pressed her temple more firmly against his and let out a gentle whimper. Jack squeezed her even closer, wishing that that the bowling ball in his throat would disappear and let him utter reassurance. An involuntary shiver passed through him and he blinked back tears, determined to maintain at least that level of control and stay strong for the kids.

Ollie broke the silence. "Eshan had a gun. He said he would kill me. Then the scary lady came and she had a gun and she shot Eshan." His whole body shuddered as he struggled to contain a sob. "And now you've got a gun too." The effort was too much as tears flowed once more and he buried his face in Jack's shoulder. Jack pulled him tight and Fi wrapped her arms round them both, as they turned inward for comfort from each other.

"I'm sorry."

"Are you? Are you really?" Fiona had stepped forward, between Ayesha and her shell-shocked son and grandchildren.

"Of course. Are you all right?" Ayesha bowed her head to better engage eye contact with the older, smaller woman. "How is …"

The blow had been seventy-two years in the making. Fiona Laidlaw was a gentle, controlled soul. She had never struck another living creature in her life – not an insect, nor a puppy being trained, or one of her own children when misbehaving as a youngster. The slap connected flush with Ayesha's cheek with a loud whip crack. The combination of total surprise and considerable force caused Ayesha to stumble backwards a step, before falling. Consciousness of the distinct lavender bouquet of Fiona's perfume heightened the surreal nature of the experience, as Ayesha's balance deserted her.

"Get out! Get out! Get out!" Fiona was standing over her, screaming. Behind her, Fi and Ollie were screaming. Jack stepped forward, wrapped both arms round Fiona from behind, and pulled her gently into his chest. He dipped his head, whispering, "It's all right, Mum. It's all right."

Ayesha reached to retrieve the Glock, which had spilled on the floor when she fell. She picked it up silently, turned abruptly and walked rapidly to the door, pushing between a phalanx of men and women in military garb that had gathered there.

The departure triggered a return of Fiona's composure. A look from Jack confirmed their mutual understanding of the need to be strong for the children. The four Laidlaws embraced in a group hug, the adults cooing comfort. A light touch on his shoulder prompted Jack to turn. Izzy fixed him with wide, concerned eyes, "I'm sorry to interrupt, Mr. Laidlaw. I wonder if I could have a word with you?"

Jack looked to his family and gave what he hoped was an encouraging smile,"Excuse me a moment, folks." He followed Izzy a few paces, sufficient for a quiet conversation to be unheard. "What do you want?"

"Mr. Laidlaw, I know how intense this whole situation is right now, but there are some practicalities that we have to deal with." She stopped, realising that Jack was looking over her shoulder, distracted by the sight of Eshan being escorted away. "Mr. Laidlaw? Thank you. As I was saying …"

"Practicalities. Yes, I heard." He was engaged now, assessing her. None of them could be trusted. She was younger than the others, with a kindly, open face. Probably sent because they felt she might be their best bet to win his confidence. "What kind of practicalities?"

"Our first priority is to have medics check your children, your mother and you to make sure none of you are physically hurt. Then we need to discuss next steps. Is it okay for the medics to check each of you over? It might be better, more reassuring for the children, if they see the adults being checked first. Then perhaps you and your mother could stay close to them when they get checked. Is that okay?"

"You said that was your first priority. What are the others?"

"Once we've had you checked out, we need to get you all home safely."

"And?"

"Sorry?"

"And that's it is it? You get us home safely," Jack resisted the temptation to make quotation marks in the air, "and then we're done?"

"Well, obviously we'll need to discuss debriefing you."

"Fuck off!"

"As I say, I recognise how intense the whole situation is right now. How hard it is to get everything straight in your mind." She smiled encouragement. "You agree that you should all be checked over? Your mother doesn't keep the best of health and this must have been traumatic for her."

"Yes!" Jack hissed the reply through clenched teeth, struggling to keep his voice low and maintain the semblance of calm for the children. She was right. "Yes, you can have us checked out. And then we can go home?"

"Assuming you are all fine, then of course you can go home. It would be sensible for all four of you to travel back in your car. We will send an escort vehicle to accompany you, and then see you safe back into your house."

"You don't think there's any danger at home?"

"No, Mr Laidlaw, we're just observing protocol."

"All right. And I suppose that debriefing me is just protocol too?" There was less of an edge to his voice.

"Yes. But that can wait until tomorrow. We really do just want to check everyone out and then get you home safe for now."

He believed her. He wondered whether he was just too drained to stay angry, too weary to be sceptical. Whatever the case, he chose to believe her. "All right, Izzy. It is Izzy, isn't it?" A nod of affirmation. "Let's have the medics check us over and get out of this place."

"Thank you. As I say, we'll escort you home. Please make sure that there is no discussion of today's events with anyone outside of the four of you. A car will collect you at eight o' clock sharp tomorrow morning to take you to your debriefing. Have you got any questions?"

"No." In time there would be questions, but for now there was just Ollie, Fi, Mum and him.

The drive home was uneventful. They watched television and ate pasta. The children went to bed early and he agreed with Fiona that she would phone their school the next morning with some pretext for keeping them home. He explained to her that he'd prefer not to talk about things just yet. He was being debriefed the next day and should be able to provide answers after that. Fiona did not protest and retired to her bed not an hour later than the kids. Jack followed suit shortly after.

## Chapter 37

The radio alarm pierced his dreamless slumber. Seven o' clock. Jack realised to his surprise that he had slept through the night. He showered, shaved and dressed before breakfasting with his mother. They agreed to let the children sleep until they awoke naturally. Jack brushed his teeth, said a quiet goodbye to Fiona and exited the front door to the navy blue Jaguar that pulled up at thirty seconds before eight. Save for a polite but perfunctory acknowledgement when he got into the car, the journey was conducted in silence. The fourteen-mile route to Thames House at Milbank took fifty-eight minutes in the rush hour traffic. Despite the "don't stop" red line on the road outside the neoclassical structure, the car glided to a brief halt in front of the huge open doors at the visitors' entrance. A tall, thin man whose grey complexion matched his business suit materialised from within, opened the passenger door and instructed Jack to follow. The Jag melded seamlessly back into the flowing traffic, the whole manoeuvre completed with zero disruption. Inside, Jack followed his guide unimpeded through what might otherwise have proven to be several obdurate layers of security. After two flights of stairs and a lengthy corridor they stopped outside an anonymous door. A grey man knocked on the door, received an instruction from within to enter, opened the door and ushered Jack in, and then closed the door from the outside.

Jack entered a small office, sparsely furnished, with opaque half-glazed partition walls to each side. The absence of anything other than basic décor and furnishing confirmed functionality rather than aesthetics was its sole *raison d'etre*. A confusing combination of mustiness and antiseptic suggested it was a venue that enjoyed only occasional use. Ayesha was seated at the corner of a rectangular table and rose as he entered. Beside her a man no older than 40, thick black hair greying at the temples, olive complexion and with sharp brown eyes also got to his feet. He was five foot eight or nine, Jack guessed, and casually dressed in navy chinos and a pale blue business shirt open at the collar. He leaned forward and offered his hand to Jack. "Good morning Mr. Laidlaw. My name is Ahmad Husain and I head up the Executive Liaison Group handling your case at MI5. I believe you know my SO15 colleague." Jack looked towards Ayesha, who met his eyes briefly. "Thank you for coming in this morning."

"It's not as if I was given a lot of choice in the matter."

"Mr. Laidlaw, why do you think that you are here?"

"I expect that you are desperate to cover things up. You want me to be schtum about what has happened."

"To a degree, Mr. Laidlaw. Our mission is to keep the country safe. Sometimes that does require … discretion. Clearly there are assurances that we would like to get from this meeting. Equally, I'm sure that there will be things that you would also like to get from our discussion."

"I need you to explain. I need to properly understand, to make sense of all of this."

"Is it not sufficient to know that your family is safe. That a potential threat to national security has been neutralised?"

"No. That's not enough. I need to understand what the hell is going on. You owe me that at least, after what you've put us through"

"You can work most of it out yourself. I can't tell you anything. This whole case is classified. You might think that you want to know everything but, trust me, you really don't."

"Don't give me that load of cock and bull. I don't give a shit about what's classified or not – whatever that actually means. None of us are leaving this room until you explain things to me. If you don't explain things properly then I'll go to the media." Jack's eyes blazed and there was an edge to his voice.

Ahmad Husain returned his stare. "Don't threaten me, Mr. Laidlaw. If my colleague or I choose to leave this room we will. You would not be able to stop us. And you would be very stupid indeed to even try."

Although a smile played on his lips, his eyes were diamond hard, and Jack didn't doubt him. "All right. I'm not threatening you. I'm simply asking you. Surely you can see that I'm struggling with all of this."

He thought he detected a flicker of something in his expression. A sigh and a softening of his eyes. "Very well Mr. Laidlaw, as you wish. But before we proceed, I must advise you that everything discussed in this meeting, and indeed all of the events preceding this meeting, are covered by the Official Secrets Acts 1911 to 1989." He paused to allow what he was saying to register. "There is a common misapprehension that someone needs to physically sign something to agree to be covered, but that is not the case. For the avoidance of doubt, you are bound by the restrictions imposed by the Act. Breaching the Act has very serious consequences and can lead to a maximum jail term of fourteen years. Do you clearly understand the gravity of this matter? Believe me Mr. Laidlaw, if I tell you what you want to know, and you repeat it – to anyone – then you could get yourself and them into very serious trouble indeed. Now, do you really want to know more, or would you rather just walk away?"

"I'm not going to repeat anything to anyone. I just want to understand. I *need* to know."

"All right then. Sit down there." He indicated the chrome and blue cloth covered office chair in front of the desk. Jack eased himself down into it while his two hosts positioned themselves back in their black faux leather swivel chairs. Ahmad Husain turned his head and locked eyes with him. When he spoke, his voice was low and calm. "There are three different classifications of government information. There's 'official', 'secret' and 'top secret'. Some of what you're asking about is 'top secret'. That means it's this country's most sensitive information requiring the highest levels of protection. 'The highest levels of protection' means exactly what it says. If it's believed that sensitive information is at risk of compromise, then the most extreme measures are considered to be legitimate."

"Are you threatening me now?"

"No, Mr. Laidlaw, I'm just trying to make sure that you fully appreciate the risks."

"I get it. You've made things pretty clear. Please, just help me understand."

"Right." Ahmad Husain leaned back slightly, still maintaining eye contact. "Six weeks ago we received credible intelligence that a plutonium based nuclear device had been purchased from rogue elements in Pakistan. That put us on to maximum alert status.The transaction was for US$200 million and the purchaser was person or persons unknown. We have been monitoring the Yekta brothers – Jalal and Idris - for two years now."

"Sorry, who's 'we'?"

"Us, the Security Service. MI5 to most people. As I say, we've been monitoring the Yekta brothers for a couple of years, and they were on the list of potential suspects for involvement with the purchase. We also had loose tabs on Mirza and Eshan, but only began to suspect that the brothers were in contact with the other two about a year ago. They were incredibly security conscious – very careful. We think Idris was particularly paranoid – rightly as it turns out – because he had a really good appreciation of how sophisticated our surveillance is. These were four very smart guys in an atypical cell. We might expect one or perhaps two really intelligent individuals in any terrorist cell, but not all four. We feared that they were capable of pulling off something really sophisticated but couldn't get close enough to figure what it might be. Jalal was always the weakest link. He's a very smart guy who thinks he's even smarter than he actually is.We suspected he was looking to recruit a female through monitoring his online activity and were able to identify the profile of the kind of woman he was looking for. We built that profile – social media accounts, official records, bank accounts, National Insurance records, health, academic and employment histories –everything imaginable that could be searched online. We created a back-story and all of the collateral necessary to 'prove' that story was real. No detail was overlooked, right down to photo-shopping pictures of her on holiday in 2012 visiting her 'relatives' before they were killed at the wedding that was bombed. Idris was able to check out images of the victims available on multiple news media and satisfy himself that they were the same people posing with my colleague in the holiday snaps."

"She was the one selected to be the female recruit." Jack cast a contemptuous look towards Ayesha.

"Yes. She was the right age and the right ethnic and religious background."

"So, she's not Ayesha Alfarsi?"

"No, she's not. That was the identity we gave to the profile we'd created."

"So, where's the real Ayesha? The kid who was in the same year as me at school?"

"Dead. When she left school in Ilford she did move with her family, but not to Manchester. He father *was* a medic, but his new job was actually in Canada. The family moved to Toronto. Ayesha Alfarsi married a Frank Green when she was twenty-two. Ayesha Green was killed in a head-on car collision when she was twenty-five. Hers was a perfect identity to use. Her father is dead, her mother retired, and she had no siblings. We were able to place appropriately dated obituaries for her father in the archives of a couple of the websites of local North West of England newspapers, just in case Idris would check – which he did. Her mother is still alive, but has absolutely no online presence at all, or certainly nothing to indicate she's in Canada. We were able to create an online address for her in Wilmslow, in Cheshire, and a bank account. The bank account has a history of regular pensions payments from her teacher's pension and from her husband's NHS pension. There is also a history of utility bill and other routine payments, as well as all of the normal withdrawals and debit card use you would expect to see on the account of a retired lady. We took great care to ensure it would appear completely authentic. That proved to be a good investment of effort, because Idris checked that out too. He even checked to see whether the records might have been artificially created recently, but our boys were able to cover their cyber tracks."

"I can see you've gone to a hell of a lot of trouble and, given Idris's paranoia, I can understand why. But why did you want to choose Ayesha's identity in particular? Surely there must be plenty of other identities that you could have chosen."

"There are other identities we could have chosen, but there

would usually be some degree of tidying up, getting our virtual ducks in a row, with most of them."

"I'll take your word for it. What I still don't understand is why you chose Ayesha Alfarsi in particular."

"Because of you, Jack. We chose her because of you." He paused; forehead creased and stared hard at Jack.

"That makes absolutely no sense. What do you mean you chose her because of me?"

"We were confident that the brothers were targeting you, so finding an identity that had some link to you might make my colleague a more attractive proposition to them."

"No, slow down. You're going to have to spell this out for me."

"As I explained, we knew Jalal wanted to recruit a female. We were convinced that female would be used to befriend you, to gain your confidence. We felt that if she had a link, a plausible way in to you, that would be more of an asset as far as the brothers were concerned."

"Don't be coy. 'Befriend' me! You mean seduce me." Jack's contempt elicited no reaction from either Ahmad or Ayesha. "But anyway, surely them recruiting a woman who turned out to be linked to me would be far too much of a coincidence? It must have raised their suspicions – surely?"

"It was a calculated risk. We had a list of five possible identities we believed we could use, including Ayesha's. When we realised that she'd been in the same year as you at school we had to decide whether the potential upside of using that outweighed the risk you've identified. Obviously, we decided it did, and so my colleague became Ayesha Alfarsi."

Ahmed glanced towards Ayesha, who took her cue. "In the event it went as smoothly as it could have. When they finally confided in me who you were, I was able carry it off without too much discomfort. I pretended that your name rang a vague bell, but that I couldn't place it. I waited twenty-four hours before finally 'remembering' that someone called Jack Laidlaw had been in my year when I was at school in Ilford. When it became obvious that it was the same Jack Laidlaw, I explained that I didn't actually know him – it was a big year group in a big school – but that I did know *of* him. Anyway, they bought it."

"Surely it can't have been that easy. Surely Idris's paranoia meter would have been registering off the scale?"

"Jalal is an extreme narcissist. It was his idea to recruit a female and, in fact, he started doing so without even telling Idris. He has such a high opinion of himself that it's inconceivable to him that an idea of his might be flawed. When Ayesha's link to Jack Laidlaw came to light, he simply saw it as a stroke of luck that reinforced the brilliance of his plan. Idris had already run his exhaustive checks on Ayesha and been convinced. He's a genius when it comes to software, but he's not so good at reading people in the flesh. He was actually quite willing to believe that it was coincidence because he'd started to find himself attracted to me."

"And you know that how?"

"I'd given a couple of subtle hints that I found him attractive, although not so subtle that he wouldn't spot them. I flattered him and, like most men, his disposition towards me became favourable."

"So, you're an expert at leading men on? Plenty of experience?" Once again Jack's barb prompted no reaction. She continued to hold his gaze, her face remaining expressionless. "Leaving that to one side, I still can't get this to add up in my head. It doesn't feel right somehow. It's all too…" Jack paused, searching for the right word, "… too tenuous."

"What do you mean?"

"It's all too big a leap. How did you know that I was their target?"

"We didn't know. Not for certain anyway. We were working on the premise that the Yekta brothers might be up to something at the bank, once Jalal made his application for the vacancy in your team. We suspected he was applying for that role so that they could get closer to you. We felt that they were interested in your access privileges – rightly as it turned out."

"I can see that. But it's still a hell of a leap."

"It's what we do, Jack. We work with fragments, scraps. We take them and weave together hypotheses and then we calculate likelihoods. We don't always get it right, and sometimes we only get it partially right. But it's what we do. And we get it sufficiently right often enough to have faith in our approach. Taking everything into account, we felt that you were their target."

Jack inhaled slowly and deeply, as their eye contact remained unbroken. She was good, he surmised. Very, very good. She had fooled him completely – fooled everyone she met. She was a consummate actress, a practiced, professional liar. And she was lying now. He felt it. "That's not good enough Ayesha, or whatever your name is. It's still way too tenuous. Why don't you just tell me? What's to be gained by not telling me?"

She broke eye contact, bowing her head slightly. A brief pause, a look towards Ahmed Husain, and then back to Jack. Calculation complete, she opened with a jab, signalling that he should be on his toes, defences ready, "There *was* another factor." Another pause. He didn't take the cue, afforded himself no protection. "Jalal and Mirza are implicated in Debs' death." The hook caught him flush on the cheek, and he could feel his balance threatened. "We know that a burned-out car driven by Mirza is the one that killed Debs." The uppercut connected with his chin, threatening to disconnect his mind from consciousness. "Our view was that Debs was killed deliberately, partly in order to make you vulnerable." The haymaker to the temple finished him. Jack crumpled forward on his chair, struggling to catch his breath, head swimming, skin blanched as the blood raced to his palpitating heart. "Jack! Jack, are you okay?"

## Chapter 38

Jack's body had switched into self-preservation mode. His automatic survival instinct had triggered an emotional detachment, a numbing of his mind so that he could feel no more pain.

It was ten past six and Debs was on the 'phone. He could hear her voice. Her beautiful voice. She was having a laugh with young Nats at the pizza joint as she ordered the large ham and mushroom and medium Hawaiian, both on standard bases. She told Nats she'd be round to collect in quarter of an hour. Then she went into the kitchen and to the fridge where she retrieved the cucumber, iceberg, rocket, spring onions and cherry tomatoes purchased from Sainsbury's on her way home from work the day before. She took the wooden chopping board from the pan drawer below the cutlery drawer and selected the second smallest sharp knife from the black stone block of five on the worktop above. She made quick work of preparing and chopping the ingredients, tossing them into the clear glass salad bowl retrieved from the same drawer as the chopping board. She put two wooden salad spoons in the bowl and placed it in the middle of the kitchen table. She returned the unused salad ingredients to the fridge and collected two small plastic bottles of salad dressing - vinaigrette that she'd share with Fi, and honey & mustard for Ollie. She placed them either side of the salad bowl, then put the glass water jug beside the vinaigrette and the salt and pepper pots beside the honey & mustard. She laid three sunflower patterned placemats, Fi and Ollie's on one side of the table and her own opposite Ollie. Three knives and forks and three white china dinner plates completed the preparations. A quick glance out of the window confirmed that the drizzle wasn't really heavy enough to merit taking an umbrella. She went through to the hallway and took her burgundy gabardine jacket from the peg, slipped it over her cotton blouse and zipped it up to the neck. The kids were playing upstairs, and she shouted up to let them know that she was just going to collect the pizzas and she'd be back soon. She closed the front door behind her, leaving it unlocked, down the short path, turned left along Roll Gardens and walked the short distance to the pizza shop in less than five minutes. The pizzas were ready and she and Nats had agreed that they thought Danny Mac had a great chance of winning *Strictly* this year. She paid the £21.40 for the pizzas using her HSBC debit card and put the till receipt in her purse. She picked up both pizza boxes, told Nats to have a good weekend and that she'd see her next week, then left the shop.

Jack could see it all clearly in his mind's eye. In the days and weeks after Debs had died, he had pored over every detail he could find of the last half hour of her life, trying to make sense of it. He had replayed this movie over and over in his head to the extent that, had Debs been alive, she would have remembered less of the details than he did. But there had always been a gap before, a scene that was missing. This time was different.

He watched Debs turn right off Woodford Avenue into Gaysham Avenue. She didn't notice the white Tesla S parked up as she dipped her head against the increasingly persistent drizzle and upped her pace slightly. She didn't see Mirza, hunched in the driver's seat, watching her progress – first in his wing mirror and then through the windscreen after she passed. She didn't see or hear Mirza start the car and pull silently into the middle of the road.

Jack wanted to call out, to scream, to warn her. Look out! He's behind you! But this wasn't a pantomime. It was a gruesome horror flick – a genuine snuff movie – and he could only watch the abomination unfold, a helpless spectator.

Debs continued along Gaysham Avenue, passing commercial premises and then houses as the strengthening wind caused leaves to dance around her like so many sprites. The lightless Tesla crawled slowly along the middle of the carriageway, some distance behind, wiper blades sweeping intermittently to ensure Mirza a clear view of his prey. He was already accelerating as she approached the cluster of telegraph pole, tree and streetlight where he knew she would cross the road. Debs stepped off the pavement without looking back, took two further steps and was struck by the murder weapon. Legs, ribs, skull and eye socket were smashed in an instant as her body bounced over the top of the car, landing lifeless in the road.

Jack saw it all again, but this time saw that Mirza's face contorted, and that he flinched at the moment of impact. Jack saw that he didn't check in the rear-view mirror, didn't see Debs' body, confident that the impact had had the desired effect. Jack saw the Tesla speed to the end of the road, flick it's lights on and turn right, before driving off. He saw Mirza behind the wheel, composed and blasé, save for a sense of satisfaction at an objective achieved. Uncaring too about the collateral damage to the lives of the whole Laidlaw family.

Everything was clear now. The vital details of the dreadful final scene had been filled in and the whole movie was complete inside his head. He knew who the assassin was and was beginning to understand the plot. Jack had agonised over this so often and for so long. His need to know who was responsible had been a craving, but now that he did know there was no satisfaction. The knowledge brought no relief.

"Are you okay?" He was mute. Ayesha – or whoever she was - was in front of him now, kneeling on the floor, one hand on each of his shoulders, peering into his eyes as though checking he was still in there. "Jack, can you hear me?"

Gradually, his eyes regained focus and he was conscious of her presence. The deafening rush of blood inside his head started to subside, the movie faded. He could hear her words, feel her eyes reaching out, offering him a lifeline. He could hear someone else's voice telling her he was all right. His own voice. Realisation, consciousness returning, awareness of where he was and what was going on. "Are you sure about this?" asking, when he already knew the answer.

She leaned back, just a few inches, realising that he was coming back, "We're sure."

"They killed Debs because they wanted to get to me." A statement rather than a question.

She took his left hand and clasped it in both of hers. "I'm sorry, Jack. I didn't want to tell you. At least not here, not like this. Not when you were so unprepared. Probably later."

"There would never be a good time to be told."

"No, you're right. There are only bad times and worse times. I'm sorry this is one of those worse times. And I'm just sorry period."

"How are you sure? Why?"

She recognised his mind's need to make sense of things, to know the detail and understand. She let his hand go, rose and returned to her seat. She exchanged a nod with Ahmed Husain. Resuming eye contact, she spoke in the same low, calm manner as before. "We have been questioning Jalal overnight. You were one of three potential targets for the group. Mirza and Eshan had broken into your home undetected, in search of copies of your security card and codes, and anything else that might prove useful to them. However, Debs arrived home sooner than they anticipated and they were concerned she saw them as they made off and would be able to ID them."

"My God! Debs did say something to me about seeing two men disappearing out of the back garden. But that was *months* before she was killed. There weren't any signs of a break in to the house or the garage. We put it down to opportunists who were scared off when they realised someone was in the house. I remember she said that she'd only seen them from behind. That she wouldn't recognise them. We didn't think it was even worth reporting." Jack's face blanched as he recalled the incident, the last sentence catching in his throat.

"Jack, if this is too painful we can stop."

"No. Keep going."

"OK, but I need to warn you that it doesn't get any easier. When they reported to Jalal, that was when the decision to kill Debs was taken. Jalal believed that killing her would remove any risk that she might identify them, and at the same time pave the way to making you more vulnerable." She paused as Jack silently appealed with moist, incredulous eyes. "I know. Jalal is clearly mad. There is no point trying to make sense of his logic. I can only tell you what he told my colleagues overnight."

"So …" Jack choked back a sob, "so what happened *that* night?"

"We haven't finished questioning Jalal, but from what he has told us and what we already had worked out, we have a pretty clear picture. They watched you and your family closely for the next six weeks, and identified your Friday night pattern as providing the opportunity they were looking for. They knew the owner of a Tesla Model S who was abroad for several months on business. They entered his home and secured the fob for the vehicle. Idris hacked Tesla's security, and they were able to use the car undetected. Quite separately, we had a tracker on Mirza's car. The day before Debs was killed it was parked just a couple of hundred yards away from where the burned-out car – the Tesla – was found. It stayed stationary there until ten past seven the following evening. It was a location where they could abandon and torch the car without being seen and had a route there from the hit that was only very lightly covered by CCTV."

Jack winced at the word 'hit'. The tiny three-letter word sounded so calculated and ruthless. And so dismissive of Debs. He could feel his emotional control being tested again, and made a conscious effort to ensure his voice didn't crack, "So if you knew all this, why didn't you move to stop them sooner?"

"We worked a lot of this out after the event, and from questioning Jalal overnight. We have two separate pieces of CCTV showing the Tesla on the precise route between where Debs was killed and Mirza's car. Mirza's car started to move at ten past seven and continued for quarter of an hour until it parked in the street around the corner from the Yetka brothers' house. We know now that Mirza went there to report back to Jalal."

"So, Mirza killed Debs."

"Yes."

"And they were all in on it?"

"No. Idris didn't know. He was a naïf. An innocent in many ways. He had no idea about Debs. He thought the Tesla was just being lined up as a fast getaway car if needed. I believe that Jalal knew he wouldn't go along with it, and that's why he didn't tell him."

"So, three of them were involved in Debs' murder?" The word came naturally. It hadn't been an accident. She hadn't just been killed. She had been murdered. All those nights of anguish, of torture, of wondering, asking himself why. Now there was an explanation, and the beginning of understanding. "They murdered her. The stupid, evil bastards thought that she was a threat to them. So they killed her. Just like that. And you said that they also did it to get at me. They killed Debs to make me … what was it you said? Vulnerable?"

"Yes, to make you vulnerable."

"Vulnerable to what? What does that mean?"

"Vulnerable to overtures from another woman, from an Ayesha Alfarsi. It was obvious to anyone who cared to look at your social media accounts that you and Debs were rock solid together. That you loved each other and had a good family life. We now know Jalal thought that, besides removing a risk, killing Debs would make it much easier for you to be seduced by another woman and then manipulated by him."

Jack could see it now, how it pieced together. "Go on."

"As I said, we worked a lot of this out after the event, and only confirmed some of the details with Jalal overnight. We knew that Jalal had applied to work in the bank, in a role in your team. We couldn't be sure he'd get the job, or even be certain that he and his brother were definitely targeting the Bank. That meant you were on our list as a potential target for them, but there wasn't enough intel to suggest you were any more likely a target than a number of others we'd identified."

"So you didn't think there was any risk to Debs even though you had identified me as one of their possible targets?"

"Good God, Jack! No, of course not. We hadn't an inkling. If we'd had the faintest suspicion an innocent citizen was at risk, we'd have had to take some sort of pre-emptive action. We hadn't a clue that there might be any risk to Debs."

Her response was spontaneous, with the merest hint of indignation that even so accomplished a performer would find challenging to feign. He believed her this time. "You said that Jalal had been looking to recruit a female into their group. Didn't that arouse your suspicions?"

"We didn't know quite what to make of it. He was clearly trying to engage with women who might have reason to sympathise with their cause, and who might also be considered sexually attractive to men." This was stated as simple fact, without vanity or conceit. "Even if we had suspected the female would be used to compromise you, there was nothing to suggest any risk to Debs' life."

Jack believed her. This part of the picture was clearer now. It made sense, even if it was horrific. Other parts of the canvas remained much less clear. "Okay, I believe that. But I'm not so sure about the rest of it."

"What do you mean? What aren't you sure about?"

"You just said that if you thought an innocent citizen was at risk, you'd take pre-emptive action. Yet you deliberately took Fi, Ollie and Mum and handed them over to these murderous bastards. You actually handed them over, put them into danger!" Jack's voice rose with his anger, articulation of earlier events bringing them sharply back to the forefront of his mind. For a split second there was a chance the fury would win control and that he would strike her, but the moment passed. Instead he stood, breathing heavily through flared nostrils, with a stare that demanded an explanation in lieu of the impossibility of any justification.

"I'm sorry for what happened to Fiona, Fi and Ollie, but the circumstances were different." She raised her left palm towards him, holding his gaze, to quell the imminent eruption of indignation. "The circumstances *were* different. By that stage we were as sure as we could be that a nuclear device was in play. Not going along with their plan, giving them any cause to suspect that things were going wrong, risked alerting them. They could have decided to trigger the nuke early. We knew that going along with them meant putting your family right into the eye of the storm, but our take on it was that not doing so would probably mean that they would die anyway, along with half the population of London."

All of this continued to be delivered in a quiet, smooth manner, although there was a hint of earnestness in her tone. A suggestion perhaps that she did care, that it mattered to her that he understood. Jack processed her explanation silently, head understanding – perhaps even accepting – the logic, heart still furious.

"There was very little chatter – these guys were extraordinarily careful about keeping things quiet and covering their tracks. But GCHQ did identify signals on the suppliers' side. Although they were pretty circumspect too, they weren't as tight as the guys at this end. There was some excited talk about a package being delivered, the payment of a second instalment and speculation about where to be to get the best view of the firework display. We were able to take that intel and link it to the clandestine money transfers the Yekta brothers were making. That, together with the information I was able to gather from the inside – which was limited – was enough for us to identify what we thought was their plan as a very plausible option."

"How could you be on the inside yet be limited in what you knew?"

"Standard protocol for these kinds of cells is that information is shared strictly on a need to know basis. So, for example, although I knew about Mirza and Eshan through SIS, Jalal and Idris only ever mentioned them to me using code names. Jalal only confirmed to me a week ago that yesterday was the day, barely enough time to make arrangements with your family – although they were on standby to make your "birthday video" as soon as the studio was available. He only finally confirmed the address of the studio yesterday morning. Before then I'd never actually met Mirza or Eshan." She paused and looked to him for confirmation that he understood, that he was taking it all in.

Jack's eyes were directed towards the carpet, but unfocused as though his brain was refusing to receive any additional inputs for fear of overload. The pause continued for a second before he gave an almost imperceptible shake of his head and looked back up at her. "So, this is all some terrorist plot, all in aid of some stupid bloody cause? My wife was killed, my kids and Mum put in danger by maniacs trying to make some kind of point?"

"We think that might be part of it, but we're not sure that's the whole story."

Jack's eyes widened. "What do you mean 'you're not sure'?"

"Until we get Jalal and Eshan properly questioned and confirm things absolutely, we really can't be entirely sure. Having said that, there is some evidence that points to this possibly being as much about money as terrorism."

"What do you mean? What evidence?"

"There are 'plane tickets booked, as you know. Three flights from London City to Paris, including one for me, and another two from Stansted to Tehran. We believe that when we go through their things that we'll find false passports for all four of them. Then there's the money. Substantial sums, into eight figures in pounds sterling, have been lodged in separate Swiss bank accounts in the names of the other four individuals booked on those flights. We think those funds were sourced from the Bank by Idris in the same way as the funds he diverted to pay for the materials for the dirty bomb."

"So, what are you telling me? That this isn't about terrorism? That it's just a bunch of gangsters? That Idris is the mastermind behind all of this?" Jack's face contorted with confusion as he tried to reconcile the image of the Idris Yekta he knew with the idea that he was some kind of criminal genius.

"No, no not at all. I really don't think that's the case. As I said earlier, I think that Idris, despite his undoubted brilliance with technology, is something of an innocent when it comes to dealing with the real world."

"Innocent! Innocent? A funny fucking word to use to describe someone involved in trying to murder people and rob a bank."

"You're right. Poor choice of word by me. I mean that he's naïve – way too naïve to be the one behind all of this. He did genuinely believe in striking back at the western world – that much was clear from speaking to him directly. But I think he really believed that it could be done by attacking the global financial system, rather than targeting people directly. I don't think that he had a clue about the bomb. When he mentioned the payment for it, he described it as a donation to a group of organised people abroad who shared his beliefs. I honestly believe that he meant that, and that he had no idea what it was actually funding. On a personal level he was quite a gentle soul.

He even expressed concerns about using your kids and Fiona as hostages and had to be reassured by Jalal that no harm would come to any of them."

Jack was listening intently, his face a stern portrait of concentration as he processed what she was saying. "So, if not Idris, it must be Jalal then."

"I agree. Jalal was the most driven and he is highly manipulative. I think that he planned it all, almost certainly in collusion with Eshan and Mirza. They are definitely complicit in all of this. I believe Jalal identified you as a key to their plot because they needed your access codes. I think that he and the other two then killed Debs and set about recruiting a female accomplice without telling Idris because he knew that Idris would be unlikely to agree with the approach. Jalal persuaded Idris to transfer funds to five different Swiss bank accounts. Four of those were to provide funds for each of them once they made good their escape. The fifth was to a front organisation that was sufficiently credible for Idris to believe in, but in reality, it was then transferred on to pay for the bomb."

Jack's face was grim, "That all seems to stack up. But you said that it might be as much about money as about terrorism. So, which is it?"

"Honestly, we don't know. We'll have a better idea after Jalal and Eshan have been interrogated. What Jalal told you about his and Idris's mother was true. I'm sure that Idris was only motivated by grief and outrage at what he perceived as the unacceptable behaviour of western democracies in the Middle East. To what extent that's the case with the others will become clearer once they've been interrogated. They certainly have experienced events in their lives that would make that a credible motivating factor for their actions. Equally, narcissists like Jalal aren't usually motivated by anything other than absolute self-interest. It seems quite plausible to me that he identified the sense of grievance the other three shared as something he could exploit to his own ends."

"You think he was willing to sacrifice his brother, kill innocent people and trigger international financial chaos just for a few million in the bank?"

"I don't think he expected Idris to be killed. But as for the rest of it, then I believe it's perfectly possible, even probable. If he had pulled it off, he'd have been rich and home free. In the chaos after he'd succeeded it's unlikely anyone would even have come looking for him. His success would have fed his ego, proof that he was smarter than anyone else. God knows what that might have fired him up to do next."

"Do you really believe that's likely?"

"Like I said, Jack, I don't know. I saw enough of Jalal at close quarters to believe it's possible. Once our shrinks are finished with him, we'll have a pretty good idea of what was really motivating him."

"Will I get to know the result?"

"Probably not. Does it really matter that much?"

Jack broke eye contact and lowered his head slowly. He didn't say anything.

"Jack, I said does it matter that much?"

A slight shake of the head and he was back focusing on her. "Sorry, I was just thinking."

"Thinking what?"

"I was remembering a TV documentary I watched a while back. They were interviewing the loved ones of military personnel who were killed in the Iraq conflict."

"And?" Eyebrows slightly raised and a small nod of encouragement.

"Well, there were two distinct schools of thought amongst the bereaved. There were those who were absolutely adamant that there was no justification for us to get involved in the conflict. They wanted revenge on the politicians who had sent their sons or daughters or partners to their death. Others could not reconcile themselves to the thought that their loved ones had been sacrificed in vain, and clung like limpets to the belief that their deaths were in pursuit of a just cause."

"Why are you telling me this?"

"Because I remember thinking at the time that it really didn't matter. The dead were dead, and nothing was going to bring them back. It didn't matter why they had died. I just didn't see the point in raking over things, reliving the pain of loss."

"I can understand that."

"But now I think differently. I understand why it mattered so much to them. I know Debs is dead and that she's not coming back. I understand that knowing all of the whats and whys and wherefores won't change that one jot.I get that. But I do still want to know why. I want to understand *why* those bastards decided to kill her." He leaned forward towards her, unblinking eyes beseeching, "Do you understand?"

She leaned forward and took his left hand in her right. "Yes Jack, I understand." Her voice was softer now, and he thought he detected a note of tenderness in her tone. "I'll see what can be done about getting a message to you."

"Thank you."

She continued to hold his hand, her body leaning forward slightly; his bowed head just a foot away from hers. The dialogue between them seemed exhausted and the almost audible silence that replaced it lasted twenty or more seconds, all eternity. Eventually, he gradually raised his head and met her eyes with his. Another aeon passed as they held each other's gaze. He could see the compassion in her eyes that he had heard when she spoke. When he finally found his voice it was strained, barely more than a whisper, "And what about us?"

She lightly lifted her hand from his and withdrew it gently back to her lap, simultaneously straightening her back by degrees until she was upright again in her chair. All the time she never broke eye contact until finally she blinked and inhaled deeply through her nose. Re-engaging eye contact, she seemed to start to edge forward again in her seat before pausing. Her reply, when it came, was in a soft register just above his. "There isn't any us." She delayed again to allow the words to land and settle, before continuing. "There isn't any us and there never was any us. But I think you already know that."

It was true, he did already know. But he still felt the confirmation stiletto his heart, like the expected death of a loved one. His drowning man despair caused him to grab desperately for any possible lifeline."But what about..."

She cut him short, albeit still gently. "Jack, I'm truly sorry for everything that this has cost you. Really, I am. I'm sorry that

Fiona, Fi and Ollie were dragged into this and I'm sorry that Debs was killed. I'm sorry that you've been deceived and that you've had to suffer all of this pain and grief."

"So, if you feel sorry, you still have some feelings for me?"

"Perhaps sorry is the wrong word. I feel regret for what this has cost you and your family, but I've no other feelings for you. You're a likeable enough man and you can sometimes be fun to be around. Your family are good, decent and likeable too. But that's as far as it goes, Jack."

"You really mean that." It was stated as a certainty, but his eyes betrayed the truth that it was a final plea for her to contradict him.

"Yes Jack, I really mean that," and, sensing it wasn't enough, continued in the same soft tone, although slightly more detached. "This was a job for me Jack. A job. It's what I do. Some jobs require people to make decisions, to behave in certain ways, because that's what's required for the greater good. Sometimes my job means that I have to do certain things, behave in a particular way, because that's what is required. You understand that, don't you?"

Jack did understand that. His mind flashed back to Jalal's rant about the death of his mother and other family members. He had railed against the description of their deaths as collateral damage. Now, he realised, Debs' death, the suffering of Fi, Ollie and his Mum, his own grief and betrayal – they were all just more collateral damage sustained in the same, pointless zero-sum pursuit. The realisation brought no comfort but confirmed that she was saying what she really believed. He held her gaze and answered in a firm voice, "Yes." Then he dipped his chin and averted his eyes.

She got to her feet unhurriedly and leaned forward, closing the already small space between them, "Good. Goodbye Jack." She closed the gap further, so that Jack could feel her breath on his face, and held his gaze for a moment. Another gentle sigh, a straightening of the back and a step to the side. She turned towards the door and in two paces had exited both the room and Jack's life.

Ahmad Husain got to his feet and looked at Jack's bowed

head as though he were going to say something. Then he turned and silently followed his colleague from the room.

## Chapter 39

"This channel is 92% secure. Adopt the appropriate protocol."
"Understood."
"Report please."
"The risk is neutralised. Two fatalities amongst the targets. One civilian with a GSW, but not life threatening. No casualties on our team."
"Yes, that's what I had heard. And what about you? Are You all right?"
"I'm fine. Thank you for asking."
"Are you sure?"
"Yes, I'm sure."
"I'm glad to hear it. I understand you were involved in debriefing the mark."
"That's right ma'am."
"Did you discuss Vic with him?"
"No ma'am. I didn't judge it appropriate."
"I see. Your call."
"One observation ma'am, if I may."
"Of course. Go ahead."
"Sometimes this job is really, really shitty."
"I know. Is there anything else?"
"No. That's everything, thanks. Goodbye."
"Goodbye."

## Chapter 40

Jack exited London Bridge underground and made his way at a brisk pace to the hospital via Tooley Street. The receptionist directed him to the third floor and he quickly located Bob's room. He hesitated before knocking and easing the door open.

"That's Jack now, Bob." Edward stood up from his chair by the bed, stepped forward and embraced Jack with a warm, firm man-hug. "Jack Laidlaw, I do believe you've brought a bunch of grapes! Look Bob – Jack's brought a bunch of grapes!"

"I should damn well think so. Better be decent grapes, otherwise he's confirmed as a walking cliché." Bob's rich voice was strong, his smile radiant, sitting up in bed, three pillows providing support. He was wearing vibrant blue paisley silk pyjamas, with the arm of his wounded shoulder resting in a fresh white sling.

"If I were a poof in silk pyjamas, I'd hardly be accusing anyone else of being a cliché. Anyway, how the hell are you? You look a lot better than the last time I saw you."

"I'm fine, Jack. All sorted. A couple more days' recuperation and I'll be back home. Sit down. Edward is going to make a diplomatic exit to go and get himself a cup of coffee, so you can use his chair."

The cue was well rehearsed. "Don't worry, Jack, Bob will give me chapter and verse on everything you pair say later on, and anyway I really am dying for a skinny latté." Edward touched Jack's shoulder and flashed a smile as he slid past, closing the door behind him.

"Come on, Jack, sit down and share those bloody grapes. Here, put them on this overbed table thingy."

Jack lowered himself into the blue vinyl chair and placed the grapes on the table. Spacious, with a second door to an en-suite, the room was an uneasy combination of luxurious domestic comforts and the trappings associated with a high-tech hospital ward. The dominant feature was the spectacular view of the Thames afforded by the large window that occupied one wall.

"I'm surprised to see you slumming it quite as badly as this."

"They took me straight from the bank to the Royal London and operated on me there. After the op Edward came to see me and we agreed that it was unfair of me to block a bed in such an excellent teaching hospital when I had the option of recovering here."

"Of course, of course."

"Now be a good fellow and pick off some grapes for me. I do have only one functioning arm at the moment." Jack did as he was bid, easing the grapes from the vine and placing them on the table within easy reach of Bob's good hand. Bob took a fruit and placed it in his mouth. "Delicious. Mmmmmmmmmm. Absolutely delicious. Go on, do have some yourself."

Jack again followed instructions and popped a grape in his mouth. It was, very delicious, "You're right. I think these could be incredibly moreish." Each man consumed two more grapes at a leisurely pace.

"Hell of a girl."

"What?"

"Hell of a girl. That new squeeze of yours, Ayesha. Hell of a girl."

"Look, Bob, I am so sorry. So sorry. You could have been killed – you damn well nearly were. I just froze. Everything seemed to be happening around me. I couldn't make sense of it as it was going on. I was preoccupied with what was happening to the kids and Mum. Then things just moved so fast. It was like I was watching some kind of play or movie, except I was in it. Except I wasn't in it either. God! That makes no sense. Then I just took off and left you, without even thinking about how you were. I am so sorry."

"Stop being an arse. Have another of these delicious grapes." Bob placed a grape in his mouth and gestured for Jack to do the same. "Now look, there is nothing – absolutely nothing – for you to apologise for."

"That's not true, Bob. I froze and you didn't. You got shot and then I left you."

"Don't be a tit. Take some more grapes off the vine for us, thank you. Now listen to me. It's clear that you're on some misguided guilt trip. The truth is that we were both lured there by some pretty smart operators and then taken by surprise."

"Yes, but you were on the ball. You acted and stopped them. You took a bullet. I simply froze."

"Jack, take the hair shirt off. Stop being such a drama queen. You'd been shown pictures of your mother and the children as hostages. They'd been threatened and your first thoughts were for them. In your situation I suspect I would have completely crumpled." He rolled a grape between his thumb and forefinger.

"You're being kind." Jack looked his friend in the eye whilst unconsciously mimicking Bob's grape rolling with his own.

"Really I'm not. I know you feel guilty. I feel guilty. If it weren't for me it's entirely likely that Idris would still be alive. So I know how you feel. I understand feeling guilty. But you have to compartmentalise it, Jack. The last thing either of us need is for the other to try and out-guilt him. Neither of us did anything wrong. We were victims of circumstance, hostages to fortune – call it what you like. We were not in that situation of our own free will and we cannot be responsible for what happened."

"Do you really believe that?"

"Yes, I really believe it. I don't feel it – not yet at least – but I do believe it. Partly because I have to and partly because it's true." Bob paused, broke eye contact, and placed the grape in his mouth. "These really are very, very good. Better quality than I'd have expected from you." Jack smiled at the jibe, allowing his friend sufficient time chewing the grape to ensure he maintained his composure. Bob sighed, equilibrium regained, and with the merest hint of concern in his voice, enquired, "And how are the children and your mother?"

"Fine, I think. Certainly the kids seem none the worse for wear. The intelligence services were concerned they might talk to their friends, but that really won't be an issue."

"They spoke to the children?"

"Good God, no! They asked how I wanted to manage it and were happy to go with my request to handle it personally."

"That's good. Everyone talks about how robust children are, but it's still reassuring to hear from you that they're well. And your mother?"

"Not quite so good I'm afraid. There's no single particular issue I can point to and say is a problem. It's hard to describe. It's more an overall impression. She just seems older, more frail, smaller somehow. She says she's fine and I don't know if she thinks she's fooling me or not, but the whole episode has clearly shaken her."

"Did they offer counselling?"

"Yes they did. But you know my mum, there was never a cat's chance in hell that she would be open to anything like that."

"Quite. She's a strong and proud woman. She's that particular type who would never complain about anything, except for extremes of weather, bad manners and a poorly made cup of tea." They both smiled at the perfect summary. "You'll just need to keep an eye on her. She'll probably get over it with time. After all, it's only been a few days."

"I hope you're right – we'll see over the next week or so. Anyway, how about you? I take it that you've had your debrief?"

"What a palaver that was. They were desperate to see me as soon as I came round from the anaesthetic. Edward insisted they wait and talk to him instead, as he judged me in no fit state to be interrogated, which is what he insisted on calling it. Anyway, cutting a long story short, I had my debrief as soon as they moved me here, with Edward present."

"And they were okay with that?"

"Edward wasn't exactly giving them a choice in the matter." Bob smiled at the recollection.

"And it went all right?"

"Nothing much to gauge it against, if I'm honest. Bit frustrating that they were more concerned about me – and Edward – keeping quiet, than answering my questions. Kept emphasising the Official Secrets Act and all that twaddle. I had to press them quite hard to learn what they knew, or at least as much as they were willing to share. Chap called Ahmad Husain did all the talking. He had a woman with him, much the same age as him, but she never spoke or even introduced herself."

"Yes, similar to the experience I had, except Husain was

accompanied by Ayesha."

"You're joking!"

"It was fine, Bob. Well – no, it wasn't fine. But it was necessary. It was kind of like I had to see her to really understand everything properly. Like we had to have that meeting in order for me to lay the ghost, if that makes any sense. It was difficult, but I came away under no illusions about her."

"Care to explain?"

"I've had a few days to process things. When I saw the grief counsellor after Debs died, she explained the grieving process. The different stages."

Bob nodded. "Go on."

"My head is there, but my heart is still struggling. I know Ayesha was never who she pretended to be. That what I thought we had wasn't real. That it never really existed and it's gone forever." A pause and a sigh. "But I'm still getting over it on an emotional level."

"I understand."

"The real horror was finding out Debs was murdered. The fact she's gone hasn't changed, but knowing the real reason has been like picking the scab off the wound. It's raw, Bob. It's like I'm right back at the beginning with Debs, and losing her." Another pause.

"Jack, I don't have any words."

"It's okay. This is the first time I've said this out loud. It helps. That thing you said a moment ago about believing something, but not feeling it?"

"Yes?"

"That kind of captures it. Ayesha wasn't real and she's gone. And I'll get over her. Debs loss feels sharper again, and I'll never get over that. But I will come to terms with it, like I was learning to before."

"I know you will."

Jack returned Bob's smile. "Thanks."

"Maybe you can tell me more some other time."

"Yes, some other time. Perhaps we can go for a bottle of wine when you get out of here. And we can exchange notes on what Husain had to say as well." He was conscious that Bob was tiring, and that recovering from a gunshot wound wasn't to be taken lightly. "Look, I really need to be getting off. This was only ever intended as a brief visit to confirm that you're malingering as usual. Let me know when you're ready for that drink – and remember it's your turn to pay."

Bob didn't feel the need to protest and they said their goodbyes. Jack caught Edward on the way out and confirmed he'd call the next day for an update and likely visit again the day after that.

## Chapter 41

The somewhat shrill background hubbub in the pizza restaurant reflected the early evening hour and the preponderance of families with young children among the clientele. Ollie stood up and turned to see over the top of the booth they were seated at. "I think I can see ours coming now!" The excitement and optimism in his voice remained as high as on the three previous occasions he had made the same declaration.

"You say that every single time a waiter or waitress comes out from the kitchen." Fi made sure her face conveyed an appropriate degree of exasperation for Jack to acknowledge.

Ollie was oblivious to his sister's barb. "No! I really think this is ours. She's coming straight towards us."

The virtue of maintaining positivity in the face of repeated setbacks was rewarded when the green-clad waitress stopped at their table. "Medium Hawaiian?"

"Here, please." Fi smiled and nodded at her plate.

"And the large pepperoni?"

"That's for greedy pig-face over there." Fi gestured in Ollie's direction.

The waitress presented Ollie with his plate and grinned at Jack. "I'll be right back with your large Margherita," then spun away back towards the kitchen.

"I am not a greedy pig-face."

"Yes you are. You ordered a large."

"Dad ordered a large too."

"Dad's a grown up. You're six and you're an oink oink."

"Am not. You're just a wuss that can't eat a proper-size pizza."

"Now, you two. Pack it in." Jack smiled his acknowledgement to the waitress as she presented his Margherita then, turning back to the kids, "No standing on ceremony now. Tuck in!"

"Stop! There's something we need to do first." Fi's intervention brooked no contradiction as she winked to Ollie and reached for her glass of cola. "Dad, Ollie, please raise your glasses." Three glasses of cola clinked together as two voices chorused *Happy Birthday, Dad* sufficiently loudly for a few diners at other tables to turn in their direction.

"Thank you both very much." There was a slight catch in Jack's throat as he suddenly remembered his birthday three years previously in this same restaurant. Fi had been Ollie's size then and Ollie had been in a high chair. Debs had kissed him. A full on, passionate smacker right in front of anyone who cared to look.

"Are you okay, Dad?" Fi was giving him a look that suggested she knew he wasn't all right. Ollie was switching his glance between Jack and his pepperoni, unsure if the *tuck in* instruction was on pause.

"I'm fine, just a little frog in my throat." He feigned a cough. "Now, what's stopping you? Get wired in!"

Ollie tore the biggest slice from his pizza and stuffed half of it into his mouth before dropping the crust end back on to the plate. "Ow! Hot!" He sucked air in to cool the burning and reached for his drink to provide further relief.

"Serves you right, greedy pig." Fi made a production out of lifting her knife and fork to cut a dainty morsel from her own pizza. Ollie ignored her as he washed his first mouthful down and reached more gingerly for the dropped, half-eaten slice.

Jack decided that he would diplomatically alternate between hand and knife & fork on each slice. He tore a large mouthful of delicious cheese and tomato bread, chewed it with relish and smiled inwardly as he noted Ollie aping his behaviour. "I must say this is a fantastic treat. But I can't help worrying that it's very expensive and that you don't get enough pocket money to be able to afford to spoil me like this."

Fi smiled and shook her head. "Don't worry about that, Dad. I can easily afford this."

Her air of sophistication morphed into annoyance as Ollie confirmed what Jack already knew. "It's no problem, Dad. Gran gave Fi plenty of money before we came out. There's even enough for us to have ice cream after."

"Oh well, that's a relief. It's a pity that Gran's cold meant she couldn't come herself."

"She could have come. Her cold's not that bad. She just doesn't like pizza. I wish she had come so I could have had hers."

His son's lack of artifice made Jack laugh out loud. "Don't you be so cheeky about Gran, you monkey. She *has* got a cold and I'll be taking you swimming in the morning so that she gets a lie in."

"Does that mean you won't be going out to The General tonight?" Fi's eyes were more questioning than her words.

"No. I mean yes, I will be going out later. Some of my friends want to buy me a birthday drink. But I won't be staying out late, I promise."

The exchange between father and daughter was cut short by Ollie's urgent stage whisper, "Look!" They both looked at Ollie and then turned to see what he was nodding towards. About twenty yards away on the far side of the restaurant a tall, dark-haired woman with her back to them was taking her seat opposite a male companion. "It's Ayesha!"

"Are you sure?" Fi's whisper was quieter than Ollie's.

"Definitely."

The atmosphere at their table was suddenly supercharged and Jack could see the children's agitation, sense their fear. "Calm down both of you. I really don't think Ayesha would be eating out around these parts. I'll tell you what I'm going to do. I'm going to get up and walk over there and see whether it really is her or not."

"You can't just walk up and stare at her!" Again, Fi's face screamed mortification even more eloquently than her words.

"Don't be silly. The Gents is over there. I'll head towards them and take a look at the lady as I go past."

"But what if it is her?" Fi's horror was unabated. "What will you do?"

Jack didn't know what he would do, but simply smiled reassuringly at the kids and got to his feet. He turned. *If it is her, I'll just ask her to leave. Be discreet. No need for a scene.* He walked forced-casually towards the toilet. He could see her handbag, which he didn't recognise, and her high-heeled shoes which did look familiar. The white skin-tight jeans looked like a pair Ayesha had, but the purple top was unfamiliar. The hair – cut and colour – were exactly as he remembered Ayesha's.

As he drew level with the table, she turned her head to the other side so that he still only had a view of the back of her head and neck. He couldn't stop and stare, so continued on into the Gents, cursing his timing whilst making a mental note that he didn't recognise the chunky ring the woman was wearing. But her neck, the hair at the nape ...

The loo was empty. Jack paused for the minimum time credible for him to have used the facilities and washed his hands. *Deep breath. Calm, calm.* He exited the door and looked straight in her direction. She had the same skin tone and very similar features to Ayesha. But she wasn't Ayesha. He could see why Ollie had thought it was, given that the boy probably only had a fleeting look at her from a much greater distance. He made his way casually back towards two pairs of puppy-dog-anxious eyes. "Relax you two. It's not her."

Fi was silent, but her face broadcast relief. Instead it was her brother who responded. "Are you sure, Dad?"

"Quite sure. I can see why you thought it might be her, but when you get up close it definitely isn't."

"Okay, that's good. I'm pleased it wasn't her. Are you pleased it wasn't her, Dad?"

"Shush, Ollie!" Fi's admonishment crashed over the table like a wave hitting rocks. "You know we're not meant to talk about her, or about any of that ... that stuff."

Jack reached across the table and placed his palms on a hand of each child. "It's okay for us to talk about it amongst ourselves. We can't talk to anybody about it outside of us and Gran, but we can discuss it with each other. Do you want to talk about Ayesha again, and about what happened?"

Fi shook her head firmly.

"Do you miss Ayesha, Dad?" Ollie looked right at him. "Sometimes Fi says to me that she wonders if you miss her."

Fi tried to glare her brother to death. Jack pressed ever so slightly more firmly on their hands and lowered his head a fraction, tilting it so that he could look at both of them at once.

"No. No I don't miss her at all." He could see in Fi's eyes that she knew he was telling the truth and they smiled at each other.

"Thought so! Good." Ollie stretched for the menu. "What kind of ice cream do you want when we've finished these?"

**The End**

## Acknowledgements

I'd like to thank the following people.

Margaret Denman, who gave me the encouragement I needed that persuaded me to start writing.

Alistair Govan, who gave me the encouragement to keep going and ensure I finished this novel.

John Ballam, for his wisdom, encouragement and advice.

Maureen O'Neill, Audrey Slade, Theresa Black, Viv Moaven, Jo Pike, Harriet David and Chris Wilson for their help and support.

My wife, Chris, for her love and support.

Printed in Great Britain
by Amazon